D1527708

FIRM HAND

NORA PHOENIX

Firm Hand by Nora Phoenix

Copyright ©2019 Nora Phoenix

Cover design: Sloan Johnson (Sloan J Designs)

Editing: Jamie Anderson

www.noraphoenix.com

THREE MONTHS EARLIER

"I can't believe that guy had such a magnificent dick and didn't know how to use it," Jonas said as he and Cornell walked back to the car. "That was utterly disappointing."

Cornell harrumphed. "That's one word for it."

He rubbed his lower back as they walked, the tight muscles informing him he'd better book a slot with both his chiropractor and his massage therapist tomorrow. God, getting older sucked. Being on his knees was a lot easier when he was twenty than it was now.

"He was clearly more turned on by watching us play together than by fucking either of us," Cornell said with a sigh.

Jonas unlocked the car, the quick double beep echoing in the parking lot. "We may have to consider finding a different club," he said.

Cornell let out a soft groan as he got into the car. Damn, his body hurt. And not in a good, endorphins-inducing way.

"Your back?" Jonas asked as he started the car.

"Yeah. And my knee." Cornell shivered in the cold car,

his breath coming out in damp clouds. "Turn the heated seats on high, would you?"

Jonas pressed a button. "You really need to make kneeling a hard limit, or at least indicate you can't do it for longer periods of time."

Cornell looked at him sideways. "It's what we do, Jojo," he said, using the old nickname for his best friend. "Subs kneel. It's kinda hard to put that down as a hard limit if I want to have a Dom take me seriously."

Jonas let out a deep sigh. "Yeah."

He didn't need to say more. It wasn't the first time they'd had this debate.

"Are you serious about finding a different club?" Cornell asked as Jonas carefully drove out of the parking lot. They'd had more snow in the last few days, another fifteen inches or so, and the lot had only been partially cleared. But they'd both grown up in the Northeast, so it wasn't anything they weren't used to. That was January in New York for you, nothing but snow, and it would stay that way for months.

"I don't know. I hate even the thought, but this isn't working. We've tried doing it separately, but that wasn't a success either."

Cornell mentally cringed. "You can say that again. Apparently, being a Dom at forty-five is fine and will make twinky subs line up out the door for you, but being a sub isn't. Where do they expect us to go?"

This, too, was not a new topic, but tonight's events had brought it home once again. Older subs were rare at the club since they were expected to have found a Dom by that point. A permanent one. A Dom who'd collared them. Fuck knew they'd both tried.

Jonas had been married for years to his Mistress—and had the son to prove it. But five years ago, they'd separated, and while it had been for the best since they'd grown apart, it had been hard on Jonas. Cassie hadn't only been his wife, but his Domme as well, and losing that stability had been a difficult transition.

And Cornell, he'd been on his own for six years now, after Arnold had left him for a younger sub who could "keep up with him," as he'd so subtly pointed out. Fuck him for not understanding that not all kinds of pain brought bliss. *Asshole.*

No, Cornell wasn't sorry anymore about the demise of that relationship, but he'd be lying if he said he didn't miss it. Not him, not Arnold specifically, but having a partner, a Dom. The intimacy. The care. The joy of obeying and submitting. Not that the whole relationship with Arnold had brought much joy in the five years they'd been together, but it'd had its moments.

"Can I stay with you tonight?" he asked, craving the companionship in bed. Out of everything he'd lost when Arnold had left him, that had been the hardest, strangely enough. He hated sleeping alone, painfully missing a body next to him. The body pillow he'd bought was a meager replacement.

"Sure," Jonas said, gently patting Cornell's thigh for a second. "I don't feel like being alone either."

"Rhys won't be home?" Cornell checked.

"Nah, he's with Cassie. He's all but done with his degree and is working a few days a week in a large physical therapy practice in Albany. He's looking for an apartment with a friend of his, but in the meantime, he moved back in with Cassie."

"Good," Cornell said. "'Cause that would be hard to explain to your kid."

"He's not a kid anymore, Cor. He's twenty-three," Jonas chided him with a laugh.

"He'll always be a kid to me," Cornell said. "I've known him since the day he was born."

Jonas rubbed his thigh again. Jonas had always been a tactile guy, often hugging and touching Cornell, and he loved the constant casual touches. "Don't make us feel even older."

They were silent for a bit as Jonas navigated the narrow, winding country road to his house. Unlike Cassie, who'd opted to stay in Albany after their divorce, Jonas had moved into the countryside. The boonies, as he called it. He'd bought an old farmhouse, a sprawling ranch with several outbuildings as well, which had been updated and modernized. The house was completely private, the nearest neighbors far away, and Cornell had to admit it was a little piece of heaven.

"So, a new club," Cornell said. "Any ideas?"

"There's more than a few in the city we could try."

Cornell scoffed. "You wanna drive three hours to New York City every other weekend?"

"No, I really don't, Cor, but what's the alternative? Boston is equally far, and we've exhausted all the local options."

He had a point there, Cornell had to admit. "Ugh, I hate it when you're right."

"We'll stay together the first few times to see if we like it and feel safe," Jonas said.

Cornell hummed in agreement. It was funny; they'd been best friends since college but had never played together till after Jonas's divorce. They'd been in the same clubs, the same parties, but never in the same scene until then. And even now, it was more out of necessity than a deep desire for each other. They were both too submissive, too needy for a strong, dominant partner—and in Cornell's case, for bottoming, since he didn't like topping—to ever be happy with the two of them. Theirs was a unique relationship: best friends with the occasional benefits, without sex ever getting in the way.

"We'll try it," Cornell agreed. "Because I know you have to be as desperate for a good scene by now as I am."

Jonas let out a half-laugh. "Honestly, I'd settle for a good, hard fuck by now. Just give me a guy with a good-sized dick who knows how to use it."

"Amen to that."

Cornell had stopped shivering, the heated seat sending a lovely warmth through his ass and back. Now that the engine was warm, the cold had been pushed out of the car, replaced by a comfortable heat. And god, how depressing was it if that was the thing Cornell appreciated most about Jonas's brand-new BMW? Jonas's big pickup truck was robust and perfect for hauling timber and everything he needed for his business, but this car, this was pure pleasure.

He noticed Jonas had slowed down. "Is it icy?" he asked. They were only five minutes out now, but the roads here were narrow.

"Yeah," Jonas said. "Felt the wheels spin a little. Must be some ice."

Cornell didn't need to tell him to be careful. They both knew how dangerous black ice could be. In the distance, headlights popped up, announcing an oncoming car.

"I love this car," Jonas said, a ring of pride in his voice. No wonder. He'd worked his ass off on his handmade wooden furniture business, creating and selling custom-made chairs, tables, picnic benches, cabinets, and more. He was good at what he did, and Cornell couldn't be more proud of him. A deep sense of gratitude filled him that despite everything he yearned for in life, he had this. This friendship, Jonas, meant everything to him.

"I love you," he blurted out. "I'm so happy we're still us after all this time, Jojo."

Jonas's laugh tinkled. "I love you too, you big sap. We'll make it, you and I. We'll find our happy ever after."

They turned the curve, and Cornell's breath caught as he felt the wheels spin, the back of the car drifting a little to the side.

"Dammit," Jonas cursed, pumping the brakes and steering to get traction again.

And then the headlights of the oncoming car were suddenly close, way too close. Cornell screamed in horror, his terror mixing with Jonas's. He screamed until the crash came, and then there was nothing but silence and darkness.

C ornell stared at his doctor, swallowing painfully. "You're saying that this is it? That I'm never gonna get more mobility than this?"

The doctor's look changed into one Cornell had become all too familiar with over the last few weeks. Professional pity, he called it. It was the look people got when they realized what had happened to him but weren't close enough to actually care.

"I'm saying you're lucky you can even walk again," the doctor said. "Your prognosis was a lot worse when you were admitted here."

Here was the rehabilitation center he'd spent the last few weeks in after being discharged from the hospital, learning to walk again, discovering that his limitations were so much more severe than he'd ever considered.

"*Lucky* is not the word I would use," he said, his tone sharp.

The doctor's face softened even more. "I can respect that, Mr. Freeman, but believe me when I say you've progressed much further than I ever thought possible."

Cornell let out a sigh. "I've always loved beating the odds."

"And that fighting spirit certainly helped your recovery. But this is as far as we can take you, I'm afraid."

"But I can't use stairs," Cornell protested. "Not without pain, at least. How will I manage in my house if I can't even handle stairs?" he asked, fighting to keep the anger out of his voice. "And I still can't walk farther and longer than a few minutes."

"There are certain adaptations you can make to your home to make it easier. A stair lift, for example. A special bathtub. But really, Mr. Freeman, considering your age, you may want to consider moving into a ranch or an apartment so everything will be on the same level. We have a consultant who will be more than happy to help you make any arrangements to make your current or future home more accessible."

Moving. He hadn't even considered that option, never realizing it would become impossible for him to return to his own home after his rehabilitation. A deep stab pierced his heart at the thought of having to buy a house without Jonas's advice. He'd always been the practical one with a sharp eye for detail. Well, Cornell was detail-oriented as well—he had to be, as an estate lawyer—but in a completely different way.

"I'll need some time to consider my options," he said, feeling defeated.

"I understand. Perhaps you could make temporary arrangements with family or friends? You will be discharged tomorrow, so you need to make sure you have a suitable place to stay."

Cornell almost choked on his own breath. "Tomorrow? I can't make arrangements on such short notice!"

The professional pity look returned. "Mr. Freeman, we've told you several times your release date was coming up. Maybe you can stay with a friend?"

A fresh wave of grief rolled over Cornell, clenching a cold hand around his throat. "My friend died," he whispered. "He's gone."

Tears welled up in his eyes all over again. He was surprised he hadn't run out by now. Lord knew he'd cried enough to end a drought in a few small countries. There had been days when he'd barely been able to see through his swollen eyes.

"Have you talked to our grief counselor?" the doctor asked.

Cornell waved his hand, not bothering to wipe away his tears. "I have. She says to allow myself to grieve and to give it time, so here we are."

The doctor shifted in his seat, apparently at a loss for words. "I don't think there's anything else we can do for you," he said, his tone changing from hesitant to conclusive. Cornell recognized when he was being dismissed. He'd done it himself with clients often enough.

"I'll make arrangements," he said.

He'd book a damn hotel if he had to. He'd probably need a live-in nurse or something as well for the first few months. There was still so much he couldn't do himself. Even getting dressed was a struggle some days, especially when his shoulder refused to cooperate.

For a fleeting second, he debated asking his sister, Sarah, if he could move in with her and her family, but he rejected that idea as quickly as it came up. He'd go mad in a house with three teenagers, two dogs, and four cats, if he remembered correctly. There might be a rabbit as well, and maybe some kind of parrot? It was easy to lose count since she kept rescuing pets. Plus, Sarah might end up killing him in his sleep, so there was that.

He shuffled out of the doctor's office, then lowered himself on a chair in the waiting room to wait for the orderly to accompany him back to his room. As he sat down with a groan, his phone rang.

"Hey," he greeted Rhys, Jonas's son, who called every day to check in on him. He was a sweetheart, so worried about Cornell.

"Any news?"

"They're discharging me tomorrow," Cornell said. "The doctor feels I've gained as much mobility as possible."

He tried to sound positive, not wanting to burden Rhys with his troubles. The kid had it hard enough, losing his father so unexpectedly.

"You can't go home," Rhys said firmly. "You don't have the mobility and functionality yet to manage living on your own, let alone in your house. It's gorgeous, but it's a death trap for you."

Right. Cornell had forgotten for a second that Rhys actually knew what he was talking about, considering he was a physical therapist who was about to get his master's degree in...what was it again? Kinetics? Cornell couldn't remember, but something about body movements. Kinesiology, that was it.

"I was thinking about trying to find a suite in an extended-stay hotel," Cornell said. "Or I could rent an apartment for the time being."

"You'll still need round-the-clock help," Rhys said, as practical as his dad had been.

"So, I'll hire a nurse?"

Rhys made a disapproving sound. "You know how much you hate having strangers around you all day."

Cornell suppressed a sigh. The kid knew him well. "I do, but I'll suck it up. Can't think of another solution that wouldn't suck just as much."

It was quiet for a few beats. "Come live with me," Rhys then said.

Cornell frowned. "What?"

"You know I moved into Dad's house. It's a ranch, so it will be much easier to navigate for you. And I'm done with my classes and only work part time, so I'm home a lot, and I can take care of you."

Take care of him? Why did that sound so damn appealing? It spoke to that deep need inside of him, even bigger after months of struggling and being alone. How he longed to surrender right now, to have someone step in and take control for a bit...but of course, that was a pipe dream.

Dozens of thoughts stormed through Cornell's head, but all that came out was, "Rhys, I can't..."

"Why?" was the immediate question. "Because the house holds too many memories? Because you'd feel guilty of taking advantage of me? Because you'd feel beholden to me?"

The quick list of arguments showed Cornell that Rhys hadn't made this offer spontaneously. He'd prepared this, had considered Cornell's possible objections in advance. Rhys had known Cornell would have a problem, and he'd already worked out a possible solution. It warmed Cornell's heart.

"For all of those reasons and a few more, yes. It sounds noble, but taking care of me is far less glamorous in reality."

Rhys sort of snickered. "You think I don't know that? It's my job, Cornell. It's what I do for a living."

He had him there. "You're not a nurse," Cornell protested weakly.

"You don't need a nurse. You need someone to help you with things you can't do yet and to be there in case something goes wrong. And I'll actually be able to help you with daily exercise, your mobility exercises, and I can even advise you on how to improve further."

He was persuasive, wasn't he? Cornell almost smiled. Rhys had always been an opinionated, strong character—much like his mother. He and Cassie had their differences, but he couldn't deny she was about as strong as they came. It was one of the character traits that made her such an excellent Domme.

"I don't know if I'll be able to handle staying at your dad's house," he said softly. "To be constantly reminded of his absence..." He had to swallow to get rid of the painful lump in his throat, something that had become almost routine by now.

"So we'll grieve together," Rhys said, his voice soft. "We both miss him like crazy, but don't you think that missing him together is better than missing him alone?"

A soft sound escaped from Cornell's lips. "Oh Rhys," he said, lost for words.

"I want you here," Rhys said. "Please, Cornell, allow me to do this for you."

I want you here. When was the last time someone had said that to him? Cornell closed his eyes, feeling himself surrender to Rhys's gentle insistence. "We'll need to get some things from my house."

"Give me a list, and I'll get whatever you need before I come pick you up tomorrow."

The joy in Rhys's voice was hard to deny. That, at least, made Cornell feel a little better about the whole thing. Rhys wanted him there, that much was clear. It might not be healthy to be swayed by that, and it totally spoke to what a needy bastard he could be and how starved for affection he was, but Cornell didn't care.

"Thank you," he said softly.

"You're more than welcome," was the heartfelt reply.

RHYS MANEUVERED his father's big-ass pickup truck through the parking lot, his eyes on the lookout for a spot in the full lot. *There.* Someone pulled out in front of him, and he whipped into the space before anyone else could grab it. He checked the walking distance to the entrance of the center, happy when he saw it was doable. That way, Cornell could walk to the car himself and keep his dignity.

He'd already packed up essentials for Cornell from his house. He could try to convince him to rent it out as long as he was staying with Rhys. He wasn't sure of Cornell's financial situation, but surely a little extra income couldn't hurt when the man would have bills the size of Mount Everest to pay. Besides, Cornell didn't know it yet, but Rhys was in no hurry to let him get back to his own house.

He rushed inside the building, determined to be on time. It was eleven on the dot when he knocked on the door to Cornell's room.

"Come in," Cornell called out, and when Rhys opened the door and stepped inside, he found him ready to go. That wasn't a surprise, since as far as he knew, Cornell had never been late for anything in his life. Rhys remembered many occasions of mutual teasing and ribbing between Cornell and his dad, who had not been quite as punctual—to put it mildly.

"What's that smile for?" Cornell asked. "You looked a million miles away."

"I had to think of Dad, who was never ready on time when you came to pick him up."

Cornell smiled as well. "Oh, I know. I always built an extra half hour in with him. Used to drive me bananas until I realized it was how he was wired."

Rhys grinned. "My mom did the same. Telling Dad my recital would start at eight when it wasn't till eight-thirty, to make sure he'd be there on time."

They both smiled at each other, lost in good memories for a while. Then Rhys gave himself a mental shove. "I picked up all the items from the list you sent me."

Cornell dropped his eyes to the floor. "Did you find everything okay?"

Rhys understood how embarrassing it must be for the man to have someone else go through his personal stuff. His thoughts went to the neatly organized drawer he'd discovered. He shouldn't have, he knew, but one glimpse had been enough to pique his curiosity. Colorful sex toys had been arranged in groups. A number of plugs. Some dildos. A few vibrating ones. And a collection of other implements, like cock rings, a spreader, and some restraining devices.

It hadn't even been that vast a collection and not that extreme. Rhys had seen much wilder than that. If you took into account Cornell was a sub and had been one for many years, a much bigger collection wouldn't have surprised Rhys either. And yet, finding that drawer, seeing that collection of toys and knowing Cornell had used those to bring himself pleasure—it had done something to Rhys. Knowing your father's best friend was a sub was one thing, but seeing the evidence was a whole other story.

Maybe he should've packed a few toys. Cornell would've been too embarrassed to ask for them, but that didn't mean he didn't need the help for a sexual release. No, that would've been too weird. Far too personal for this stage of their relationship. Cornell was already on edge about staying with Rhys—no need to make things awkward and risk him pulling the plug on the whole idea. He wasn't risking the best opportunity he'd ever get to get close to Cornell.

"Rhys? You okay?" Cornell asked.

Rhys realized he'd been lost in thought again and had forgotten to answer Cornell's question. "Yeah, sorry. I've got everything you asked me for, no problem at all. Are you ready to go?"

Cornell pushed himself out of the chair he'd been sitting in, a painful wince flashing over his face. He pointed toward the weekend bag sitting on the bed. "One of the orderlies packed up all my clothes and things from here. So if you could grab that, we're good to go."

"Sure," Rhys said, slinging the strap over his shoulder.

"So you have my things?" Cornell asked again, and Rhys realized he was either nervous or stressed. He couldn't remember ever seeing Cornell that way, and it was a stark reminder how much had changed.

"Yes, I have everything," he assured him, then added, "Nothing for you to worry about."

Cornell turned toward him, those gray eyes burning with intensity. "Young Rhys, the list of things I worry about is so long that this barely makes the list in the first place."

Ah, Cornell's infamous sarcasm. It was somehow reassuring that no matter what had changed, some things had stayed the same.

"Please forgive me," he said lightly. "One less thing to worry about."

Cornell studied him for a few beats. "Okay, let's go."

Rhys had to refrain himself from offering help when

Cornell walked beside him, his gait slow and unsteady. The man had to learn to ask for help—not an easy feat considering how proud he was. And age probably played a role as well. Admitting you needed help was one thing. Admitting it to someone so much younger and healthier was much harder. Rhys would have to give him time. But not too much time.

Cornell stopped, his right hand white-knuckling the metal bar that lined both sides of the hallway. He was panting slightly, and Rhys spotted sweat pearling on his forehead. Rhys bit his tongue.

"I'm sorry," Cornell said, his voice soft. "I'm slow as..."

He stopped, but Rhys added, "As a snail in heat." It had been one of his dad's idiosyncratic expressions, and Rhys smiled. "I've always wondered about that one," he said. "First of all, do snails even experience heat, and if they do, wouldn't that make them faster?"

Cornell chuckled. "I asked that once as well, and he said that even in heat, snails are still slow. Or even slower, because they use up their energy for sex instead of speed. No idea if there's any truth to it."

"Knowing Dad, probably not," Rhys said, "But I love that expression anyway."

It was still surprising, how fast that wave of grief would roll over him, making his throat clench and his breaths painful. His eyes burned, and he took a few slow, deep breaths.

By the time he had composed himself, Cornell had caught his breath. It took forever to reach the car, and Rhys didn't like how pale and sweaty Cornell was when he finally made it to the passenger seat. Pride was all well and good, but he would only allow it for so long.

It didn't surprise him when Cornell fell asleep during

the ride home. He stole a glance sideways every now and then. The lines he'd always thought of as laugh lines had deepened. God, Cornell could laugh, a full belly laugh that was infectious as hell. Rhys hadn't heard that laugh since the accident.

Cornell's usual tan had been wiped away by a pale grayness that worried Rhys. Cornell was not okay. Not even close. No wonder, after what he'd been through, but Rhys still worried. Not so much about his physical state, though he certainly had a long road ahead of him there as well, but more about his mental state.

He'd known the man since the day he'd been born, and he'd always been full of life. Cornell possessed a wicked, sharp sense of humor that had caused those laugh lines, that had made Rhys laugh on many occasions, even inappropriate ones. At the funeral of his grandmother—his dad's mother—Cornell had cracked a joke that had them in stitches, scrambling to compose themselves before they got out of the limo. His grandmother had always been a mean woman, and Rhys hadn't even felt guilty about laughing so hard.

Cornell had always sparkled, but the Cornell Rhys saw now was the furthest thing from that. It was like his inner light, his fire, had been extinguished, and that worried Rhys. He'd have to monitor his mental state, make sure he was okay.

He let him sleep until he'd parked the car in the driveway, as close to the front door as possible. Thank fuck his dad had moved into a ranch after the divorce. It hadn't been for any other reason than he'd fallen in love with the house and, more importantly, with the location. Rhys had loved the house as much as his dad had, the tranquility of the country setting with acres of lush green surrounding them.

But now it was a godsend, this house, because it would allow him to take Cornell in. And take care of him, whether the man wanted it or not.

Cornell let out a soft groan when Rhys shut off the engine. "Are we there?" he asked, his voice sleepy.

He was adorable like that, Rhys thought, not that he'd utter that sentiment. Cornell would call a cab right then and there, and he'd lose his one opportunity to spend time with him. "We are. Do you think you can make it inside?"

Please say no. He'd hate to put his foot down on the first day, but Cornell really shouldn't walk any more. He'd already pushed himself far beyond his limits for the day.

Cornell hesitated. "I'm not sure," he said, his voice soft.

"Do you want me to help you?" Rhys wanted nothing more than to help, but Cornell would have to come right out and say it. Rhys wanted clear lines of communication from day one.

It took Cornell a little while to make up his mind. "Yes, please," he said, his voice barely audible.

"Okay."

Rhys got out of the car and walked around to open Cornell's door. The man managed to turn his body and get out, leaning heavily on Rhys's arm.

"How are you gonna..."

Cornell's question transitioned into a rather undignified squeal when Rhys simply bent over and picked him up, careful not to touch him where it hurt.

"Rhys, you can't..."

"Lean against me," Rhys told him. "Don't fight it."

God, he'd lost weight. Cornell had always been lean, with the build of a runner, but he'd lost too much weight since the accident. Muscles too, Rhys guessed. He'd have to make sure Cornell ate well. Lots of protein, to replenish what his body had lost.

He was surprised when Cornell stopped protesting and instead relaxed his body and put his head against Rhys's shoulder.

"Thank you," the older man said softly.

Something rushed through Rhys at those words, a sweet sense of victory. How he wanted to take care of Cornell, much more than the man was ready for. He'd have to be patient. "You're welcome."

They were both quiet as Rhys carried him inside, where he took Cornell straight to his bedroom. It was the guest room Cornell had always stayed in when he'd spent the night. At least, when Rhys had been home, because he was pretty sure Cornell had spent many nights in his father's bed when Rhys had been with his mom or at college. Those two had been inseparable.

"I want to stay up for a bit," Cornell protested, and Rhys had to bite back a laugh because he sounded like a tired toddler.

"It's been intense," Rhys said, keeping his tone warm and friendly. "Don't you think a nap would be smart right now?"

"I feel like I've done nothing but nap the last few weeks," Cornell said, his eyes darkening. "I want to stay up for a change, watch some TV."

"You can watch TV when you wake up," Rhys said, gently putting him down on the bed. "Do you want to sleep in this, or do you prefer pajamas?"

"You're strict," Cornell complained, shooting a dark look in Rhys's direction. "Are you getting back at me for all the times I was strict with you when you were a kid?"

You have no idea how strict I can be, Rhys thought, keeping the emotions off his face. "Pajamas or no?" he asked, ignoring Cornell's comment and question.

"I can sleep in this," Cornell capitulated, and Rhys helped him get comfortable in bed. "And how long should I nap, oh bossy ruler of everything?"

Nope, Rhys didn't mind being called bossy at all. "Let's do two hours. It will take you a little to fall asleep, and once you do, you can nap for one sleep cycle."

Cornell looked at him questioningly.

"Research has shown that there are ideal lengths for naps. You can either do a short power nap or nap in full sleep cycles, which on average last an hour and a half."

"Huh," Cornell said, sinking deeper under the covers." I didn't know that."

Rhys smiled. "They actually taught me some practical stuff in college. Imagine that."

Cornell's mouth pulled up on one side into a crooked grin, his eyes fluttering shut. "Smart ass."

Rhys didn't answer but stood there, watching Cornell fall asleep. When he did, his breathing leveling out into a deep pattern, Rhys let out a slow exhale. Hurdle one was accomplished. Cornell was here, safely under his roof. Now he had to make sure the man got better. Rhys vowed he would take care of him. He owed that to his dad's best friend, right?

And if he enjoyed having the man near for different reasons, why, that was just a bonus.

Cornell was embarrassed to realize how tired he was, even after his nap. God, he was like a senior citizen, dozing off on the couch while watching a Netflix series on unsolved murders. His belly was full, courtesy of the pasta Alfredo Rhys had made. Talk about unexpected talents. Cornell hadn't even known the kid could cook.

When he'd mentioned it to Rhys, the guy had merely smiled and said something about Cornell not knowing him as well as he thought he did. Whatever that was supposed to mean. Cornell had to admit that Rhys kept surprising him, and that was weird, considering how long he'd known him for.

"Time for bed, maybe?" Rhys's voice startled Cornell awake when his eyes had once again drifted shut. He forced them open, but it was hard, so hard, to stay awake.

"Yeah," he said, admitting defeat. "I can't seem to stay awake."

"Allow me to share a bit of professional advice," Rhys

said, his eyes nothing but kind. "Stop trying to. Listen to your body and what it needs."

He had a point, Cornell acknowledged to himself. As a sub, he was well aware of his physical limitations, maybe more so than those who weren't in the lifestyle. He was trained in recognizing his limits, in communicating them even, so why was it so hard under these circumstances?

It wasn't like Rhys was a stranger. He'd seen the kid grow up, for fuck's sake. He couldn't claim he'd ever changed his diapers, but that was more because he'd been clear from the start that wasn't in his description as his godparent. Buying him presents, taking him on fun day trips? Yes, absolutely. Getting up close and personal with human excrement? Hell no. Not even from a baby, no matter how cute he'd been.

"Cornell, you with me?" Rhys asked, and Cornell realized he'd closed his eyes again.

"Yeah. Getting up now."

He couldn't hold back the low groan of pain as he pushed himself into a sitting position, swinging his legs over the side of the couch. His injuries had been extensive, he knew, but the amount of pain he'd been in had unpleasantly surprised him. Even now, three months after the accident, his body still reminded him daily.

The other car had hit them head-on, and it had been a massive RAM pickup truck, driven by an eighteen-year-old with not enough experience on icy roads to drive a vehicle that size. Jonas's sleek BMW had been horribly outmatched. The impact had sent them flying and had crushed the front of the car, killing Jonas instantly and shattering Cornell's legs. At first, they'd told him he'd be lucky to ever walk again. He'd managed to beat the odds there, but pain had become his constant companion.

His knees were the worst. They hurt all the time, a low-grade, throbbing pain, but especially when he bent them and put weight on them. Getting up, walking up or down the stairs, hell, even sitting down on the damn toilet had become something to fear.

And worst of all: he would never kneel again. That, more than anything, was almost unbearable since it meant the end of his days as a sub. He'd already struggled before the accident to find Doms willing to play with a sub his age, but one who had limitations like he had now? One who couldn't kneel? His chances of ever having a scene again were now zero. As if losing Jonas hadn't been enough of a blow.

Maybe Rhys had a point. Maybe giving into this bone-deep tiredness was better. Maybe he should stop fighting for a bit, because god knew he'd tried. He groaned and grunted as he shuffled to the guest bedroom, Rhys following him at a distance close enough to grab him, he noted. Cornell stopped to look at him.

"I forgot to ask, but are you sleeping in the master bedroom now? In your dad's room, I mean?"

For the first time, Rhys looked insecure as he shoved his hands into his pockets. "No. It feels sacrilegious, you know? That room, it smells like him, even now. I don't want to lose that last connection to him."

A wave of grief barreled through Cornell, and he leaned his hand against the wall for support. "Yeah," he said when he trusted himself to speak again, when that hard choke-hold on his throat had relented. "I understand."

Something else occurred to him. "Did you go through your dad's things already?"

Jonas's will had been straightforward, as he'd left every-thing to Rhys. He'd only asked Rhys to duplicate personal pictures for those who wanted them, like Cornell. Cornell was well aware of Jonas's will, since he'd been the one to craft it for him years ago. God, neither of them had even figured they'd need it anytime soon, but after the divorce, Jonas had wanted to make sure Rhys would be taken care of. So they'd spent a good day setting it up, going over all the options, and then they'd stuck it in a drawer, so to speak. Yet here they were, much too soon.

Rhys shook his head. "No. I left everything as it was and moved back into my old room. Mom offered to help me go through Dad's stuff, but that felt wrong to me. I was hoping you might help me when you got better."

Relief filled Cornell that all of his friend's things were still there. So many memories were stuffed into this house, into Jonas's furniture and his clothes, his personal effects. Oh god, his *very* personal effects...

"I'd be happy to help," he said quickly. "Also because I'm sure there are some things your father would rather keep private."

Rhys gestured at him to move it into the bedroom, and Cornell took the last few steps—with effort. He was tight from exertion and pain when he reached his bed. Before he could collapse on top of it, Rhys grabbed his arm.

"Night routine first," he said with a hint of a smile.

"Night routine? What am I, six?" Cornell protested.

"Dude, that's what you always called it," Rhys said, laughing now. "Even when I was a teen and I would stay with you when Dad was traveling and Mom was out, you still told me to do my night routine."

Cornell couldn't help but smile. "You're enjoying this way too much," he told Rhys.

Rhys wiggled his eyebrows. "You have no idea. Now, get a move on. It's time for bed."

The smile wouldn't leave Cornell's face as he used the toilet, washed his hands, then brushed his teeth.

"Don't forget your meds," Rhys called out from the bedroom, and Cornell dutifully took the painkillers and sleeping aids he'd been prescribed. When he shuffled back into the bedroom, Rhys held out his hands. "I'll help you undress."

Cornell stopped in his tracks. "Erm, thank you, but I can manage that myself."

Rhys didn't move an inch. "I'm sure you can, or rather, that you think you can, but that's not the point. You're staying here so I can help, so I can make things easier for you."

Cornell swallowed. "With some things, yes. Things I can't manage on my own. But this, I can do myself."

Rhys slowly shook his head, and the disappointed look on his face did funny things to Cornell's belly. Like he had failed somehow.

"Are you gonna fight me on everything?" Rhys asked, and his tone stirred uncomfortably in Cornell's stomach.

He felt himself slink, his shoulders dropping. "I'm sorry."

Now why on earth had he almost tacked on *Sir* to that statement? Probably because he was responding to Rhys's tone like he would to a Dom. The kid had no idea what that quiet, authoritative tone did to him, but Cornell felt himself react to it. He'd better cut that shit out right fucking now. That part of his life was over, and he'd do well to remember. And even if it wasn't, that was not a side of him Rhys needed to know about. It would lead to too many embarrassing questions about his dad that Cornell would never answer.

"I'll try to be more cooperative," he said. "Just... It's hard, okay? It's hard to ask for help, to acknowledge I need it. I'm a grown-ass man, and it's infuriating to have to ask you for help."

Rhys cocked his head. "Me specifically? Or help in general?"

Cornell hesitated. This was getting a lot more personal than he'd intended it to. Still, he didn't want to lie to Rhys either. "It was a struggle in the rehabilitation center as well, but it's even harder with you."

"Why? Am I making you feel bad about it?"

Cornell felt small now for making Rhys feel like he'd done something wrong after everything the kid had done for him. "No, this is not on you. This is me being proud and a little stubborn, maybe."

The corner of Rhys's mouth curved. "You, stubborn?"

Cornell sighed. "Yeah, yeah, I know. It's hard, Rhys. I've known you forever, and I've always been the one to take care of you. Asking you for help, it..." He gestured, unable to find the right words for his frustration.

"It makes you feel like the roles have been reversed, and that makes you feel dependent and old."

Rhys's words were calm, carrying no judgment, and Cornell let out a breath. "Yes. I wasn't ready for this yet. For any of it..."

Much to his dismay, his voice broke. He fought back the sadness that threatened to overtake him. "I wasn't ready to lose my best friend. We were supposed to grow old together and terrorize nursing homes until we'd get kicked out."

He lost the fight, tears streaming down his face. Rhys's hand landed on his shoulder, gentle but strong, and for some reason that broke the last hold Cornell had on himself. He wasn't sure if he'd stepped forward or if Rhys had, but Rhys was holding him, pulling him tight against him, and Cornell surrendered to the grief.

It felt so good to be held. God, he had missed that these past months. He put his head against Rhys's shoulder, inching even closer to him, and closed his eyes. He let it come, the tears and the aching sadness, the gaping emptiness inside him where Jonas had been. And Rhys held him, those strong, young arms surrounding him like a sea wall that protected him from the battering waves in king tide.

Minutes passed, but it could've been hours, and Cornell just let go. Rhys had him, and right, now, it was the best feeling in the world. He'd go back to feeling old and guilty tomorrow.

Rhys didn't say a word until Cornell had calmed down and was about to step out of his embrace. "Are you ready to let me help you now?"

Cornell sniffed inelegantly. "Yes."

He held back the honorific that had almost followed. Again. What the fuck was wrong with him?

"Okay. Let's get you into your pajamas."

And as Cornell finally brought himself to let go of those sheltering arms, he realized that there were a lot of things wrong with that statement, but what was most wrong was how much he loved it. Rhys crouched as Cornell untied the thin laces of his sweatpants, then gently worked them down. Even before Cornell could tell him to be careful, Rhys used his hands to spread the pant legs wide as he eased them down, not once touching the many scars on his legs.

Cornell could've cried all over again at the sweet care Rhys showed, gesturing Cornell to lean on his shoulders with both hands as he stepped out of the pants. He'd already put out a pair of pajamas, Cornell saw, and his heart did a little skip. How he had missed this.

He stepped into the pajama pants, then stood still as Rhys pulled them up with the same care as before.

"Raise your arms," came the quiet order, and up went Cornell's arms.

"I can't raise this one farther than this," he said, almost apologizing.

"Hmm. That was your torn rotator cuff, right? We'll work on that."

"Do you think you can improve my range of mobility?" Cornell asked.

"We haven't even gotten started…"

Rhys's intonation was off, as if he'd wanted to say more but then changed his mind. Cornell waited for him to continue, but he stayed silent as he helped Cornell out of his hoodie and into his pajamas. Together they walked to the bed, Cornell's exhausted body leaning heavily on Rhys's. He turned when Rhys gestured, allowing him to guide him down onto the bed, where Rhys gently lifted his legs and positioned them. Once Rhys pulled the covers over him, he realized how intimate this was.

"Are you comfortable?" Rhys asked.

"As comfortable as I'm gonna get."

"We'll settle for that for now, but the goal is to get you truly comfortable again," Rhys said, his voice brimming with promise.

Cornell closed his eyes, too tired to keep them open. "Thank you," he mumbled, feeling himself drift off. The meds were kicking in.

"You're welcome," Rhys said, his voice soft and tender as a whisper, a feather that danced over Cornell's skin, "…sweetheart."

Surely he was asleep and dreaming already?

3

R hys slept like crap that night, too excited about the notion of Cornell in the house, sleeping down the hallway from him. He shouldn't be this pumped about it. It was a little embarrassing, and it made him appear young, which was exactly what he didn't want. Cornell was already way too aware of Rhys's age, or at least the age difference between them.

Rhys could see it in his eyes, his face. *A kid*, that's what he still considered Rhys. Well, he'd prove him wrong. He'd show Cornell he wasn't a child anymore, that he was all grown up. In which case, it would help if he got over that giddy joy inside him he always had when Cornell was near him and manned the fuck up. He was on a mission, after all.

He woke up still tired but jumped out of bed anyway, eager for the day to start. He took a quick shower and dressed in dark-blue chinos and a polo shirt—comfortable and yet mature, he figured. His usual attire of his funny T-shirt with ripped jeans wouldn't cut it, since Cornell was always dressed to a T. The rather casual clothes the man was wearing now looked somewhat out of place on him. Too sloppy.

He listened at Cornell's door, a soft snoring rhythm telling him his guest was still asleep. Good. That would provide Rhys with the opportunity to prepare breakfast. Cornell had lost too much weight and muscle definition. Time to get him healthy again.

Rhys cut fresh strawberries in chunks, then a banana. He put them in a little bowl, then added some almonds and hazelnuts. Next, he measured out full-fat Greek yogurt and put it in another bowl. There, that looked picture perfect, right? Meanwhile, the Nespresso machine was done making Cornell's favorite morning blend: a smooth, mild coffee. Rhys added a drop of milk, then put everything on a tray and headed for Cornell's bedroom.

He knocked, surprised when Cornell actually answered. He must've woken up in the meantime. "Come in."

"Good morning," Rhys said, smiling when he saw Cornell's adorable bed hair sticking in every direction. His right cheek still showed the creases of his pillow, and Rhys wanted to hug him something fierce. "I come bearing gifts."

Cornell's eyes lit up. "Coffee. You sure know the way to my heart, kid."

I'm not a kid, Rhys wanted to tell him, but he bit it back and kept smiling. It was only their first full day. He had time.

"It's not that hard, Cornell," he said. "Your addiction is well known."

"I prefer the term 'strong affinity,'" Cornell said. "Now shut up and give me my fix."

Rhys, who had held out the cup to him, pulled it back slightly. "You getting bossy on me now? Say the magic word."

It might all be joking and jesting, but he wouldn't tolerate Cornell giving him orders. That, at least, had to be clear from the start, even if Cornell wasn't aware yet of their dynamic.

Cornell laughed. "May I please have my coffee, oh great, almighty king Rhys?"

"You may."

Rhys handed him the coffee. The little sound Cornell made as he took the first sip shot straight to his cock. He watched him as he emptied the little coffee cup, the size tailored to the Nespresso lungo he'd prepared.

Cornell licked his lips as he handed the cup back. "I wouldn't mind another cup."

"You'll get it when you've finished your breakfast," Rhys said.

"You getting bossy on me now?" Cornell joked, using Rhys's own words against him.

He had no idea, Rhys thought, but he didn't say that, of course. "I prefer to think of it as encouragement," he said instead. "If you finish this lovely, healthy breakfast I prepared for you, you'll get another cup of coffee."

Cornell studied him, his eyes narrowing. "That sounds an awful lot like blackmail to me."

Rhys sent him a beaming smile. "Blackmail is such a big, ugly word. As I said, think of it as encouragement, me wanting to take care of you and help you get healthy again."

He almost held his breath as he awaited Cornell's answer. Had he picked up on Rhys's subtle reference? Was his deep desire to be taken care of strong enough to overcome his stubbornness and inner resistance to Rhys?

"Okay," Cornell said finally. "But I need to use the bathroom first."

Right. Rhys should've thought of that. "Do you need a hand?" he asked.

Cornell raised an eyebrow as he lifted back the covers.

"I've been peeing on my own since I was three years old, kid. Pretty sure I can manage it."

"Don't get smart with me," Rhys snapped. "The vast majority of accidents with recovering patients at home happen either in the morning when people are stiff from sleeping and their muscles aren't warmed up yet, or at night when they're tired."

Cornell's eyes widened. Rhys knew his reaction had been a bit abrupt and harsh, but Cornell's disrespectful tone was grating on him. It was as if the man wanted to use every opportunity to make it clear he didn't need help. That needed to stop right now.

"It... it was a joke, Rhys," Cornell said. "I meant no disrespect."

"Well, it is disrespectful. You're mocking my sincere offers to help. And stop calling me a kid, for fuck's sake. I'm twenty-three, not some child."

Cornell's Adam's apple bobbed as he swallowed. "Sorry. I'm truly grateful for your help, Rhys. I'm sorry for being difficult."

Sweet relief rushed through Rhys's veins. This was more than he'd counted on, this sincere apology. "Okay," he said, making sure his voice was warm and affirming. "I appreciate you saying that. Now, do you need help?"

Cornell's cheeks colored. "Just to get up and to the bathroom. I can do the rest myself."

You don't want me to watch you while you pee? It was on the tip of Rhys's tongue to say, but he couldn't. It was much too fast, too soon. But when he looked at Cornell, it was as if his thoughts had followed a similar path, as the blush on his cheeks intensified and his pupils were dilated. *Oh, interesting*, Rhys thought. Cornell *liked* that, the idea of someone watching him do his business. The man definitely liked a little humiliation. Rhys filed that information away.

"Of course," he said smoothly. "Whatever you need."

And someday soon, he'd help Cornell with his other needs as well. The man didn't realize it yet, how much he needed Rhys, but he would.

He helped Cornell get up, steadying him until his body had adapted and he was ready to walk. It didn't take long, bringing him to the bathroom and back. Cornell wanted to head back to bed, but Rhys pointed at the desk where he'd put down the breakfast.

"No eating in bed," he said.

"Oh, okay," Cornell said and allowed Rhys to guide him to sit at the desk, where Rhys set up everything for breakfast, including the *Washington Post* Cornell liked to read in the morning.

"Enjoy your breakfast. Call out when you're done. I'll leave the door open, so I should hear you."

"Don't you have to work?" Cornell asked.

Rhys shook his head. "I took two weeks off from work."

"For me?" Cornell's voice held a mix of awe and disbelief.

"Yes," Rhys said, meeting his eyes.

"But... but that's too much," Cornell protested, his hands moving in agitated gestures.

"No, it's not," Rhys said. "I wanted to make sure you're okay, and I wasn't comfortable leaving you by yourself right now for such long stretches."

"I can't believe you did that," Cornell mumbled, still fidgeting.

Rhys put a hand on his shoulder—his good one—and noticed Cornell stilled instantly. He wasn't tensing up, more calming under Rhys's hand. He was very sensitive to touch, apparently. Rhys filed that, too, away for later.

"Stop worrying about it. It wasn't your decision to make anyway. Now, eat your breakfast."

Cornell held his eyes for a few seconds, a flash of surprise visible before it disappeared again. Rhys wondered if he would say anything, would comment on the subtle commands Rhys was giving him. Was he even picking up on them consciously? But Cornell stayed silent, though his eyes were alert.

Rhys left him to it, retreating to his dad's study—he couldn't think of it as his own yet—to work on his business plan for his private practice. He worked part time for a large practice that offered a broad range of physical therapy. It was a great opportunity for a young guy like him, but after working there for a year, he knew it wasn't where his heart was. He'd already thought about starting his own practice before his father had died, but the costs involved had made it a long-term goal.

Now everything had changed, and while he'd a million times rather have his dad back, the money he'd left Rhys from his life insurance and savings would allow him to realize his dream. It wasn't how he had planned it, but at least something positive would come from losing his dad. And so he opened his spreadsheets—the bane of his existence right now—and started analyzing the latest numbers he'd come up with.

"That deep thinking frown is gonna give you wrinkles," Cornell spoke, and Rhys's head jerked up from his screen.

Cornell leaned against the doorway, his pajamas replaced by a fresh pair of sweats and a Patriots hoodie Rhys had bought for him as a joke years ago. The man knew diddly squat about football, but Rhys was a fan, and he'd bought the hoodie for him as a Christmas gift.

"Must be some serious stuff you're working on," Cornell said.

"My business plan," Rhys answered, almost automatically, since he was a little distracted by the fact that it seemed Cornell wasn't wearing any underwear. There was an outline visible, a not-so-subtle swell under the fabric, meandering down his right leg, and Rhys swallowed.

"Business plan? For what?" Cornell asked, pushing himself off against the doorway and slowly walking into the room. Rhys was glad to see him walking correctly, not favoring his good leg. Even his upper body was straight, which would help prevent other injuries like back pain. But then his eyes got drawn to that slightly bobbing bulge in the man's sweatpants, and he had to avert his eyes and focus on Cornell's inquisitive gaze.

"For my own practice," Rhys said, getting up from behind his desk because he wanted to be on eye level with Cornell. It would help keep his attention off the man's cock. "I'm taking the money Dad left me and opening my own practice."

Cornell's eyes widened in surprise, and then Rhys watched as he struggled for composure. He felt himself get misty again as well.

"It's gonna be like this for a long time, isn't it?" Cornell finally said, his voice pinched. "Us tearing up every other minute over something that reminds us of him...or even at mentioning his name."

"Yeah," Rhys said softly. "I think that's how grieving works."

Cornell grabbed his arm, hanging on to it with a firm grip. "I don't like feeling this way."

"I don't think we're supposed to like it. It's...life."

Cornell let out a shaky sigh. "You're handling this far better than me."

There was such profound sadness on his face that Rhys couldn't help but step close and press a soft kiss on his cheek. "Everyone grieves differently. And don't forget that we both lost someone else. I've always known I would lose him at some point, because that's how life works. Sons bury their fathers. But you, you lost your..."

He hesitated, not even sure what word to use. *Best friend* didn't even come close to covering it, but Cornell had no idea Rhys knew what they had been. Well, maybe it was time to open up about that.

"You lost your soul mate. It's different. Not more or less, but different."

Cornell's hand on his arm tightened. "S-soul mate? We were friends, best friends."

Rhys scoffed. "I'm neither stupid nor blind, Cornell."

"I-I don't know what you're talking about."

Rhys stood close enough to drill into his eyes, and he loved that he was taller, even if by less than an inch. "Yes, you do. You two haven't been mere friends for a long time, probably since my parents divorced and you split with what's-his-name."

Of course he knew the name of the Asshole Arnold, as his dad had dubbed him, but that didn't mean he had to dignify him by mentioning him by name. Rhys had over-heard a conversation between his mom and dad when his dad had been catching her up on what had happened. It had been crystal clear Arnold had cheated on Cornell before "trading him in for a younger model," his dad had said. Even at age seventeen, Rhys had been furious about that betrayal.

Cornell's tongue peeped out to lick his lips, a little

nervous tic Rhys had spotted before. "I-I don't know what to say."

"Oh, I bet you don't," Rhys said, feeling more than a little smug. "And by the way, don't you worry about going through my dad's personal things in his bedroom, 'cause I already saw his entire collection of sex toys."

Cornell paled. "I need to sit down."

Rhys thought he was joking at first, but when Cornell actually started to walk, he helped him get to the desk chair and lower himself, his face wincing. That must hurt his knees, Rhys thought. It was a hard move to make on your knees since it required so much control in your muscles.

"You okay?" he asked, a little concerned when Cornell butted his face in his hands.

Cornell's head shot up. "Of course I'm not okay! I just discovered my godson knows about his dad's sex life."

"And quite a bit about yours as well," Rhys supplied helpfully.

Cornell's face disappeared behind his hands again. "Oh god," he groaned.

Rhys perched against the edge of his desk, crossing his arms. "Why is that so embarrassing? Did you really think I thought you were virgins? Or not having sex?"

"Can you please stop saying words like *virgins* and *sex*? They're disturbing coming from your mouth."

Rhys grinned. If Cornell thought that was disturbing, he was in for a surprise. "Why? I rather like both."

Another groan, deeper this time, and what a beautiful sound it was. "Please, kill me now."

They both froze, and then Cornell slowly raised his head. "I'm sorry," he said, his whole face depicting shock. "I wasn't thinking. God, what a horrible thing to say after... I'm so sorry, Rhys."

"It's okay," Rhys said, breathing in deeply to get rid of the instant tension in his body that ill-timed joke had caused. Still, he understood. It was a joke, nothing more. Cornell would be the last person in the world to make light of his father's death.

When Cornell's face kept showing horrified shock, Rhys closed the distance between them and put both his hands on the man's shoulders, taking care to keep the right one light so it wouldn't exacerbate his injury or cause him pain. "It's okay. I know what you meant. It was a joke."

As before, Cornell seemed to react to his touch, relaxing under his hands. Rhys felt his shoulders drop lower and his face lost the expression of deep shock and regret. He gently squeezed his good shoulder, not willing to let go yet, and to his satisfaction, Cornell leaned into his touch. It was such a minor movement that he probably didn't even realize himself, but it pleased Rhys.

"Why don't you go take a shower while you still have energy? It'll help warm up your muscles as well. Make sure you leave the door open so I can hear you in case you need help. After, we'll do some exercises, okay?"

Cornell nodded, and Rhys let go of him. Then, because the man still looked a bit forlorn, he bent over and pressed a kiss on his forehead. "You'll feel better after a long, hot shower. You always do."

4

The hot water pummeled down on his back, his muscles relaxing in joy, and Cornell thanked Jonas silently for installing such a great shower in his guest bathroom. The one in the master bathroom was even better, but he wasn't ready to enter that room yet. Too many memories there.

His head was a mess after that confusing interaction with Rhys. Okay, his joke had been stupid. He'd been so damn embarrassed that his brain hadn't been working properly when he'd cracked it. It had been insensitive as fuck, and he should thank god on his knees—not like that even was an option—Rhys had taken it so well.

But in his defense, he'd been completely flustered that Rhys apparently knew about Jonas and him. How much did the kid really know, though? Rhys might suspect his dad and Cornell had been intimate—there was an understatement—but not how often or in what roles. Maybe not all hope was lost yet, and he could maintain a shred of dignity?

Then his mind went to Jonas's vast collection of toys—toys that Rhys had alluded to seeing, and if that was the case, he was screwed. God, Jonas had been a total toy-whore, an addict to the latest and the newest, and Cornell had made endless fun of him for buying yet another new shiny object. He had more dildos than a sex store, a broad assortment of cock rings, spreaders, butt plugs, and even an impressive collection of handcuffs, rope, and various instruments to inflict pain. You know, for when he had a guy stop by who didn't bring his own whip.

Hell, he'd built a damn playroom in the basement, a room that was locked at all times to prevent Rhys from seeing it, but if he had moved in here... Cornell groaned all over again. If Rhys had seen the basement with the toy cabinet... Embarrassed didn't even cover it, and he felt his cheeks heat up all over again—and not from the hot shower. He would never live that down, though he had to admit Rhys had been pretty cool about it.

But what was up with that weird vibe between them? Was he imagining things, or had there been some *moments* between them? There had been that awkward exchange about needing help or not in the bathroom. God, the thoughts that had gone through his mind. It wasn't that he had *wanted* Rhys to watch, but he'd always loved a little humiliation, and it had created a picture in his head. And he could've sworn Rhys had picked up on it, too, though he hadn't said anything.

Then there were these things Rhys told him to do, these subtle commands that fell so easily from his lips...and that Cornell so willingly obeyed. Did Rhys know what it did to Cornell, that warm, authoritative voice? Of course he didn't. He probably didn't have a clue, since Jonas and Cassie had kept that part of their lives hidden from him.

God, he was so much like his mother. Cassie was a phenomenal Domme, and there had been times where

Cornell had wished he was bi, like Jonas. But he was about as gay as one could be, he supposed, one hundred percent on the Kinsey scale, if that was even possible. Well, ninety-nine percent then. He loved women, appreciated and respected the hell out of them, but not as a romantic partner or even as a Domme. He needed that male strength, the harshness of a male body, the firmness and hairs and muscles.

And now he was hard, because of course he would be, thinking about that. He sighed, even as his hand automatically slipped around his dick, pumping it a few times, aided by the soapy shower gel that was still on his body. Then he stilled, remembering the open door, not just to the guest room but to the hallway as well. He'd left both open, even though he'd been a little apprehensive about it, because Rhys had made a good point about being able to hear him.

Now, that could backfire on him. He'd have to be oh so quiet. So he squeezed tighter, making small but intense movements, steadying himself against the wall with his other hand. His dick grew even harder, excited to finally get some action again. It had been, what, weeks? Cornell's movements stilled as he realized he hadn't jerked off since the accident, then resumed again with fervor.

No wonder he'd been picturing someone watching him pee. Or imagining sparks between him and Rhys. He was simply horny. Hell, he'd already been horny when the accident happened. That last scene Jonas and he had done together had been a total bust. Oh god, the Dom—or the guy pretending to be one, rather—had been blessed with such a perfect cock. It had been a fucking work of art, probably eight inches of solid flesh, rock hard, and perfectly curved. Too bad the idiot hadn't had a clue how to use it and had even less experience in domming.

It had been the last conversation he and Jonas had ever had, discussing whether they should find a different club. Well, that question was moot now. He'd never find another club...and he'd never have another session with Jonas. It would be him and his right hand, maybe a Grindr hook up if he was lucky. Then again, most of those assumed he was a top and a silver daddy, and he was neither.

He let go of himself, his erection wilting as if it had never happened. It was for the better. He had no business going there, not while staying in what was now Rhys's house. He looked at the open door, the part of the room he could see, the slight draft making him shiver. And then it hit him all over again that this was his life now, this painful, recalcitrant body and this heavy, grieving mind. This blackness inside him that was supposed to get lighter and better over time, but that felt as oppressive as the first day.

He rinsed himself off, exhausted suddenly, and shut off the shower. Toweling off took ages, his shoulder refusing to cooperate, and by the time he was done, he was too tired and in too much pain to get dressed. He slipped under the sheets, too hot after the shower to cover himself fully, and let the sadness overtake him. When he fell asleep, his pillow was wet from tears.

RHYS STOOD IN THE HALLWAY, his hands balled into fists, his nails cutting deep into his flesh. Was there anything worse than listening to Cornell's intense grief? Finally, the man had fallen asleep. How Rhys had wanted to storm in there to console him, to take him into his arms and tell him things would get better. But he couldn't.

Oh, he'd slipped into the room with every intention of

being there for Cornell, but one glance at the man's body had confirmed he was buck naked. And that, Rhys couldn't do. Not for himself, but especially not for Cornell. That was a level of intimacy the man was nowhere near ready for, and to be honest, neither was Rhys.

This thing they had, this connection or spark or whatever you wanted to call it, this was too fragile, too precious, to recklessly endanger by making a bold move like that. No, this required patience and a light touch, even if Rhys's hands ached to hold him, knowing his touch would make Cornell feel better. The man responded to touch like nothing else.

He'd relaxed when he heard Cornell's breathing even out, then deepen. Luckily, the door was still open, and he all but tiptoed inside. Cornell was sleeping on his stomach, the sheets covering him only partially. Fiery scars painted his shoulder and the leg that was visible. God, Rhys had come so close to losing Cornell as well, and that made it hard to breathe at times.

Cornell's face was turned sideways, subtle stubble covering his skin. He'd have to help him shave, Rhys realized, because Cornell preferred to be clean shaven. His hair was too long as well, a dark lock falling over his forehead. Rhys brushed it back, his heart doing a funny little jump at the sight of Cornell sleeping. He gently pulled the covers over him, hesitating only briefly before pressing a soft kiss on his forehead.

"Sleep well, sweetheart," he whispered. He closed the door behind him as he walked out, and that was good, because he'd barely stepped out when his mother called.

"Hi, Mom," he answered.

"Hey honey, how are you holding up?"

He walked back to the living room so he wouldn't wake Cornell up. "Good. Better," he corrected himself.

"Have you been back to school yet?"

"No. I only have one paper I have to finish and one final exam, but I've postponed both. I've talked to my profs and they understand."

She made an appreciative sound. "Good. Glad to hear it. And work?"

He took a deep breath. Here we go, he thought. "I've taken off work for two weeks."

"Why?" his mom asked, audibly baffled. "Is there something going on you're not telling me? Are you sure you're okay?" she then asked, her voice filling with worry. "If you want to stay here for a bit, then—"

"Cornell is staying here," Rhys interrupted her.

"Come again?"

He installed himself on the couch. This wasn't gonna be a quick conversation. "I asked him to move in here while he's recovering. He can't live on his own, Mom. He's nowhere near ready for that. His ability is still limited, and his house is a death trap with all the stairs."

"Rhys…"

He waited, too experienced in her little tricks now to succumb to the temptation to keep talking and defend himself. That was what she did, either stay silent with quiet disapproval or say a few words, and he'd feel almost forced to fill that silence. He no longer did.

"I'm surprised he agreed," she said finally. "He's a man who's attached to his independence and privacy."

"He's also a man who knows when he needs help," Rhys pointed out.

"Does he now? And did he come to that conclusion himself, or did he need a little help getting there?"

"I didn't put pressure on him in any way," he said stiffly,

offended that she would even suggest it. "You know I would never do that."

It only took her a second to cave. "I know, I'm sorry. Does he know?"

"About me? Hell no." Rhys laughed. "Do you really think he would've moved in if he'd known?"

He heard her let out a sigh. "No, he wouldn't have. It would've made him way too uncomfortable. It still will when he finds out, Rhys. This is not something you can keep from him for long."

He forced himself to not get defensive. "I know, Mom. I have zero intention of keeping it a secret. It hasn't been the right time yet. The man is grieving deeply."

"So are you, honey," his mom said, her voice soft and warm.

"I know, but it's so hard for him. I just…"

"You wanna take his pain away," she completed his sentence. "You want to take care of him."

She'd always seen right through him, even as a kid. Rhys didn't know if it was because she was a Domme and so experienced in reading body language and picking up on subtle clues or if it was a natural talent. Then again, he was the same way, often sensing people's emotions way before they showed them.

"I do," he confessed, almost holding his breath at her reaction.

"Oh honey," she said, and he waited, slowly counting in his head to refrain from saying more. "You know this has disaster written all over it, right?"

He pushed out a breath, already regretting saying anything to her. Of course she wouldn't support him in this. She, too, thought he was still a child. The only person who'd treated him as an equal had been his dad. "Possibly."

"Not possibly, Rhys. It *does*. He's more than twenty years older than you, the same age as your father."

He leaned forward on the couch, gesturing with his left hand as if his mother could see him. "And you're telling me this, why? Do you think I don't know how old he is? How far we're apart in age? You've told me yourself, over and over: a D/s relationship doesn't necessarily mean you're in a love relationship as well. It doesn't even need to include sex. Or have the rules somehow changed now that it concerns me?"

"No, of course they haven't," she said, sounding tired and much older. "But it's hard for me to know that you're making such a colossal mistake."

Rhys's jaw ticked. "It's my mistake to make. And don't you dare butt in. This is my private life, and you stay the hell out of it."

"Hmm," she said, and Rhys almost cringed at the iciness of her tone. "I suppose you're right. Maybe it's for the better. Maybe you need to fuck that man out of your system once and for all so you can move on."

Before Rhys could say anything, she hung up on him, and he closed off his phone with an angry gesture. Few people infuriated him as much as his mom at times. He loved her, but he'd always been more drawn to his more introverted dad, a man who had been a solid rock for him for as long as he could remember.

He'd been gentle, kind, a man who loved hugging and touching. Rhys remembered endless nights of watching movies on the couch as a kid, plastered against his dad. Stability, that's what he had been. A safe space of endless love and acceptance, no matter what Rhys had struggled with.

He'd told him his big secret only months before his death, begging him not to tell Cornell, and he hadn't. His dad hadn't liked it, but he'd made it clear that his loyalty to Rhys surpassed his loyalty to Cornell, and if that didn't say everything Rhys needed to know about how much his dad had loved him, he didn't know what did. And he'd been proud of him, so endlessly proud.

"God, I miss you, Dad," he whispered, and then it was his turn to fall apart, sobbing quietly into the cushions of the couch to muffle the sounds until he once again ran out of tears.

When his tears had run dry, he took a few minutes to compose himself, splashing some cold water on his face. There was no denying he'd cried, but then again, he didn't feel the need to hide that from Cornell. He was not ashamed of his emotions, especially of his grief and sadness.

It was at least two hours later when Cornell came stumbling out of his bedroom, looking adorable, even if his eyes were still red and swollen from his crying fit.

"I fell asleep," he said, looking apologetic.

"That's okay," Rhys told him. "You needed it, apparently."

He wanted to ask so badly if Cornell was okay, wanted to soothe his pain more than anything, but it was too much, too soon. But there was something he *could* do.

"You look like you could use a shave," he said.

Cornell sighed. "Yeah. It's hard with my shoulder, because the precise movements make me tense up and it hurts. In the rehabilitation center, I had an aide help me."

There was his in. "I'd be happy to help you."

Cornell stilled. "You'd help me shave?"

The man had no idea of the things Rhys wanted to help him with. "It would be my pleasure."

He bit his lip for a few seconds, clearly thinking about it. "Okay," he said finally, and Rhys's heart did a little jump.

"Come with me," he said, smiling when Cornell immediately obeyed and trudged after him into the room Rhys was using as his bedroom. He installed him on a chair, then got the shaving kit from Cornell's room.

"You do know how to use this, right?" Cornell said, eyeing Rhys a little suspiciously. "Because shaving yourself is different than shaving someone else."

Rhys grinned. Cornell had no idea how much experience he had with sharp objects—not that he was about to tell him that. "I promise I won't cut you."

Cornell didn't look entirely convinced, but he allowed Rhys to start wetting his cheeks and covering his chin with shaving foam. "You can close your eyes if that's easier," Rhys told him, but Cornell's clear blue eyes stayed focused on him as he stepped in with the razor in his hand.

It was strangely intimate, shaving someone else. Rhys had worked summer jobs in a nursing home and as such, had plenty of experience with shaving others, but none of his patients had ever looked at him as intensely as Cornell did. With slow, confident moves he started scraping off the foam.

"Put your head against my stomach," he told Cornell as he took position behind him.

Cornell let his head sink back, resting it against Rhys's body. How crazy that such a simple gesture had such an impact on him, Rhys mused as he steadily worked on Cornell's face. The way Cornell had submitted to his care... It shouldn't mean as much as it did, feeling that surrender in his body, that trust. God, he longed so much to touch him, much more than this simple act.

They were both silent as Rhys shaved him, but Cornell's eyes never left his face. When he was done, he wiped Cornell's chin off with a warm towel. He finished by rubbing on some calming shaving balm he always used himself. There was something strangely arousing about making sure Cornell would smell like him. "There," he said. "Handsome as ever."

Cornell slowly sat up, touching his chin as if to double check Rhys hadn't nicked him. "I'm way past handsome, but thank you. This feels good."

Rhys bit his tongue to avoid blurting out how handsome he thought Cornell was. Instead, he gave Cornell a quick rub through his hair, because he couldn't resist it. "You're welcome."

5

After the shave, Cornell installed himself on the couch, watching Netflix. He kept rubbing his chin, loving how clean and smooth it felt. He smelled of Rhys, he thought, and wasn't that a strange realization, that he knew what Rhys smelled like. It was so quintessentially him, that slightly spicy, subtle scent that Cornell now knew came from his shaving balm. He liked it, he decided, and he kept breathing it in the rest of the day, comforted on a level he couldn't even explain.

He spent the rest of the day doing nothing but lounging and doing his exercises in between. It was amazing how tired he could get from that, but remembering Rhys's earlier advice to not fight his body, he gave in and went to bed early.

He was getting dressed the next day when Rhys knocked on his door. "Come in," he called out before realizing he was wearing only boxer briefs.

Oh well, it wasn't like Rhys hadn't seen him in those before. Besides, the guy was a physical therapist. He constantly saw people half-dressed. And it wasn't like

Cornell's aging and battered body had any chance of evoking a reaction in Rhys, even if he knew the guy was gay.

"Morning," Rhys said with a friendly smile, his eyes flicking over Cornell's body. "I brought you breakfast again."

Cornell breathed in, the smell of coffee hitting his nose. "And what do I have to do today to get my coffee?"

Rhys put the tray down and his smile widened. "Funny you should ask."

"Uh oh."

"I want you to take two minutes and do some stretches with me, okay?"

"Two minutes and that's it? 'Cause I'd hate to see that lovely coffee go cold."

"Two minutes," Rhys promised.

"Let me get dressed," Cornell said.

"No, do it like this. It will help me see if you do it right."

"Oh," Cornell said, feeling strangely vulnerable to have his body on display. That feeling increased when Rhys took up position next to him and showed him a stretch Cornell was supposed to emulate, tight muscles rippling in that young, strong body. Cornell clenched his jaw as he copied the movement as best as he could.

"Try to relax your muscles," Rhys said. "You're tensing up, and that's pulling your shoulders up."

"It's not that easy," Cornell said, a little more snappy than he had intended to, and he felt horrible right after. Rhys was only trying to help him, and it wasn't his fault that Cornell was a bitter old man who was envious of his youth. Ugh, when had he become that guy?

Then Rhys's hands gripped his shoulders, gentle but firm, and the tension melted away. A soft sigh tumbled from his lips and he closed his eyes for a second, leaning into that touch.

"That's so much better." Rhys spoke in that soft, warm tone that curled around Cornell like a fuzzy blanket, one of those weighted ones that made you feel hugged and safe. Cornell wanted that tone all day, yearned to earn that praise. He needed to be a good boy and earn favor from his...

His eyes flew open. What the ever-loving fuck was he doing? Why was his mind going there? Again? There was something wrong with him when he started seeing the twenty-three-year-old son of his best friend, his *soul mate* as Rhys had so perfectly described it, as a...as a Dom. Because for a few seconds, that's how it had felt, as if Rhys was his Dom, praising him. And god, Cornell craved that.

"Something wrong?" Rhys asked, his hands still on Cornell's shoulders.

Cornell had to clear his throat before he could speak. "I think it's been two minutes, no?"

Rhys let go of him. "You did well. Enjoy breakfast. Don't take a shower today, because I want to do some exercises with you later to see your range of mobility and make a plan for further improvement. So don't get dressed, just throw on a bathrobe."

And with those kind but clear commands, he left the room. Cornell put on the bathrobe Rhys had gestured at and lowered himself into the chair with shaky limbs. What the hell was happening? He had to get a grip on himself, because this was insane. Maybe he should've jacked off yesterday anyway, because clearly, he had some unresolved sexual tension or something in his system that made him react this strongly to...to nothing, really.

There was nothing between him and Rhys. It was all in his head, because there was no way Rhys could ever be interested in a man more than twenty years his senior, and even if he was, Cornell could never go there. He was his godson, for fuck's sake. His best friend's kid, who he'd watched grow up. Granted, he'd grown up into one hell of a man, but he was barely that, way too young for him, for anyone.

And those commands, the way he reacted to his voice, that was all because he'd been without a Dom too long. God, he couldn't remember the last time he'd had a scene that had left him fulfilled emotionally as well as physically. He tried to think back as he ate the yogurt with fresh fruit Rhys had prepared for him.

The last time had been with that Dom who'd given a demonstration in the club and who had taken a liking to Cornell and Jonas. He'd used both of them in his scene, and he'd made them fly so high it had taken hours before the high had worn off. Sub drop had been severe that week, but the guy had even checked in on them after a few days, wanting to make sure they were okay. Now that had been a worthy Dom.

Maybe he should find out if the guy would be visiting anytime soon. Then he caught himself. What was the point? He was useless as a sub now, unable to kneel, unable to perform even basic physical services for his Dom. And as for any kind of pain infliction, he couldn't imagine himself being able to take on anything, not with the constant pain he was already in. Sure, it was a different pain, and the endorphins from deliberate pain might help, but even the thought left him shaken. They wouldn't know his limits, and it would be all too easy for him to get hurt even worse. No, he had to accept that part of his life was over.

He ate his breakfast and read the newspaper that Rhys had thoughtfully supplied again. He really was a sweetheart, wasn't he?

Sweetheart.

It triggered something in his brain, that word, as if he'd heard someone use it recently. He frowned. It must have been on something he watched on TV, because he couldn't have heard it anywhere else.

He waited for a bit after breakfast, strangely nervous about the exercises Rhys had proposed. He had to find a way to get out of his head, to forget about these strange thoughts, because it would get awkward soon if he didn't. Should he jerk off first? But why would he when this wasn't even sexual? Besides, his dick wasn't showing any interest.

He shrugged it off, a stab of pain reminding him that was not a move he should do, and padded into the house, looking for Rhys. He found him in what used to be a room where Jonas had some gym equipment, but that had been transformed in a physical therapy room. Cornell whistled between his teeth as he looked around.

The carpet on the floor had been replaced by shiny vinyl, and there were mirrors on two walls, as well as a long rail that looked like a ballet barre. There were two different treatment tables, a treadmill, and an exercise bike, as well as a range of small fitness equipment like kettle balls and yoga blocks and more.

"This looks amazing, Rhys," Cornell said, impressed with how professional it appeared.

"Thank you. You're the first to use it, so you get to be my guinea pig."

"Thank you?" Cornell said, half-joking.

"Okay, so I want to do some tests today to check your range of motion, especially for your shoulder, but if we still have time and you're not too tired, we can look at your legs as well."

Cornell cocked his head. "I would've thought my legs would take priority?"

Rhys shook his head. "No, not for me. They're still healing, and you have some residual swelling. I think the plan there is to slowly build up in non-strenuous exercise, like walking and swimming. But your shoulder is my first concern, since it didn't heal as well as I would've expected it to. Can you take the robe off and hop on this table for me?"

"Don't expect any hopping from me," Cornell joked as he reached for the belt of his robe, feeling that same strange embarrassment again. "Crawling will be more like it."

"I'll take you whichever way I can get you," Rhys said, and boy, that sounded way more sexual to Cornell than it should. He groaned as he managed to sit on the table, his legs dangling over the side.

"Okay, raise your good arm for me. Now your bad arm," Rhys said, and over the next minutes, he let Cornell do a series of movements that tested both shoulders. Rhys made notes on an iPad, and Cornell smiled at his focus and professionalism. Hell, he did more tests than the rehabilitation center had ever done, that was for sure.

"What's the verdict, doctor?" he joked when Rhys was done and was studying the notes he made with an adorable frown between his eyebrows.

"Can I touch you?" Rhys asked, and Cornell was almost surprised he'd ask for permission.

"Sure."

Rhys put his iPad down. "Lie down for me on your stomach. I want to try something."

It was far from elegant, the way Cornell managed to lie down, but he did it, a sigh of relief flying from his lips when he could relax again.

"I want you to put both of your arms on these arm rests, okay?"

Rhys pointed at two arm rests he pulled out of the table

that were at a 45-degree angle from his body. Cornell moved his arms and discovered it was a comfortable position because there was no tension in his shoulders and he didn't have to put any weight on them. His face fit perfectly into the oval hole in the table, so he could look down at the floor and keep his head relaxed.

"This is very comfortable," he reported back.

"Good. That's the goal. Now, I'm gonna try massaging your shoulder, which may hurt. I think you have connective tissue that formed after your injury. It's gotten too much and too immobile, and it's preventing your shoulder from functioning well. My hope is that by massaging this, we can stimulate the circulation and get it to become supple again."

Cornell tried not to think about that one word he'd so casually dropped. *Hurt.* He was so damn tired of his body, of the pain. Still, he mentally fortified himself. "Sounds good."

He heard a cap open and then warm oil dripped on his back. "It's warm," he said, surprised.

Rhys laughed. "I use a little warmer for the oil so it's not so cold to the touch. That way, patients don't tense in shock."

Cornell heard him rub his hands together, and then they landed on his shoulder. The touch was gentle, strong hands warming up the muscles with steady, systematic moves. That felt good, actually, and just when he thought that, Rhys's thumbs dug in.

"Holy fucking..." Cornell swallowed the rest, needing his energy to keep breathing.

"Yeah, it's as I thought. I'm sorry, because I know this hurts. The good news is that this will give you improvement soon, especially if we do this regularly."

Oh god, he wouldn't survive this on a regular basis. This fucking *hurt.* Then he checked himself. Yes, it hurt, but not more than what he'd been through already. Much less, in fact. He could do this, and when Rhys said it would help in the long term, he'd suck it up and bear it. It would be worth it. And so he tried to relax into the pain as Rhys kneaded and massaged with amazing strength in his hands.

"Good, I can feel the tension leaving," Rhys said, and the pleasure center in Cornell's brain lit up like a fucking Christmas tree. He was such a pathetic pleaser, willing to do anything for a little affectionate praise. Still, he couldn't help himself, and he focused on his breathing, willing his muscles to slacken even more.

"Yes, you're doing great. This makes it so much easier for me to reach the areas where I need to be," Rhys said, his voice taking on that warm affirmation. "Do you feel the pain lessen as well? It won't hurt nearly as much if you manage to stay relaxed."

How about that? The kid was right. And so Cornell focused on relaxing and breathing, soaking up Rhys's casual words of praise like a dying plant soaking up the sunlight.

THIS WAS a special kind of torture, Rhys felt. Not so much touching Cornell, because that was too clinical and focused on helping him to be sexual. No, it was the way Cornell responded to his every word of praise. The man was so hungry for it, and it was hard for Rhys to find the right balance. He wanted to give him what he needed but without taking it too far. Cornell couldn't realize yet that Rhys was on to him, though the question was how long he could keep that up.

His mother's words came to mind, about Cornell becoming uncomfortable when he found out. They were far beyond uncomfortable now. If Cornell discovered it and knew that Rhys had used praise on purpose to subtly steer him, he'd be livid. And maybe he'd have a right to be. It did feel like manipulating him, even if he was doing it with the very best intentions.

No, he should tell him. Soon. Cornell needed to know so they could at least be open about that. And maybe, just maybe, he'd be open to playing together. It wasn't like he had a ton of options right now, not with him being confined to the house, way out in the boonies, as his dad had always called it. Not many Doms would be willing to come all the way out here, not for a sub who had so many limitations.

Cornell's shoulder reacted wonderfully to the massage, the tissue already becoming more supple under his administrations. Good. That meant he responded well to massage, which he could've predicted, considering how quickly he always reacted to even the simplest touch. Rhys rested his hands on Cornell's body.

"How does that feel?" he checked.

"Good," came the somewhat drowsy answer. "It hurt at first but it got much better."

Rhys's heart swelled. "What do you say about a little relaxing massage as a reward? You know, me kneading a bit of tension out of your body?"

He held his breath. Had he gone too far?

"Erm, yes, please? Your hands feel amazing," Cornell said, his voice still dreamy.

Rhys smiled as he poured more oil on the man's back, then rubbed it in with slow, deep moves. He doubted Cornell was even fully aware of what he was saying. It had sounded like he'd been half asleep, his body relaxed and his mind someplace else. Well, Rhys could help there and make him relax and fall asleep completely.

"I've got you," he said, keeping his voice soft, his hands finding knots and massaging them until they became fluid and warm. It was routine for him, usually, but this time, he couldn't look away from the body he was working on. What was it about Cornell that drew him in? He wasn't even sure, and he'd had years to think about it by now.

He wasn't overly muscled; on the contrary. He had a lean runner's build, thanks to the marathons he used to run before a torn ACL in his left knee made him stop. Toned, definitely, but not like a six pack. It was more about an innate grace he had, a magnetic energy that pulled Rhys in. Every time he was in the same room as Cornell, the man would draw him in, like a helpless bee to a flower.

His mind wandered until a small movement under his hands caught his attention. Cornell's hips shifted. Maybe he was becoming a bit uncomfortable? He'd been on the table for a while now. Rhys wanted to shrug it off, but then Cornell did it again, a subtle move with his hips. Then again, and Rhys's breath caught as he realized the truth. Cornell was seeking friction. He was rubbing his cock against the table with slow but deliberate movements. Was he doing it in his sleep?

"Cornell?" he asked softly.

The answer was a soft moan and increased hip move-ment. Cornell was asleep, the massage apparently turning him on and making him react unconsciously. Oh god, what should he do now? Cornell would be so embarrassed when he woke up. Should he wake him?

His touch changed, his fingers no longer kneading but stroking now. Caressing. Touching that hurting body that he wanted to explore in so much more detail. Cornell stirred again, a sigh releasing from his lips as he leaned into Rhys's touch, wordlessly begging for more.

Rhys had no doubt that if they kept this up, Cornell would have the classic happy ending to his massage. But he couldn't keep going, could he? Should he? His mind was at war with itself, wavering between the desire to make Cornell experience sexual release and the more practical thought that it would change things between them forever. And if Cornell woke up and discovered Rhys had known, had encouraged him, there would be major embarrassment. What was the right course of action here?

In the end, not making a decision turned out to be a decision in itself, as Cornell started moving carefully but in an undeniable rhythm, rubbing his cock against the massage table. Rhys almost held his breath, scared Cornell would wake up. But the man's body stayed relaxed, his breathing speeding up only slightly under Rhys's continued ministrations.

He was tempted, oh so tempted, to go lower, to caress those globes that were only covered by a thin layer of cotton from his underwear. They would feel so good, but even more importantly, he would make Cornell feel so good. God, one hand, one finger even, and he could make him fly. But he couldn't, not without his permission. So he kept massaging his neck, his back, teasing the lines of his underwear until he was practically squirming on the table.

He battled with himself, knowing what Cornell needed to fly over the edge. All he had to do was tell him to come, but he couldn't. What he was doing was already crossing a line, one he maybe shouldn't be crossing, but he wanted Cornell to have his orgasm. The man deserved that release.

But that's as far as he could go, and so he kept his mouth shut, waiting until Cornell's body would override his deeply ingrained need to have permission to come. It took another minute or two, but then the man's body sped up, clearly chasing his release.

Cornell's moan was anything but soft as his body jerked with his orgasm, and Rhys rushed out of the room before the man would wake up and realize what had happened. He walked straight into his own room, where he locked himself in the bathroom and used his hands that were still slick from the massage oil to jerk himself off furiously. His release left him panting and shaking, slapping his oily hand against the tiles to hold himself up.

A smile curved his lips, transforming into a big grin. Holy fuck, that had been hot as hell. And they were only getting started.

6

Cornell jolted awake, seconds before orgasming. His whole body was tight, his muscles fully contracted in anticipation of what was coming— pun intended. In his confused state, he tried to hold back, attempted to veer off the ledge, because he wasn't sure he had permission to come, but it was too late. His body jerked, his eyes pinching shut as his release overtook him.

He'd dreamed, he realized as he came down from his high, still panting. A highly erotic dream where Rhys had been massaging him again, only this time, it had been a different type of massage. His talented hands had roamed all over Cornell's body, making it sing. And for as long as that glorious dream had lasted, he'd felt whole, not in pain, and it had been everything.

What the hell was going on with him that he had spontaneously orgasmed not once, but twice? Yesterday, there had been that whole incident in the massage room. Apparently, he'd fallen asleep during Rhys's massage, and that, too, had developed into a dream. And when he'd woken up, he'd come in his underwear, something that hadn't happened since he'd been in college. He had been absolutely mortified, and only the fact that Rhys had not been present had saved him from feeling utterly and completely embarrassed and humiliated.

And now this? Another sexual dream with an orgasm as a result? What was his subconscious trying to tell him? He'd dated a guy once who had believed dreams could explain everything about what was bothering your subconscious. He'd even gone as far as claiming they could predict the future. To humor him, Cornell had played along, even trying to deliberately create lucid dreams, as the guy had called it. He'd never been much good at it, but the relationship had fizzled out before the guy's obsession with dreams had become a point of frustration.

But Cornell had done some reading on dreams, because his curiosity was piqued, and he did know they tended to latch on to signals your subconscious picked up. Not always accurate, but one had to wonder where his erotic dream about Rhys had originated from. Was it a sign that Cornell was sexually frustrated, that he had needed a physical release and his body and mind had found a way to realize that? Or was there something else going on?

After all, he *had* imagined for there to be some kind of sexual tension between him and Rhys, which was ridiculous, of course. The kid was over twenty years his junior, and there was no fucking way. Men like him weren't attracted to men like Cornell. They could be, if they thought Cornell was the silver daddy type of guy, but even twinks rarely made that mistake anymore. His body language was too demure for that, too submissive, as it should be.

Rhys didn't know all that, not being in the scene, but

even if you took that out of the equation, there was no way a guy like him would be sexually attracted to Cornell. He was too old, too broken, too damaged. No, Rhys felt sorry for him, and that was all it was. And Cornell's subconscious might have a blast imagining that to be something more, but it wasn't. At least he got a good orgasm out of it. Or two, if you counted yesterday's.

He was about to slide the covers back when there was a knock on the door. That could only be Rhys, of course, and there was no way he would show him the undeniable wet spot in his underwear. So he slid back under the covers before calling out to Rhys he could come in.

He came in carrying a breakfast tray, but one peek at the contents revealed it wasn't the usual yogurt and fruit.

"No yogurt today?" Cornell asked, a little disappointed.

"Nope. Oatmeal today, the super healthy kind."

"Yay," Cornell said, piling on the sarcasm.

Rhys merely smiled, not taking the bait. Hmm, he'd have to be more direct, perhaps. "I really liked the yogurt," Cornell said, hopeful.

"I know," was the calm answer.

Still not getting anywhere. Even more direct, then. "I'm not a huge fan of oatmeal," he tried.

This time, it earned him a chuckle. "Did you think I didn't pick up on your previous three attempts to get you yogurt?"

Busted. He let out a sigh. "I'd hoped you were being slow on the uptake, yes, rather than mean for taking away my yogurt."

"Have ever known me to be slow on the uptake?"

Rhys's tone was light, but there was an edge to it, as if he was warning Cornell not to push much further. Well, that was reasonable, he supposed. Rhys did deserve gratitude and respect for taking Cornell in. Plus, the massage the day before had made a difference—a big one. He was sore now where Rhys's strong hands had dug into his flesh, but the tension in his back and especially his shoulder was so much better already. No way was Cornell losing that privilege, though perhaps that was a funny word to use in this context. It wasn't like it was a privilege extended by a Dom to a sub, a privilege that could be taken away if the sub misbehaved or displeased the Dom.

Rhys had carried that edge to his tone, though, that warning signal that he was not amused and on his way to displeased. And maybe it was because it was so ingrained in Cornell, but he didn't like the idea of Rhys being displeased or irritated with him. Twenty-plus years of being a submissive were hard to ignore.

"Cornell, where did you go?" Rhys asked, still with that zing of sharpness.

"I'm sorry, S—Rhys. Got lost in thought. I'll eat the oatmeal and stop complaining."

Oh, he'd come so close again to calling Rhys *Sir*. He could only hope he'd covered it up fast enough.

Rhys's smile was back. "Good," he said, and it took Cornell a second to realize *boy* wasn't to be expected to follow *good*. Why did that leave him feeling somewhat bereft?

"Are you getting up?" Rhys asked. "No eating in bed."

Crap. What could he do now? "I need to use the bathroom first," he said quickly.

"So?" Rhys asked, his brow furrowing in confusion.

Cornell ground his teeth. "Can I have some privacy, please?"

Rhys's eyes narrowed. "What's going on with you? You're being weird."

"Why is me wanting to have a shred of privacy weird?" Cornell snapped, unable to hold it in.

"Then there's this," Rhys said, his tone icy. "You snapping at me for no reason. What's going on? Did something happen?"

Yeah, I had a spectacular orgasm while dreaming about you touching me, Cornell thought. *That's what's wrong. Plus the fact that I can't get out of bed because you'll spot the evidence.* But of course, he didn't say any of that, not even when Rhys's eyes narrowed further and frustration rolled off him in waves. It took effort, Cornell realized, to not crumble under that glacier-like look, to not give in when everything in him wanted to.

"There's nothing wrong," he said, making sure his voice was calm despite his inner turmoil. "And I do apologize for my snappy tone."

Rhys's expression warmed. "You do know you can talk to me, right? If something is bothering you?"

Cornell tried a careful smile to test the waters. "If we started talking about everything that bothered me, we'd need a few weeks."

Rhys slowly shook his head. "Don't make light of it. I could say I know what you're going through, but I really don't. I do know that you must be worried about stuff and sad and hurting and a whole lot more."

"You forgot angry," Cornell said, strangely comforted by Rhys's words. "Pissed off. And grieving, which is an emotion that's hard to describe, I've discovered."

Rhys's hand came down on his good shoulder. "Yeah, grieving is ten emotions wrapped into one. But no matter what you feel, you can talk to me."

God, he had such a big, kind heart, Cornell thought. How sweet was that, this urge to take away Cornell's pain. He couldn't, of course, but no one could. Cornell had talked to the grief counselor in the rehabilitation center. She'd had some good and practical tips, but it hadn't taken away the pain or ever lessened it. It was always there, the pain, both the emotional and the physical. Nothing and no one could take that away, but Rhys was so sweet for even trying.

"You're gonna be my shrink in addition to being my cook, cleaner, physical therapist, and nurse's aide?"

He'd meant it as a joke, partially anyway, but something sparked in Rhys's eyes. "I'll be whatever you need," he said, and the funny thing was that it didn't sound like a joke at all.

WHAT HAD *that* been all about? Rhys had decided to give Cornell the privacy he apparently needed—for whatever reason—and walked back into the kitchen. What had gotten into Cornell? That snappy tone, the attitude, it puzzled Rhys.

Had something happened he was unaware of? That seemed almost impossible, considering how much time they spent together. It wasn't like Cornell could hide much from him. And yet that had been what it felt like: Cornell hiding something from him. And boy, Rhys did not like that at all.

Why didn't Cornell trust him enough to tell him what was going on? Was he still embarrassed about his body, his injuries? *Building trust takes time*, he heard Ford tell him in his mind. *You're going too fast*, he always told Rhys. He'd learned tons from the Dom who had trained him, who was still mentoring him, but Ford hadn't been able to impart patience in Rhys. Yet. But it looked like he would need it with Cornell.

On impulse, Rhys called him, knowing the man was always up early anyway. Ford didn't believe in sleeping in.

"Rhys," Ford answered the phone. "What vexes thee, my young grasshopper?"

That was something else Rhys loved about the Dom: he knew when to skip the pleasantries and focus on the good stuff. "What do you do when a sub is hiding something from you?" he asked.

"Like what? "Ford asked.

"Like they ask for privacy without telling you why they need it."

"Privacy how? Like, for a phone call? To do something? To jack off?"

To jack off. Rhys's brain fired on all cylinders all of a sudden. Why hadn't he thought of that? It had to be something sexual, something Cornell didn't want Rhys to know. Had he been playing with himself when Rhys had knocked? That was an option, though he would've been taking a big risk at that time of day, considering Rhys had brought breakfast at the same time the last couple of days.

"Rhys, you still with me?" Ford asked.

"Yeah, sorry. I figured it out just now."

"Figured what out, what he's hiding?"

"Yeah. Something you said helped me connect the dots."

Ford hummed. "Good. Now tell me about him, because the last time we spoke, you didn't have a sub. In fact, last time we saw each other, you got drunk off your ass and waxed poetic about some older guy you had the hots for."

Oops. He should've known better than to spill his beans to Ford when they'd hung out a few weeks back. The guy had a memory like an elephant and the tenacity of a bulldog. In his defense, Rhys had been overwhelmed with grief and frustrated with how little he could do for Cornell, who was clearly struggling with everything in the rehabilitation center. So he'd gotten drunk—*off his ass* was still a charitable description, most likely, since he'd had the mother of all hangovers the next morning—and had dumped on Ford, who'd always been a good listener.

"Well, he's not my sub exactly," Rhys said, feeling his cheeks heat up even though Ford couldn't see him.

"Either he is, or he isn't," Ford said. "This is not an area where you want ambiguity."

"He's a sub," Rhys said. "An experienced one. He's just not my sub... yet."

"Rhys, I'm starting to get worried here. You're gonna need to give me more context, kid."

He couldn't blame him for that last word, not when he was acting like one. "He's the guy I told you about, the older sub. He got hurt in the same accident that killed my dad and is staying with me to recover."

Ford whistled between his teeth. "Sneaky. And you're hoping the close proximity will help him see what an amazing Dom you are."

Rhys winced. He could lie, but experience had taught him that wasn't smart with Ford. "I haven't told him I'm a Dom," he said, bracing for the storm he knew was coming.

What the fuck had he been thinking, calling Ford? This was what happened when he did things on impulse: they never ended well. Wasn't that something Ford had tried to teach him as well?

"Rhys," Ford said, and Rhys shrunk at the authoritative tone. "I take it you're not abusing his trust and violating his boundaries?"

Rhys thought of the massage's happy ending. "No?" he

said, but it came out a question. "I don't think I am," he corrected. "But I'm aware he responds well to commands from me, even subtle ones, and to touch. I can calm him with a simple touch, center him."

"Part of me is proud that you read him so well, but a much bigger part is concerned about his consent. If he doesn't know you're a Dom and he's been a sub for a long time, he may be subconsciously responding to you. That leaves him vulnerable for abuse by you or to the feeling of being used or abused. I know you'd never abuse him, Rhys, but this is a gray area you're navigating in."

Rhys felt his mentor's reprimand in his soul. "I know. It's... I don't know how to tell him. What if he laughs me out of the room because I'm too young?"

"You like him," Ford said. "You want him to take you seriously."

"Yeah," Rhys said softly. "I really do."

"So be the Dom he needs, the Dom he deserves. If you want him to take you seriously, then act in his best interests. That means being open and transparent, as you damn well know."

He felt so small, so infinitesimally small. "I know. I'm sorry."

"Don't apologize to me, kid. Suck it up. Find the balls I know you have and have a conversation with him. He deserves that... and so do you. This sneaking around isn't good for either of you."

"I know," Rhys said again, and the truth was that he did know. With anyone else, he wouldn't have dreamed of being this secretive about something that was such an important part of his life. But it was Cornell, and he was so damn scared of losing him. "I'm scared," he confessed. "Scared he'll reject me out of hand, laugh at me."

"Trust me, I understand," Ford said, much kinder now. "But if he does, he's not the sub for you. Respect and trust, Rhys. Respect and trust," he repeated the club's motto.

Rhys nodded, even though Ford couldn't see it. "I'll tell him today," he promised. "And I'll prove to him I'm the perfect Dom for him." He heard a noise behind him, a gasp, so loud it froze the blood in his veins. "Ford, I gotta go," he said and ended the call.

He turned around slowly, knowing who he would face. But the devastated look on Cornell's face crushed him. "Did you say Dom?" Cornell whispered, taking a hesitant step toward Rhys.

"I can explain," Rhys began.

"You're a Dom?" Cornell asked a little louder.

Moment of truth. "Yes," Rhys said, his voice surprisingly stable despite his inner turmoil. "I know I'm young, but—"

Cornell made an abrupt gesture with his hand. "I don't care about your age. If I was old enough at twenty-one to know I was a sub, you're old enough to know you're a Dom," Cornell said, flooring Rhys with that casual assessment.

That was where he'd expected Cornell to protest, to insist he was too young. "Then what..."

Cornell's eyes spewed fire as he took a few shaky steps closer. "How the hell could you keep this from me? How could you keep something so... so monumental from me?"

Rhys's soul hurt at the accusation that echoed through the room. "I didn't know how to tell you, not without you pulling back from me or laughing at me."

Cornell frowned, his eyes still blazing. "Laughing? Why would I laugh?"

"Because I'm twenty-three. A baby Dom, I've been called more than once. It's funny how no one questions a sub my age, but when you're a Dom, there's a minimum age, apparently."

"Try being a forty-five-year-old sub. Doms may have a minimum age, but I've long since passed what's considered the maximum age," Cornell said, the bitterness dripping from his voice.

Rhys couldn't hide his surprise, and he cleared his throat. "That's the first time you've told me you're a sub."

Cornell waved his hand. "Like you didn't know. If you're half as good a Dom as your mom is, you spotted me from the moment you knew D/s was a thing, and your dad, too."

Rhys sighed. "I've known for years," he admitted.

"So why didn't you ever tell us?"

Now came the hardest part, but before he could say anything, Cornell must've read it from his face. "Jonas knew," he said with a sigh. "You told your dad."

"Yes, but only a few months ago. And I made him promise not to tell anyone, including you."

"Why?" Cornell asked, the anger slowly dissipating from his eyes and his face. "Why didn't you tell me? What were you so scared of?"

"That you'd see me differently," Rhys said quietly.

"Of course it changes how I see you. I'm already seeing our interactions in a whole new light."

Rhys opened his mouth to say something, then thought better of it. Anything he said, Cornell would use against him. He might be an estate lawyer, but he was still a lawyer who could argue your socks off to the point where you happily handed them over so you could end the discussion.

"Did you manipulate me?" Cornell asked, his eyes laser-focused on Rhys's.

"No. I wouldn't do that. But I will admit to using subtle

commands and appealing to your submissive nature to get you to do what I wanted."

Cornell cocked one eyebrow. "And how is that not manipulating me?"

Oh god. "Because I had your best interests at heart?" Rhys offered. "You know I'd never make you do anything that would hurt or harm you."

The sheer disappointment on Cornell's face was like a dagger to Rhys's heart. "You did it without my consent. That's pretty manipulative, if you ask me. It leaves a bad taste in my mouth."

Rhys could barely swallow, so closed up was his throat. "I'm sorry," he said, his voice hoarse. "I never meant to hurt you. All I wanted was to take care of you."

"Forgive me if I question everything right now, including your motives. I'm gonna need some time to think about all of this and decide what I'm gonna do."

Rhys was terrified to ask, but he had to, even if the potential answer scared him. "Are you leaving?"

"The thought did cross my mind. I'll have to weigh my options."

This couldn't be happening. Cornell could be leaving, and Rhys would have only himself to blame. He'd blown it, his one chance with Cornell.

He straightened his back and forced himself to meet Cornell's eyes. "I will support whatever decision you make, both emotionally and practically," he said, his voice only wavering a little near the end.

"Thank you," Cornell said. "I will apprise you of my decision."

He carefully turned around, and Rhys watched help-lessly as he walked out. There was nothing he could do now but wait. And hope, but even though he was an optimist by nature, he realized with heart-crunching realism that his chances here were slim. He'd fucked up so badly, and he had no one to blame but himself. His body was shaking as he lowered himself in a chair, then buried his head in his hands. Four days, Cornell had been here. Only four days, and Rhys had fucked it all up, risking him leaving.

So. Fucking. Stupid.

7

To his credit, Rhys left Cornell to himself that morning, only checking in every now and then but not attempting to start a conversation. Good, because Cornell wasn't in the mood, his head still spinning from the mind-blowing discovery that Rhys was a Dom. A trained one, by the sounds of it.

Cornell had caught the name of the Dom he'd been on the phone with—presumably his mentor. Ford. Cornell knew only one Ford in the scene, and if he was Rhys's mentor, that spoke volumes. Ford was not only a good guy, but a good Dom as well, one who took what he did seriously. He wouldn't take on anyone, so him agreeing to mentor Rhys meant the kid had talent and the right attitude.

Kid. Somehow that word felt wrong now to use for Rhys. His age hadn't changed, and yet something inside Cornell now protested at that term. If he was a Dom, he deserved enough respect to treat him like a grownup.

Rhys was a Dom. Cornell kept trying to wrap his mind around that. The gorgeous young man with his warm brown eyes and a body that made you sit up and take notice was a

Dom. Jonas's son was a Dom. Cornell felt stupid, not being able to get past it, but it felt so big, so momentous.

And maybe it also felt like something he should've known, should've picked up on. How had he missed the signals? He thought back on their interactions the last few days. Rhys's subtle commands. His deep care for Cornell. The way he'd reacted when Cornell hadn't shown respect.

Cornell's cheeks flushed as he realized the signs had been there. He hadn't missed them, exactly, because he had noticed Rhys's behavior. He just hadn't come to the right conclusion because he'd never considered the possibility. That, of course, was not only woefully naive, but somewhat stupid as well.

Cornell had known he was submissive since his first encounter with domination in college. He'd taken to it like he was born for it—and so had Jonas. And Cassie had been a Domme already, a few years older than them. She'd known as well. So why had he never considered Rhys might be interested in the lifestyle? After all, he had parents who'd been involved their whole lives.

Maybe it was because deep down, he'd expected Jonas to tell him. It hadn't occurred to him that Rhys would keep anything secret from his father, considering how close they were. And Cornell had also never counted on the fact that his best friend—his soul mate, as Rhys had called him— would keep something so big hidden from him.

Of course, now that he knew, he understood. Confidentiality was a cornerstone in the scene. Aside from that, as much as it hurt, Cornell understood that Jonas's loyalty to his son had outweighed his loyalty to his best friend. So, here they were, and now Cornell had to find a way to work through this.

God, how he missed Jonas right now. He would've been

able to help him make sense of it. He had so many questions. In fact...

He called out to the kitchen, where Rhys was making lunch. "Can I ask you something?"

Rhys looked up, meeting his eyes. "Anything."

"How did your dad react when you told him?"

"He was fine with it. A little surprised, but positive and supportive. He did check I was training under someone respectable," Rhys said.

"You're training with Ford, right?" Cornell asked.

"Yeah. I've completed my two-year training with him, but he's still mentoring me."

Cornell nodded, happy with that answer. "He's a good Dom. A great one, in fact. At least you trained with..."

He stopped talking, not happy with how that had sounded. Rhys had ceased cutting veggies or whatever the hell he'd been doing and looked at him, clearly awaiting his response.

"That came out wrong, like you being a Dom is a bad thing, something negative. It's not," Cornell said.

Rhys lifted an eyebrow. "It's not?" he asked, sounding surprised.

"Not inherently. Clearly you have talent, or Ford wouldn't have taken you on."

"Thank you."

"Don't thank me yet," Cornell warned him. "The fact that you may be suitable as a Dom doesn't mean I've forgiven you for lying to me and manipulating me."

"Duly noted," Rhys said solemnly, but with enough relief that Cornell felt his rush of hope.

So Jonas had supported his son. No surprise there. It would've been majorly hypocritical of him to object to his son being in the D/s lifestyle. Still, it did mean that Jonas, too, had recognized his potential. He would've never supported Rhys if he was a bad Dom, no matter the fact it was his son. They'd both gotten burned by bad Doms enough times to be highly critical and selective in who they graced with their seal of approval.

"And your mom?" Cornell asked.

This time, it took longer for Rhys to answer. "Her reaction has been mixed," he finally said.

Cornell considered it. What would Cassie's main objection have been? "Did she feel threatened by you?" he asked. That wouldn't be out of the question, since some Doms had professional jealousy toward other Doms, especially those who seemed highly gifted and intuitive.

Again, Rhys took his time. "A little, maybe, but I think she questioned my motives, mostly."

Questioned his motives? That sounded rather ominous, as if Rhys had another reason to do it besides finding his identity in domming, just like much of Cornell's identity and self-worth was wrapped up in submitting.

Now there was a depressing thought, and the deep sigh escaped him before he could swallow it back. Rhys looked up instantly, meeting Cornell's eyes, making him realize he'd been staring at him that whole time.

"Why *did* you want to be a Dom?" he asked to cover up the strange satisfaction it provided that Rhys was so tuned into him.

Rhys held his gaze for a second or two, then went back to what he was doing. "I visited a club, and it felt like coming home."

Cornell waited, but when Rhys didn't say more, he asked, "Not something you're comfortable talking about?"

"That's not it. It's more that it's a long story, far more complicated than I can explain while making our lunch, which is done by the way." He hesitated, avoiding Cornell's eyes. "Do you want to eat together, or would you prefer to eat by yourself?"

They'd shared every meal except breakfast, which Cornell had eaten in his room. But lunch and dinner had been served at the kitchen table over easy conversation. They'd never lacked topics to talk about, and Cornell had loved how natural it had felt. If he were honest, he'd started looking forward to it a little. More than a little, even. Did he want to give that up? Then again, the odds of conversation flowing easily weren't exactly stellar.

"I'll take that as a no," Rhys said, and it wasn't hard to detect the pain in his voice.

"Rhys..." Cornell started, but he didn't know what to say. He shouldn't apologize, seeing as how he had nothing to be sorry for. But he didn't want to hurt him on purpose either by not eating together.

"It's okay, Cornell," Rhys said as he walked over and put a bowl of salad in front of Cornell, the dressing on the side, exactly the way Cornell preferred it.

"I'm not punishing you," Cornell said, grabbing Rhys's arm when he started to walk away.

"No?" Rhys asked, but there was no meanness to it—more like he was checking with Cornell how he had meant it.

"No," Cornell assured him. "But I need more time. There's a lot to consider."

Rhys blew out a slow breath, and a little of the tension in his body seemed to seep out. "I can understand that, and I certainly respect it," he said. "I'll be here."

Cornell ate his salad, his mind working as he appreciated the healthy lunch. He hadn't been lying; there was a lot to consider. How much Rhys had manipulated him, for example. That evasive answer when Cornell had asked Rhys about his motives. Why Cassie suspected his reasons for wanting to be a Dom were wrong. The list was endless. But the biggest question was the one that kept playing in his head, like the famous song from The Clash on repeat: *Should I stay...or should I go?*

RHYS KEPT HIS DISTANCE, leaving Cornell alone as much as he could. He only reminded him to do his exercises, then brought him his meds when he saw Cornell had forgotten them. Dinner was grilled salmon and pasta, eaten in front of his iPad in his office, watching some documentary.

He hurt. God, he hurt. More than anything else, including the fact that Cornell didn't want to see him, was the knowledge that he'd wounded him. As much as it pained him to admit it, his mother had been right. He should've never kept this from Cornell, and now he was paying the price for his arrogance. He'd been such an idiot.

When his phone rang, for one stupid second he thought it would be his dad, since he'd called so often this time of day. Then it hit him all over—his dad would never call him again.

He answered the phone, his eyes veiled by tears. "Yeah?"

"It's Ford. You okay?"

And that was why Ford was such a good Dom. He not only picked up signals, but he acted on them as well, followed up when his gut told him something was wrong.

"No," Rhys answered honestly. "But I will be."

"He found out?"

Rhys sighed. "Yeah, and he wasn't happy. I fucked up badly, man."

"You did. So now you show him that you own that and that you'll do better next time. Because you won't make this mistake again, now will you?"

Rhys cringed at the Dom-tone Ford was using. "No, Sir."

"Good. You busy tonight?"

Rhys considered it. He didn't like to leave Cornell alone out of some deep protective instinct, but the truth was there was no medical reason why the man couldn't fend for himself for a bit.

"Not really. But I can't stay away long," Rhys said.

"Can you spare two hours? I have a session I'd like you to observe."

The way Ford asked it made Rhys curious. "What kind of session?"

"You'll see... but it could come in handy someday."

Rhys found himself agreeing on the condition Cornell would be okay with him leaving, and so he found himself approaching the man after all. He looked tired, the lines on his face more pronounced than usual. It reinforced the guilt Rhys was already feeling heaps of anyway.

"Would it be okay with you if I go out for a few hours?" he asked.

Cornell's face tightened. "Going clubbing?" he asked, his tone barely civil. "Or going to a different kind of club for a scene?"

Rhys's heart hurt. This distrust, this was what he had caused. "Neither," he said. "Believe it or not, but I'm not a fan of clubbing or hookups. And I wouldn't dream of doing a scene right now, not with how emotional and upset I am. I've been taught better, and Ford would have my ass."

Cornell lowered his gaze. "Sorry," he mumbled. "That wasn't very nice of me."

"No," Rhys agreed, seeing no reason to deny it or pretend. "But I can understand where it's coming from."

"So where are you going?" Cornell asked, looking at him from between his lashes.

All of a sudden, Rhys could see what a handful he could be as a sub, how bratty he would be at times. God, he itched to correct him, but he couldn't. Before, it had been delicate, correcting him enough to communicate his boundaries but not so much it would raise suspicion. But now that Cornell knew, it was impossible. He didn't have the right to say anything, and yet everything in him protested at Cornell's tone and impudence.

In the end, he settled on a what he hoped would be a subtle correction. "I'm not entirely sure why I owe you this information, but I'm going to Ford's. He's doing a scene he wants me to observe."

"What kind of scene?" Cornell asked, and both Rhys's eyebrows shot up.

He reached for his phone and pulled it from his pocket, holding it up. "Would you like me to call Master Ford and tell him you'd like to know?" he asked, drilling into Cornell's eyes.

"No, Sir, that won't be necessary," Cornell said, and then they stared at each other in shock. "That was... I didn't mean to say that. Not that you don't deserve... I misspoke," Cornell stammered.

"No harm done," Rhys said, but on the inside, he was practically doing a victory dance. Cornell had called him *Sir*. That had to mean something, right?

He mulled it over in the car as he drove to Ford's, who lived about twenty minutes away. Why had Cornell called him that? He'd almost done it before, Rhys knew, but then he'd been able to swallow it back. What made him want to say it? Was it because he was so used to it? Or was Rhys connecting with him on a Dom-sub level? He knew that the best scenes, the best pairings, resulted from an intuitive, genuine connection. You couldn't force that, but it was hard to define when it happened.

When he arrived at Ford's, putting his car in the garage he had the remote key code for, he still didn't have an answer. He forced himself to park the thought. Ford demanded full concentration in scenes, as distractions could have disastrous effects, he'd taught Rhys.

He found Ford in the basement, also known as the dungeon, where the man had a playroom set up that made Rhys drool.

"Hey, kid," Ford greeted him. Rhys bristled inside, but he didn't call the Dom out on it. Not his place, even though the Dom knew damn well how much Rhys hated being called that.

"Thanks for inviting me over."

"You're welcome, kid."

Rhys clenched his teeth. "Are you trying to get a rise out of me?" he asked, unable to keep himself from speaking up.

"It's an easy way for me to see where your temper is. The more emotional you are, the more you react to this. On a good day, you can take at least five *kids* before you react visibly and another five before you speak up," Ford said calmly.

Rhys felt like a balloon that was being deflated. "Sorry," he said. "It's been a long day."

Ford's strong hand clamped down on his shoulder. "Just be aware. That's all I'm asking. Be honest with yourself about how you feel and where your temper is at. Learning to control it is the next step, but you can't do that until you've learned to check in with yourself."

Rhys nodded. "Thank you."

It was frustrating, the reminder of how much he still had to learn. He'd been impressed with Ford from the first time he'd met him. At just shy of forty, the man was the single best Dom Rhys knew: steady, calm, very organized, and as ethical as they came. It made him sound like a total school boy, but he wanted to be Ford when he grew up.

When he'd told Ford that, he'd smiled. "Don't aspire to be me," he'd said. "Aspire to be the best version of you."

Days like today, with the painful reminder of how much growing he still had to do, brought the wisdom of that advice home. "I'll do better next time," he told Ford, who shot him what could only be described as a proud smile.

"I know you will."

The doorbell rang, and Ford nodded. "That will be Shawn."

Rhys stayed in the dungeon, taking his usual spot on a comfy chair in the corner. The sub who walked in a minute or so later was not at all what he'd been expecting. First of all, he was African American—a bit of a rarity in a club that was predominantly white, sadly. But aside from that, with his broad frame and well-developed muscles, Shawn defied every preconceived notion and stereotype of subs. If Rhys had met him somewhere, he would've never guessed him to be submissive.

Despite his impressive physique, there was something slightly off about his gait, the way he walked. He wasn't so much favoring one leg as he seemed out of balance.

"Shawn, this is Master Rhys I told you about. He'll be watching only," Ford said. Shawn dipped his head in Rhys's direction, not meeting his eyes. Rhys appreciated that sign of respect. "You can ignore him from now on," Ford said. "Focus on me."

"Yes, Master," Shawn said.

"Let's start by getting you naked," Ford said.

As Shawn started undressing, the Dom shot a look of warning in Rhys's direction. He didn't understand it until Shawn dragged down his pants and revealed a prosthetic leg. He'd had a transfemoral amputation on his left side, and the remaining thigh and his other leg were covered in thick scars. Their redness suggested this was a relative new injury that was still healing. That explained the slight imbalance he'd spotted, then.

Rhys was grateful he'd seen much worse so his face wouldn't show any reaction. Not that Shawn even glanced in his direction as he neatly folded his clothes with a precision that suggested a military background.

When he was done, Shawn presented himself to Ford: his hands clasped behind his back, his posture ramrod straight, and his head bowed. He couldn't kneel, Rhys guessed, and yet everything in his posture communicated respect and submission to his master.

Ford studied Shawn, then walked around him to inspect him from every angle. He let out an appreciative hum. "Beautiful, Shawn. Perfect posture."

From his viewpoint, Rhys had a perfect view of Shawn's face, and it lit up at that simple praise. Any doubt Rhys had left about him being submissive vanished.

Ford took Shawn through the scene he'd planned, which was centered on sensory play, Rhys discovered, and made him state his safe word. Rhys watched in fascination as Ford tied Shawn down to his table in a relatively comfortable position on his back, double checking to make sure the straps he'd used weren't too tight. Then he blindfolded him, and the scene began.

Feathers were followed by pencils sharpened so much

they looked like dagger points, then ice cubes, a hot breath blown over his body, a Wartenberg wheel, and velvety soft fabric until Shawn was squirming under the assault. His body responded to every little touch then, his cock leaking copiously. It was beautiful to see him brought to the brink again and again, and then have Ford back off.

And as he watched, his own dick iron hard in his pants, Rhys realized why Ford had wanted him to see this. If Cornell ever agreed to sub for him, their scenes wouldn't be conventional either. Cornell had too many physical limitations for that. No, Rhys would have to come up with scenes that he could do, like Ford had adapted to Shawn's abilities. That amputation had to have been mere months ago, his skin and the amputation wound still too painful to endure much standing. Ford had made it work, and that's what Rhys would have to do as well.

When he drove home that night—after watching Shawn have the orgasm of his life after an hour and a half of edging —his mind was already plotting and planning. The chance of Cornell ever submitting to him was low, but if he ever did, Rhys would be ready for him.

8

Cornell woke up before his alarm went off, his morning wood in full glory after yet another dream with Rhys in the lead role. Only this time, he'd been full-on dominating Cornell, teasing him and edging him, then telling him he couldn't come. The result was a hard-on that could pound nails, and this time, Cornell didn't even hesitate to wrap his hand around himself, sneaking underneath his pajama pants.

He'd only gotten a few jerks in when the all-too-familiar knock on the door came. It was almost a repeat of yesterday's scene, except he'd come already then, but everything had changed now, hadn't it? He stilled, debating what to do. Should he tell Rhys to put the breakfast in front of the door? That seemed somewhat harsh. Besides, he'd have a hell of a time picking it up, so no.

But letting him come in? It would be the same awkwardness as yesterday, only now with him trying to cover up his arousal rather than a wet spot. Except, why should he have to cover it up? If Rhys wanted to be treated like an adult and all that, he could damn well learn to deal with that as well, no? And the fact that on some level, it felt like getting back at him a little didn't hurt either.

Feeling positively rebellious, Cornell called out, "Come on in!"

He watched Rhys as he came in, a hesitant smile on his face that was instantly wiped off when his eyes dropped to Cornell's hand, which was still wrapped around his dick. Only the crown of his cock peeped out from underneath his underwear and pajama pants, but it was enough to make Rhys swallow visibly.

"I see you're off to a good start of the day," Rhys said as he finally tore his eyes away and put the breakfast tray on the desk, as he'd done for the last few days. "I'll leave you to it," he said, avoiding Cornell's eyes as he walked out.

"You're not gonna try to stop me?" Cornell asked him.

Rhys slowly turned around. "Do you want me to?"

Cornell harrumphed. "You're not my Dom."

"You know, I'd never pegged you for a bratty sub," Rhys said, and Cornell's eyes widened.

"I'm not a brat," he said with all the indignity he could muster, considering he still had his hand wrapped around his dick.

"Deliberately baiting and challenging a Dom? That's bratty behavior in my book," Rhys said calmly.

Oh, how Cornell wanted to fire back that Rhys couldn't possibly know jack shit about things at his age, but he couldn't. It was mean, hitting him where he knew it would hurt, and untrue to boot.

"I'm not baiting you," he said, and much to his own chagrin, he could hear the pout in his tone.

Rhys folded his arms across his chest. "Do I need to point out that you were jerking off in front of me? Not sure what else to call that but baiting me."

The fact that Rhys was so calm about it took Cornell's thunder away. "You keep interrupting me in the mornings," he said, pouting even more. God, what was he, a teenager again? "That's why I asked for privacy yesterday, but you made such a big deal out of it."

Rhys shook his head. "I made a big deal? All you had to do was tell me you wanted to jack off, and I would've walked away."

"Like you would've given me permission," Cornell said, and his cheeks flushed as he realized what he had blurted out.

To his credit, Rhys looked like he was trying not to grin, though he failed miserably. "I didn't know you wanted or needed my permission."

"I don't," Cornell said. "I don't know why I said that. Besides, I had already come yesterday anyway, but I didn't want you to see that."

"And you're telling me this, why?"

God, he was infuriating. He was so calm and collected when Cornell felt like he was losing it by the second, stammering and making a complete fool out of himself.

"I wanted to let you know I need some privacy in the mornings," he said, unable to come up with a more plausible reason. Well, there was one, but no way was he sharing that with Rhys. He'd shown enough of his hand already. Then again, he'd always sucked at playing poker.

"I suggest you wake up earlier, then," Rhys said. "I'm here every morning at eight sharp. You wanna jack off before breakfast, set a damn alarm."

He had a point there, Cornell had to admit. Again. He finally let go of his cock, which had lost interest anyway, and tucked himself back in. "Okay," he said, surrendering to the inevitable.

"Yeah?" Rhys asked, clearly surprised.

"What do you want me to say?" Cornell snapped. "You're right, okay. I was baiting you."

"I know. I recognize a bratty sub when I see one."

"You don't like bratty subs?" The question was out of Cornell's mouth before he even realized it, and his cheeks heated up all over again. How infuriating that in his forties, he still hadn't gotten over that insane habit of blushing. "Forget I asked that," he said quickly.

Rhys merely grinned at him. "Go eat your breakfast before your coffee gets cold. And wash your damn hands first."

"Yogurt again, I hope?" Cornell asked.

"Yes, but with some added flax seed, which I know you're not a fan of. But if you eat all of it, I have a reward for you later."

Cornell felt himself respond to it, the promise of that reward for good behavior. How he longed to please Rhys, even if he wasn't his Dom. Then he caught himself. "That's what you've been doing the last few days," he said slowly. "Getting me to do things by promising me a reward."

"Yes," Rhys admitted instantly. "And I figured I'd keep doing it until you tell me to stop, to show you that I can be open about it."

"It feels like being manipulated," Cornell said.

Rhys cocked his head in a gesture that was so much like Jonas that a wave of emotion barreled through Cornell. "Why?" Rhys asked. "You're wired to respond well to rewarding good behavior. Why is that manipulation if I recognize that and use it to help you?"

"Who says you won't use it to make me do something I don't want to?" Cornell said. "If you know what I respond to, you could abuse that."

Rhys looked like Cornell had slapped him. "I guess that's where trust comes in," he said. "The faith you should have in me that I would never abuse that knowledge."

Cornell hesitated, but then decided honesty was the only way if they had any hopes of moving past this. "I'm not sure I have that level of trust in you right now," he said softly. "Not after what you did."

Rhys's shoulders dropped even lower. "I can understand that. I'm sorry for suggesting the reward. It's what I've been doing for the last few days after seeing how well you respond to it, and I figured that if I stopped now, it would be like admitting I had been manipulating you...which I haven't."

"I can see that," Cornell said. "But I don't know yet how I feel about it, okay? Let's just take it one day at a time and be open about this."

Rhys nodded quickly. "Open communication is always good," he said. Then he met Cornell's eyes. "Does that mean you've decided to stay?"

Cornell sighed. "No. It means I haven't decided to leave."

RHYS WASN'T sure if his conversation with Cornell had been a victory or a defeat. Maybe a little bit of both? He thought he'd been on the winning side, until Cornell had dropped that little bomb at the end, about not trusting Rhys. And if that hadn't hurt enough, he'd added the bonus of not being sure yet if he wanted to stay.

Well, Rhys should've known better than to think Cornell would just get over it, that one day was enough to move past it. He wouldn't, and frankly, it wasn't fair to expect that of him. This would take time, which was hard considering Rhys's lack of patience. He'd have to learn.

He was almost tempted to text Ford and ask him how to grovel to a sub, but he wasn't sure that would be smart. Ford tended to expect him to actually do something with his suggestions, so he would follow up, expecting a detailed account of what would no doubt be a massive humiliation for Rhys. Yeah, better not.

Then again, he had already asked Ford something similar, or Ford had given advice himself, Rhys couldn't remember how he'd worded things. He'd told Rhys he should show Cornell he was trustworthy by being the Dom that he needed. So, that's what Rhys would do. As much as Cornell would allow him, he would take care of him the best way he could.

When Cornell walked into the living room after having showered, Rhys was ready for him. "If you're up for it, I'd love to do some more massage and exercises with you," he said. "I know we're still working on trust, but I hope you do trust me as a physical therapist."

Much to his relief, Cornell hesitated only briefly before nodding and saying, "Yeah, I do. And I'd appreciate that because the massage you gave me before provided relief already."

Then his eyes narrowed, and Rhys had no trouble guessing where his mind had gone. Still, he waited to see if Cornell would bring it up. It was a strange thing to say about a man Cornell's age, but he truly looked adorable when he was flustered, like he was now. The way his teeth troubled his bottom lips, the slight blush on his cheeks, his eyes that only dared to peek at Rhys.

It was as if knowing Rhys was a Dom had made him behave more like a sub, interestingly enough. Before, Rhys had caught glimpses of it, but they'd been mixed in with the professional Cornell, the detail-oriented, put-together lawyer. Or friendly, almost avuncular Cornell, who'd tried to behave like Rhys's godparent. But now, he saw more of the unfiltered Cornell, and he loved it.

"Did you..." Cornell started, then stopped again, and Rhys took pity on him.

"Did I know you had a happy ending to the massage two days ago? Yes, I did."

Cornell groaned. "Oh god. What happened?"

Rhys shrugged, determined to keep it light. "You fell asleep, or something close to it, and in that dreamlike state, you started humping the table. I let you."

Cornell looked at the floor. "Did you...help me?" he asked softly.

"I didn't touch you," Rhys said, anger flaring up at the suggestion. "Well, I touched your back, obviously, but that's it."

"Then how...?"

"You respond well to touch," Rhys said. "When I switched from a deep tissue massage to a relaxing one, you...reacted. That's all. And it happens to a lot of male patients, so no need to feel embarrassed."

"Out of curiosity, do people ever stop feeling embarrassed when someone tells them not to?" Cornell asked, a flash of his humor back. "Because for the love of everything holy, it has never worked on me."

Rhys couldn't help but chuckle. "True. It's like telling people to calm down. At no point in the history of mankind have people calmed down when being told to."

Cornell laughed too, but then his face sobered. "So maybe let me decide whether or not to feel embarrassed, no?"

Rhys nodded. "Point taken. Let me rephrase it then and state that it's normal for the male body to respond like that, especially for someone who's as sensitive to touch as you are."

Cornell looked at him funny. "What do you mean?"

Rhys frowned. "You know you're super responsive to touch, right?"

The puzzled look on Cornell's face only intensified. "I have no idea what you're referring to."

How was it possible that he'd been a sub for so long and had never realized that? Hadn't his Doms ever picked up on it? Or they had, and they'd assumed he knew, like Rhys had. Either way, this was not a conversation he wanted to have on the go.

"Can you sit with me for a bit so I can explain?" he asked.

Cornell nodded, then carefully sat down on the couch. "It's funny, but now that I know about you being a Dom, I can't believe I missed it. It's so obvious," he said.

That was a compliment, right? Rhys decided he'd take it as one. After all, it meant Cornell was responding to it, so clearly, he was doing something right. "Thank you."

He sat down across from him, then searched for the best way to broach the subject. "I know I haven't earned the right to ask you anything, but for this particular conversation, it would really help if you could humor me and share a little about your experiences and preferences as a sub," he said.

Cornell blinked a few times. "Okay," he said slowly. "I wasn't expecting that."

"Only if you want to," Rhys stressed again, a little worried he was making things worse. It was just that he didn't know where to start if Cornell truly didn't know this about himself.

"You'll have to forgive me, but it's still a little weird to be talking about this with you," Cornell said after a long pause. "I've known you since you were a baby and now you want me to talk about sex and spanking and stuff with you."

Rhys heard him, but he also heard the two things Cornell mentioned first. Sex and spanking. *Interesting.* "I understand. It's gonna take some getting used to."

"It's not weird for you?" Cornell asked.

Rhys almost wanted to laugh, because how could it be weird when he'd stopped seeing Cornell as his godfather, as some kind of sexless avuncular type, ages ago? God, he'd had his first erotic dream about the man when he'd still been a teen. "No," he said. "But I've had more time to get used to it."

Cornell was stalling, he recognized, but he let him. Pushing would only have the opposite effect, as Cornell was not a man who liked to be pushed. Bribed with a reward, yes, but not forced or put under pressure. So he sat as Cornell watched him in that semi-stealthy way of his, where he peeked from under his eyelashes while pretending to look down. He was good at that, Rhys had noticed. Probably years of experience of secretly watching his Dom when he was told not to.

"I like being tied down," Cornell said, his voice soft. "Shibari, too, but only with an experienced Dom who allows me to place myself in a position I can hold for a long time. Otherwise, it takes forever and gets too uncomfortable."

When he stopped talking, Rhys realized it had been an opening move, to speak. The rest, he'd have to ask. "How about pain and impact play?" he asked. "Whipping, flogging, that kind of thing?"

Cornell shook his head. "I like spanking," he offered,

and Rhys had to blink back a lovely vision of Cornell offering himself for a spanking on his lap.

"Knife play?" he asked, his voice a tad hoarse.

That resulted in a firm head shake.

"Water sports?"

Another resolute no.

"Sensory play?"

Cornell thought about that one for a bit. "I don't think I have much experience with that. It's too tame for most Doms."

"What else do you like, Cornell?" Rhys asked, and if he let a little Dom slip into his voice, well, that couldn't be helped, now could it?

"Sex."

The word was so soft that Rhys would've missed it had he not been watching Cornell so closely. "You like sex?" he asked.

Cornell's cheeks were stained with a gorgeous flush now, and he studiously avoided Rhys's eyes as he nodded.

"Penetrative sex or...?"

"All of it. Blow jobs, giving and receiving. Hand jobs. Edging. Coming. The cuddling afterward."

Ah, there it was, Cornell showing himself. The urge to reward him with a *good boy* was strong, but he had no idea how Cornell would react to it. Still, he had to give him something.

"Thank you for sharing that," he said, making his voice warm, and Cornell's face lit up.

"It's what made your father and me..." he started, then stopped talking. Rhys watched him as myriad emotions flashed over his face. "Touch," he finally said, his voice choked up. "That's the common element in all of it. I like to be touched."

"Yes," Rhys said simply.

"With Jonas, that's why we shared a bed," Cornell said, and Rhys's heart skipped a beat. "For the cuddling. Not because we had sex, because we didn't. Well, in a scene sometimes when we played together. Jonas was..." he stopped again, and Rhys could see the realization on his face of who he was talking to.

"It's okay," he assured him. "You can talk about my dad. It doesn't weird me out. Also, I know he was vers, because he and I actually talked about that."

When his dad had mentioned that, Rhys had filled in the blanks. His dad had fucked Cornell sometimes in scenes, that was the conclusion. Rhys understood. It was the almost inevitable consequence of them playing together with one Dom. Of course, watching two subs pleasure each other would be gratifying.

"You're okay with all of this?" Cornell asked.

"Yeah. Talking about this shouldn't be weird, you know?"

"But it's your dad we're talking about. With me."

Rhys smiled. "Yes, and I thought I'd made clear I've known about you two for a long time. I was okay with it when I found out, and that hasn't changed."

Cornell studied him for a bit more, then let out a sigh. "So, touch... Would you believe me if I said I never realized it?"

Rhys's smile widened. "I gathered as much, yes."

"How the hell did you find out that quickly?" Cornell asked, and it was almost an accusation.

"By paying attention?" Rhys said. "I noticed how well you responded when I touched you."

"Huh," Cornell said, and that one word was stuffed with meaning. "To the massage, you mean?"

"Not just that, but in general. You calm down if I put my

hand on your shoulder. You relax when I massage you." He hesitated, then decided to go all in to build Cornell's trust. "Hell, you lean into my touch whenever you have the opportunity. You crave it, Cornell. There's nothing wrong with that; it's how you're wired."

Cornell's mouth had dropped open a little before he closed it, then opened it again to speak. "And after all that, you're asking me to submit myself to another massage. Isn't that asking for trouble for me?"

9

He knew better, and yet Cornell found himself on the massage table again, face down, his body tense in anticipation.

"Try to relax, Cornell," Rhys said. "It's not a test. You have nothing to prove, neither to me nor to yourself."

Cornell let those words sink in. Rhys was surprisingly wise for his age. And he certainly was perceptive. Cornell still couldn't believe how quickly Rhys had picked up on that whole *sensitive to touch* thing. Now that he thought about it, it made total sense, but he'd been a submissive since he was twenty-one, and he'd never quite put it together. It had taken Rhys only a week. Cornell wasn't sure if that spoke more about how oblivious he had been to his own body or how tuned in Rhys had been. Probably a little of both.

Rhys massaged his shoulder again, and Cornell had to bite his lip from groaning in pain. This stage certainly wasn't arousing, thank you very much.

"I'm sorry," Rhys said. "I know this hurts. Massaging

connective tissue is one of the most painful things, especially in a spot like this, but I can already sense the difference from two days ago. We're not there by a long shot, but your body is responding well."

And that, right there, was one of the reasons why Cornell had agreed to the massage after all. Even knowing that he might react again, become aroused, it hadn't deterred him from submitting himself to Rhys's hands again. As much as he could try to fool himself that the slight improvement he'd experienced in his shoulder was a fluke, what Rhys had said confirmed it. The massage *did* help, and Cornell would do anything to get his body into the best state possible. He had to do whatever he could to reduce the constant pain if he ever wanted a shot at having his life back.

Rhys kneaded his muscles, and Cornell and endured it, trying to focus on his breathing and staying relaxed.

"You're doing great," Rhys said, his voice dropping a little to that wonderful, rich tone that reached deep inside Cornell and made him feel things. Things that he had no business feeling with Rhys, and yet here they were.

He didn't respond, but he felt himself relax even more into Rhys's hands, as if his body wanted to prove even more that the guy had been right. Even when Rhys was hurting him—and not the good kind of hurt—Cornell was responding and obeying. Submitting, basically, even if it was a different kind of pain.

It was a little shocking to realize how much he *wanted* to obey him. That part, more than anything else, was a struggle for him. Even with how ingrained his need and desire to submit was, he shouldn't be persuaded that easily to obey just anyone. The fact that Rhys was so much younger, that they had never played together, that there was the whole entanglement of having known him since he was a baby, all those reasons should make him be cautious.

And yet he wasn't. Well, maybe his mind was, but his body, his soul, yearned to submit to him. Hell, he'd obeyed him even before he'd been aware Rhys had been commanding him.

He allowed himself to sink deep into his thoughts as Rhys worked his shoulders and back. The pain grew less and less, and Cornell felt the tension seeping from his muscles, responding to Rhys's touch. Still, that part could be explained as reacting to physical therapy. That didn't mean he'd been right about the rest, though if he were honest with himself, Cornell knew Rhys's analysis had been spot on.

"I'm slowly going to move into a relaxing massage, to help your muscles recover from the beating they took. Is that okay with you?"

Cornell knew why he asked. He wanted to make sure Cornell was okay with the possible consequences. Well, there was the second reason he had agreed to the massage, after all. Sure, his primary reason had been to alleviate his pain and discomfort and improve his range of mobility, but the second, that was about to happen right now. Would he react again? Even knowing that it had happened before, even with him aware of Rhys's theory, would his body respond anyway?

"Yes," he said, once again biting back the honorific he wanted so desperately to tag on.

That part, more than anything else, was concerning to Cornell. Obeying Rhys, responding to his tone and commands, that was one thing. Reacting to his touch, still all explainable. After all, it had been a long time since he'd been touched, and even longer since he'd had a good scene. But him constantly wanting to call Rhys *Sir*, that was plain fucked up. That spoke to a connection on a level that made Cornell very uncomfortable.

Rhys's touch changed, from the strong, almost bruising strokes to lighter ones. He ventured lower, too, close to the waistband of the simple cotton boxers Cornell was wearing. Cornell's skin tingled, recognizing the difference.

"That's good," Rhys said. "I can feel you relaxing. The hurting part is over. Now we're getting to the good part."

Cornell couldn't help but tense up at those words. What did Rhys mean, the good part? Was he deliberately trying to get Cornell aroused?

Rhys chuckled. "That got your attention. Relax. Nothing's going to happen that you don't want, okay?"

Nothing's going to happen that you don't want. Did that mean something could happen if he wanted it? Did he want something to happen? Cornell's head was spinning, even as his body relaxed again. Seconds later, he felt himself move against Rhys's touch, seeking more. Ah, that was what Rhys had been talking about, about him leaning into the touch. Dammit, why did the kid have to be right about everything?

"Stop thinking so hard," Rhys said. "Allow yourself to feel."

Allow yourself to feel. It was easier said than done. Then again, he'd managed the last time, hadn't he? All he had done was feel to the point where he'd drifted off, completely relaxed and immersed in Rhys's touch. He had to have been, because if his mind had been at work, there was no way he would've allowed himself to come.

So he could try that, maybe. How did it feel? He concentrated on Rhys's hands, which were now stroking his back with slow, soft strokes. He would venture out to Cornell's upper arms every now and then, turning his muscles liquid. It felt good, relaxing, a welcome change from the previous massage.

Rhys was right, Cornell really did like being touched. Even after mediocre scenes, he'd loved the aftercare. Being held by someone else, the cuddling part, that could make up for not getting much out of the scene itself. There had been this one Dom, years ago, who'd had hands much like Rhys's. Firm hands that could alternate between the best spanking he'd ever had and hugging and cuddling him as if there was no tomorrow. Cornell had almost mourned when the guy had found the love of his life in a sweet boy and had collared him. He'd been happy for them, but he'd felt the loss of not being able to play with him for months.

God, Rhys's hands really were perfect. He had power in them for sure. Cornell wondered how they would feel hitting his flesh. Spanking seemed like such a basic concept, but he could count on one hand the number of Doms who were good at it. Many of them considered it below their skill level or merely regarded it as a warm-up, something they had to get through to get to the good parts. But when done right, spanking could be everything Cornell needed to fly.

And as Rhys's touches slowed down even more and became gentle caresses, like velvet on his skin, he had no trouble imagining what they would feel like on his ass. Oh, Rhys would hit him good, slapping his cheeks until they were all red and swollen, just the way he liked it. And then when Cornell was all hot and bothered, Rhys would deny him his orgasm, of course, because things were never that easy. Then he would play with him, teasing his hole, making him fight back what his body so desperately wanted. He would be begging by then, moving against Rhys's hands, seeking that friction that would send him over the edge, at the same time knowing that he couldn't displease his Dom.

His eyes flew open, his body tensing up as he stilled the movements he'd been making. He had been humping the table. Again. The combination of Rhys's touch and the thoughts they had triggered had been enough to make him rock hard. Oh god, now what?

"Stop," he said.

Rhys's hands immediately let go of him, and he could've cried at how empty that lack of touch made him feel.

"It's okay," Rhys said. "I'll stop if that's what you want, but whatever you're feeling, it's okay."

"It's not okay," Cornell said, his voice barely more than a whisper. "I shouldn't react this way to you."

"So, with anyone else, it would have been okay?" Rhys asked, and Cornell realized the truth of that question.

Did he have a problem with getting aroused in the first place or because it was with Rhys? After being a sub for so long, he knew that how his body reacted was never something to be ashamed of. Most of it was instinctual anyway and had little to do with choice. He could fight it, and of course, sometimes he had to if that was what the Dom wanted, but at the end of the day, the body decided its own way. He could only control how he handled it, not the reaction itself.

"I don't know," he said. "I know I shouldn't judge myself for how I respond physically, but it's kinda hard not to."

"What if I give you permission?" Rhys asked.

Cornell was eternally grateful that he didn't have to look him in the eyes, his face hidden from Rhys's scrutiny on the table as it grew hot and undoubtedly red. "What do you mean?" he asked.

"You're struggling with your own thoughts that you're

not supposed to react to me, right? My guess is that with any other Dom, you would've been fine with it. Just not with me. Am I right?"

"Yes," Cornell said after a short pause. "Though I'm pretty sure I would've felt the same with any other physical therapist."

"But the way I'm touching you now, that's not a physical therapist's touch. You didn't react this way during the initial massage. I deliberately moved into something else, and we both know this."

"You transitioned from being a therapist into a Dom," Cornell said, understanding where Rhys was going with this.

"Exactly. So, you can skip the thought that it's not okay to react to a massage like this, because what I did was almost guaranteed to evoke a reaction in you. Now it's about you giving yourself permission to react to my touch, and I'm telling you, I am granting you that permission."

Cornell's breath quickened. It shouldn't make a difference, Rhys giving him permission, but it did.

"Tell me as a Dom."

TELL ME AS A DOM, Cornell had said, and Rhys realized immediately what he meant. "Yellow to slow down, red to stop," he said.

"Yes, Sir," Cornell said, and hearing those two simple words fall from his lips sent a rush through Rhys like he'd never experienced before.

"I'm going to touch you now," Rhys said, his hands shaking a little. This was it, what he had been hoping and dreaming for for such a long time—permission to touch Cornell in a different way.

"Yes, Sir. Green, Sir," Cornell said, his voice dropping to a different tone, one that pushed all those buttons inside Rhys.

"You have my permission to come," Rhys said, struggling to keep his voice as level and steady as he wanted it to be.

"Yes, Sir. Thank you, Sir."

Was there anything sweeter than Cornell's submission to him? He was almost drunk with the feeling of it. Luckily, his hands knew what to do, and they resumed their exploration of Cornell's body. Instead of focusing on his back, he started with his head. This wasn't something he usually did, but he knew from experience how wonderfully relaxing a good scalp massage could be. Hell, he still drove forty-five minutes to his favorite hairdresser because of the way the guy massaged his head after washing his hair. Best. Thing. Ever.

So, he did the same to Cornell, smiling when the man let out little groans and sighs of appreciation. Even there, tension was seeping away, and Rhys smiled, the joy of making Cornell feel good rolling through him.

He moved from Cornell's head down to his neck, getting rid of the last bit of tension there, before moving further down. Cornell let out another muffled moan when Rhys trailed his spine, teasing him by stopping just short of his boxers.

"Don't hold back," he told him. "I want to hear you."

"I can get embarrassingly loud," Cornell commented softly, which made Rhys chuckle.

"First of all, there's no one here to hear it but me. But more importantly. If I tell you I want to hear you, that's all you need to know. There's no such thing as embarrassing when it comes to sounds and noises. You know how you respond to touch? That's what sounds are to me. The more I hear you, the more you please me."

"Yes, Sir," was Cornell's quiet but happy response.

To test him, Rhys slipped a finger underneath his waistband and trailed it from one side to the other. Cornell shivered in response, his skin breaking out in goosebumps, but even more beautiful was the little gasp he let out.

Rhys wanted to go further, but despite mentioning the color system briefly, he needed to make absolutely sure Cornell was on board with this. But outright asking him would break the scene. "You know, your ass looks really tense too," he said, keeping his voice light. "Maybe I should massage that a little as well."

Cornell took a few seconds to answer. "Maybe you should, Sir."

That was it. He had his permission now, and joy rushed through him all over again. That first time, Cornell had done much of the work himself, simply reacting to the sensual massage Rhys was giving him with seeking friction. This time, Rhys could give him a little more help, even though he doubted Cornell needed much. He'd already spotted the telltale movements of the man's hips subtly grinding against the table.

He dropped his hands lower, massaging Cornell's ass cheeks through the thin cotton fabric of his boxers. Cornell let out short groans, and Rhys smiled. "Something wrong?" he asked innocently.

"No, Sir."

Just when Rhys thought Cornell wasn't taking the bait, the man added, "I thought you might be able to do a better job if you took my boxers off. Sir."

"You telling me how to do my job now?" Rhys asked.

"I wouldn't dare, Sir. It was merely a suggestion."

Rhys smiled as he slipped his hands underneath the fabric, touching Cornell's bare skin on that gorgeous, strong ass. He was rewarded with a loud moan. He teased first, light caresses, and even those got a response from Cornell every single time. Then he started stroking him for real, finding those globes that fit so perfectly into his hands.

The funny thing was that he hadn't even been lying. There was some tension in there, but it melted away as he kneaded and stroked, caressed and touched. And oh, the wonderful concert of sounds that Cornell was producing. Little gasps and moans, grunts when Rhys was teasing him too much, sighs when he found a spot he hadn't reached before.

Cornell had spread his legs as wide as he could on the table, even pulling them up a little bit, the clearest invitation he could give, Rhys felt. "Do you like it when I touch your ass?" he asked.

He knew the answer, but he wanted Cornell to admit it. No matter where they would move after this. He had to have this experience.

"Yes, Sir."

"Are you an ass man?"

"I'm not sure what you mean, Sir."

Rhys loved how respectful Cornell was. Sure, he'd had years of experience and training, but the way he consistently addressed Rhys as *Sir* was intoxicating.

"Do you like it when someone plays with your ass? Does it turn you on, boy?"

That last word had tumbled out of his mouth before he realized it, and Rhys held his breath as he awaited Cornell's response. Had he gone too far? Would Cornell object to being called that by someone who was so much younger than him?

One, two, three seconds, and then Cornell spoke up. "Yes, Sir. Very much."

As if to underline his words, Cornell pushed his ass up at Rhys, and his fingers, still slick with massage oil, bumped against Cornell's hole. Rhys waited for him to freeze up, but instead, he moaned as if it was exactly what he'd been hoping for.

"Cornell," Rhys said, as much in warning as in want.

"Green, Sir," Cornell said, and he couldn't have given a more perfect answer. The fact that he was still aware this was a scene of some sort was encouraging. That meant they had boundaries and safeguards in place. All Cornell had to do was use his safe word, and everything would stop. Rhys had no intention of pushing him even close to his boundaries, but Cornell had all but invited him to do this, hadn't he?

To test him, he put his slick middle finger at the top of Cornell's crack. He felt him hold his breath in anticipation, but he didn't say anything. Very slowly, Rhys dragged his finger down, and when he was about to reach his hole, Cornell lifted his ass again.

Rhys couldn't help but chuckle. "Am I going too slow for you, boy? Or do I need to tie you down?"

Cornell breathed out audibly, bringing his hips back down. "No, Sir. Sorry, Sir."

Rhys heard genuine regret in his voice, mixed in with a tinge of fear, probably because he was scared Rhys would stop. He had absolutely no intention to, but wasn't it beautiful to see Cornell respond like this? One day, he would make him beg. If he was already so beautiful like this, how amazing would it be to hear him plead and beg?

"You know how this works, don't you, boy? Who's in charge here, me or you?"

"You, Sir," came the quick reply.

"If I'm not mistaken, your job is to take whatever I decide to give you, right?"

"Yes, Sir," Cornell said, subdued.

"Well, technically, I didn't tell you to keep still, so that was an error on my part. Since I'm feeling magnanimous, I'm going to give you permission to move now, okay? And remember, you have my permission to come."

As soon as he touched him again, Cornell's hips rolled, first in a downward move that brought his cock—which Rhys couldn't see but assumed was aching for more friction —into close contact with the table. But then he brought them up again, seeking Rhys's touch. And Rhys obliged, giving him exactly what he was searching for. He pressed his thumb against Cornell's hole, putting pressure on it without trying to breach him.

It took Cornell a few tries before he had a rhythm going, and Rhys moved with him, watching in rapt attention as the man pleasured himself. He now regretted he couldn't see his face, but he could picture it, those high cheekbones stained with a blush, those eyes glazing over as he started to chase his orgasm for real.

The rhythm increased, and so did Cornell's breathing, interspersed with little gasps and moans. He was getting close, and Rhys helped him by using his other hand to keep caressing his ass, teasing his crack, even as he held the thumb of his right hand firmly planted against that hole. God, he wanted inside him something fierce, his own cock protesting it wasn't being let in on the action, but that was way too fast, too soon. This was about Cornell, about giving him pleasure. His own dick could wait till later.

"Do you want me to stay, or do you want privacy to finish?" he asked when it was clear Cornell was about to come. The man hadn't said anything, but after everything that happened between them, Rhys wanted to make sure he was on board with this sudden escalation of intimacy between them.

"Stay," Cornell gasped, panting hard now. "Please, Sir."

And there it was, the word Rhys didn't think he'd be ever able to resist from Cornell. *Please.* He'd been right, the man was irresistible when he begged.

With his thumb still pressed against him, Rhys grabbed his neck with his other hand, then brought his mouth less than an inch away from Cornell's head. "Come for me," he commanded him.

The result was instant, Cornell's hips jerking twice, and then a long moan flew from his lips as his whole body shuddered. "Ungh!" he called out, a sound that hardened Rhys's cock even more.

He removed his thumb from his ass, then started caressing his back with slow, gentle moves to bring him down. "That was beautiful," he said. "You are beautiful."

He was saying too much, maybe, but then again, he hadn't said enough for a long time, so maybe he was overdue. He kept mumbling sweet encouragements as he felt Cornell's body come down from its high.

"Do you want me to clean you up, do you want to do that yourself?" he asked when Cornell's body had stilled and his breathing had returned to normal.

He knew the answer before Cornell spoke, but couldn't help being disappointed when it was as he had expected. "I'll do it myself."

He could hear the distancing in his voice, and while it

made total sense after an experience like that, it somehow hurt as well.

"Rhys," Cornell said, as if wanting to signal even more that as far as he was concerned, the scene was over. "Thank you."

As he walked out, Rhys decided that it was enough for now. They'd taken another step. A big one.

10

Cornell kept his distance from Rhys the rest of the day. What was supposed to have been an experiment had turned into something far more. Sure, he'd known on some level he'd been playing with fire, allowing Rhys to massage him again. But he hadn't expected *that*.

His own reaction to Rhys's touch had still managed to surprise him, even after what Rhys had told him about how sensitive he thought Cornell was to it. Knowing it was one thing, but experiencing it was another. And he couldn't blame it on being sex-starved or something either, considering he'd come two days before. From the exact same thing, no less.

No, this could only be explained as him responding to Rhys, to his touch. What was even more sobering was that it wasn't merely his touch either. The way he had handled it, his voice, the things he had said to Cornell, it had all been exactly what he needed. He hadn't even realized how much he needed to get permission to chase that orgasm, to allow himself to feel it, and then to come, until Rhys had granted it.

Now everything had changed. Considering how relatively vanilla this had been, one could argue if it had constituted an actual scene or not, but Cornell's instincts said it had been. Rhys had presented himself as Dom and Cornell had responded as sub. There had been mentions of safe words. All the core elements were there, even if the actions themselves had been relatively innocent.

No, things would never be the same between them ever again. They'd crossed a line that was impossible to uncross. The only choice that was left was how to move forward, which brought his previous dilemma back to the front of his mind again. Should he stay or should he go?

He sipped the Earl Grey tea Rhys had brought him before he'd headed out to do some grocery shopping. Cornell had settled on the couch in the living room, somewhat relieved to have an hour or so to himself. Not that Rhys was bothering him in any way, but he had a big decision to make, and knowing that he had uninterrupted alone time helped.

There were plenty of reasons to go. He was slowly doing better, and he didn't think he needed round-the-clock care anymore, though he didn't trust himself to be on his own yet. The thought of having to climb stairs scared the crap out of him, so going home was not an option. But there were alternatives he could think of, even ones that didn't include moving in with his sister and her busy household.

Another reason was to give both himself and Rhys their privacy back. The incident yesterday morning when Rhys had almost walked in on him jacking off spoke volumes about how limited he was in his activities here, especially sexual ones. It wasn't like he could see himself engaging in anything serious soon, but he might want to start using some toys again. A man had needs, even if he was a little older and still recovering from surgery.

And Rhys, at his age, had to have needs as well that were hard to fulfill when Cornell was staying with him. Sure, he could go out to score, but maybe he felt he couldn't leave Cornell alone for so long. Granted, he had gone out to watch that scene with Ford, whatever that had been about. But Rhys's sense of responsibility was strong, Cornell knew.

There was the sense that he was imposing on Rhys, unintentionally requiring him to adapt his life to Cornell's presence. For fuck's sake, Rhys had even taken a leave of absence from his job. That had never been Cornell's intention. He couldn't stay so long that Rhys would start to resent his presence. He'd been here five days. Now, maybe that was a good time to leave.

He blew out a slow breath, allowing the truth to settle in his mind. All these reasons, they had nothing to do with the decision to stay or go. They were excuses, reasons his mind came up with to avoid thinking about the real issue at stake here. Him staying or going had zero to do with inconveniencing Rhys or being well enough to leave. The only deciding factor was what had happened between them.

After the way Rhys had deceived him by withholding the truth about being a Dom, Cornell had thought it impossible to ever trust him again. And yet today, he had given him that trust. Granted, it had only been a very limited scene, but he'd felt safe with him. The fact that Rhys had checked consent every step of the way had surely helped.

As much as Cornell wanted to deceive himself and focus on all those bogus reasons for leaving, he couldn't deny the truth. Something was happening between him and Rhys, something he had never expected or even considered. There was a spark between them, attraction. How the hell that was possible, Cornell had no idea, but he could at least acknowledge it.

And that was the bottom line, the sole reason for him to stay...or go. If he stayed, he knew where this chemistry between them would lead. You couldn't put a Dom and a sub who had this kind of spontaneous connection in the same house, in forced proximity, without expecting them to act on it. If he were to stay, he would end up playing with Rhys, submitting to him.

The question wasn't if the many reasons he could think of to leave were valid. The question was whether or not he had good reasons to stay. Was the connection between him and Rhys worth exploring?

His first instinct was, of course, to say no. How could it be, what with the age gap between them and more importantly, the fact that Rhys was Jonas's son. Technically, Cornell was Rhys's godfather, no matter how limited he had executed that role over the years. He had known Rhys since the day he'd been born, and that was not so easy to brush off.

If only he could ask Jonas. That was the thought that made his heart clench painfully, bringing tears to his eyes. How was it possible that the one time where he needed his friend's wisdom more than anything, his friend wasn't there? He needed Jonas's blessing, his approval, before he could do this.

Cassie, she would have an opinion on this, no doubt. Cornell liked her and certainly respected her as a Domme, but her opinion carried little weight with him. She'd been critical of choices Jonas had made before, and Jonas had ignored that as well. He'd always been crystal clear to Cornell about that, saying that the day she filed for divorce was the day she stopped having a say in his life and his choices. And he'd been right.

No, Cornell was pretty sure Cassie would have an opinion on it, and it wouldn't be a favorable one. But what would Jonas think? If he had been alive, what would he have said to Cornell? Would he have objected to the idea of his only son domming Cornell? It was easy to imagine he would've disapproved as well, and that was certainly Cornell's first emotional reaction, which almost made him decide to leave right then and there.

But then his mind prevailed, and he wiped the tears off his eyes, took another sip of tea, and leaned back on the couch again. Seriously, what *would* Jonas have thought? He closed his eyes, imagining his friend sitting right next to him. At first, the grief was so strong that he couldn't even think, too overcome with the sheer size of the empty place Jonas had left in his life.

"God, I miss you so much," Cornell whispered into the room. "How I wish you were here to tell me what to do."

He smiled at his own words, knowing that Jonas would never tell him what to do. All he would do was offer alternative viewpoints, playing devil's advocate at times, but he would never straight up tell Cornell what to do. They both trusted each other enough to know the other one would make the right decision in the end.

Yes, Jonas would've trusted him to make the right decision. But what was the right call here? What if it hadn't been Jonas's son, would Jonas have had an opinion then? He'd never had an issue with an age gap, not even a reversed one. Hell, at their age, they had both constantly played with Doms that were younger than they were. Granted, not many who were in their early twenties, but they'd had a ten-year age gap more than once. That had never been an issue for Jonas.

So, the question was whether Jonas would've had a problem with the fact that it was his son. Would he have trusted Cornell to treat his son right? Now there was a question that brought a soft smile to Cornell's face. If Jonas had known Rhys was a Dom, he would've also known that it wouldn't be Cornell who took care of Rhys It would be Rhys who took care of Cornell. That was the role they would both be looking for, and Jonas would understand that.

Cornell remembered a couple they had met, years ago. It had been an older Dom with a young sub, the two beautifully in sync. Jonas and Cornell had watched a demonstration they gave, both enraptured at the Dom's skill and the sub's complete submission. Only later had they found out the two were father and son.

When that news had broken, they had been banned from many clubs. Jonas had brought it up with Cornell, saying that while he understood that legally, the clubs had little choice, morally, he didn't have an issue with their relationship at all. "As long as they're consenting adults, it's all good with me," he had told Cornell, who had agreed with him.

Wasn't that true for everything they did? No matter what someone's kink was, their fetish, the thing that got them off, there was no shame in it, as long as it was between consenting adults. They had both watched many things over the years that they themselves would never engage in, but that didn't mean they judged them. Just because it wasn't his kink didn't mean he had to judge or shame someone else for liking it.

And there was his answer. If he and Rhys started something, if they entered into a Dom/sub relationship,

Jonas would've been okay with it. They were two consenting adults, both more than legal age, both with the knowledge and the experience in the scene to make an informed decision. Sure, Jonas would've needed some time to get used to it, probably, but Cornell couldn't imagine him judging it.

There was, of course, the added complication that Jonas had fucked him on several occasions. Never outside of scenes, because neither of them had any desire for that, but they'd certainly played plenty of times with the same Dom. If he and Rhys were to move into a sexual relationship within their D/s one, it would mean he would've shared a bed with both father and son. He had to admit that was a little weird, but not weirder than a lot of things he'd seen and even done over the years. Hell, weird was a relative term, the eye of the beholder and all that.

He had one more piece of information he needed before making a decision. It only took one phone call to get the information he needed, Master Ford's phone number. He decided to call him right away.

"Hello?" Master Ford answered. Cornell recognized his deep baritone immediately.

"Good afternoon, Master Ford. This is Cornell Freeman. I don't know if you recognize my name?"

"I do. How are you doing? I was so sorry to hear about your accident and especially of Jonas's passing. It's a loss for the community, but especially for you, seeing how close you were. And for Rhys, of course. You have my deepest sympathies."

Cornell took a steadying breath. "Thank you, Master Ford. It's been...rough without him, but I'm surviving. Thank you for asking."

"I have a suspicion what this phone call is about, but

why don't you ask me your question?" Master Ford said. Cornell was happy to hear his tone was warm and patient.

"I know you mentor Rhys, and as such, you can't tell me anything about your conversations with him. I totally respect that, but I wanted to ask your opinion on whether or not he is a good Dom. I need to be sure that he is not going hurt me, Master Ford. I don't think I could take that, not after what I've been through already."

He'd ended up revealing a lot more than he'd intended to, but maybe it was for the better. Master Ford needed to know that he wasn't trying to get him to share gossip. Cornell needed to know if he could trust Rhys.

"I completely understand the question, Cornell, and I have no trouble answering it. The quick and dirty answer is that yes, he's a great Dom. One of the best I've ever seen at that age."

Cornell let out a breath of relief. "Thank you, that's great to hear."

"That doesn't mean he doesn't fuck up every now and then, as you have discovered already."

"He told you what happened?" Cornell asked.

"Yes. And I wasn't amused. But he also told me he took full responsibility."

Cornell's first instinct was to confirm, but then he thought better of it. "I'm sorry, Master Ford, but that's something between me and him."

A chuckle sound through the phone. "Great answer, boy. You already have loyalty toward him. That's a great start."

How he loved it that Ford, who was younger than him, so easily called him *boy*, signaling his acceptance of Cornell's status. "Thank you, Master Ford."

"Look, Cornell, I'm not saying he's never going to make another mistake. We both know he will, if only because he's young. But his heart is in the right place, his instincts are unlike anything I've ever seen in a man his age, and he's eager to learn. He won't hurt you on purpose, that I can promise you."

With that said, Cornell's decision was made. "Thank you, Master Ford. I appreciate your taking the time to talk to me. Could we please keep this between us?"

"Absolutely. And if you ever need me again, you know where to find me."

Cornell ended the call and sat on the couch for a long time, finishing his tea. A strange sense of calm came over him now that he'd made his decision. He was staying.

RHYS WAS on his way back from grocery shopping when his mom called. For a few seconds, he debated not answering, but he knew that wasn't gonna work. His mom would keep calling until he did pick up. Worst-case scenario, she would show up uninvited. No, he'd better face the music.

"Hi, Mom," he answered.

"Hey, baby," his mom's voice echoed through his car's speakers. "How are you?"

"Good," he said. "On my way back from grocery shopping."

"Is Cornell still staying with you?"

Well, at least she was getting to the point of her call right away, Rhys thought wryly. "Yes, he is."

He wasn't offering more than that, figuring she would have to ask if she needed more details. He had no doubt that she would.

"How much longer is he going to stay?" she asked, predictable as always.

"I don't know. We haven't agreed on an end date for this arrangement."

He could've said *until Cornell is better*, but he didn't want to. That would mean she had a yardstick to measure by, and he had no intention of handing her that power.

"But he's not staying for weeks, right?" The horror in her voice was palpable.

Rhys was tempted to say he hoped it would be a lot longer than mere weeks, but that, of course, was the exact wrong thing to say. "As I said, Mom, we haven't set an end date. But I'm fine with him staying, so there's nothing for you to worry about."

Any hope that would make her let go of the topic was in vain, as she proved with her next question. "Please tell me you're charging him rent of some kind?"

And there, in a nutshell, was the core of the conflict between his mom and his dad. She wasn't a bad person, not by any standards, just a very calculated one. She didn't do anything without expecting something in return. It had made her a successful businesswoman, but it was at times hard to deal with when Rhys's life philosophy was more like his dad's.

His dad had always been generous, kind to a fault, always giving people the benefit of the doubt. Rhys remembered a trip he took with his dad to New York City, years ago. His dad must've handed out money to at least fifty homeless people in one weekend. And when Rhys had questioned him about how smart it was, suggesting they might be addicted or use the money to buy booze, his father had shrugged it off. Always err on the side of kindness, he'd taught Rhys. "What they do with the money, that's their responsibility. My responsibility is to be generous to those I think need it," he'd impressed on Rhys.

"No, Mom, I'm not charging him anything," Rhys said with a sigh.

"He's taking advantage of you, baby. He's using you."

Rhys felt his frustration rise, not merely over his mom once again butting in on his business, but about her whole tone and attitude. "I've asked you this before, but would you please stop calling me *baby*? I'm not a child anymore, and I've told you it irritates the crap out of me when you call me that."

Her huff of annoyance came through the phone loud and clear. "I'm your mom. I can call you whatever I want to."

"No, that's not how it works, and you know it. Let me put this in terms I know you will understand. This is a hard limit for me, okay? The next time you call me baby, I'll hang up the phone. I've asked you at least five times before, and I'm not going to ask again."

He might not be able to stop her from asking about Cornell, but he sure as hell could make her stop calling him by that stupid nickname. Not that the nickname in itself was stupid, but it was something he would want a lover to call him, not his mother. That, of course, led to him imagining what it would be like to hear Cornell call him that, and he had to force himself to clue in to his mother again, just in time to catch the tail end of a rant about ungrateful kids who didn't appreciate a mom looking out for them.

"There's a big difference between looking out for me and telling me how to live my life," he said, tired of having the same conversation with her over and over again. "The first is appropriate with your child, the second is appropriate with your subs. Please try to remember I'm in the first category."

Her tone was pure ice when she replied. "I don't appreciate your sarcasm."

"Well, I don't appreciate you disrespecting my boundaries, and yet here we are. Was there anything else?"

He knew he'd crossed the line into being downright rude, but at this point, he really didn't care anymore. He'd had so many similar conversations with her, and they all ended the same. He'd refrained from saying something often enough, but she had disregarded every time he had pointed out that she was crossing a line he didn't want crossed, so it was time for more drastic measures.

"I hope you're not doing all of this in some desperate attempt to get him interested in you. It's never going to work, him and you. You're far too young for him. He needs someone with much more experience. Besides, it's inappropriate, what with him being your godfather and all."

Rhys's blood was boiling, and the only thing that kept him from blowing a gasket was the realization that was exactly what she was after. It would give her more ammunition to accuse him of being immature and not ready to be a Dom. So instead, he swallowed back his temper and focused on the contradictions in her statement.

"Which one is it, him not being interested in me or being inappropriate? Because if he's not interested, as you claim, there's nothing inappropriate."

He could almost hear her clench her teeth. "I see you're not being reasonable about this. We will talk at a later time."

Rhys's "I'm looking forward to it" came after she'd already hung up. God, he hated these kinds of confrontations with his mother. Sadly, they had become more frequent since his father had passed away. Rhys wasn't sure if it was some kind of misguided reaction on her part to protect him out of fear that something would happen to him as well, but he didn't appreciate it. Or maybe it was her way of grieving, though that didn't make a whole lot of sense either. Whatever it was, it needed to stop.

He hated that she'd been able to ruin his good mood after that morning's scene with Cornell. Cornell had kept his distance afterward, but Rhys had felt his eyes on him the entire time. He'd snuck a few quick glances in his direction, confirming the man was as much staring at him as staring into space, clearly thinking about something. It wasn't hard to figure out what he was thinking about. He still hadn't made a final decision whether or not he was going to stay after what had happened. And of course, after their encounter that morning, the stakes had only been raised higher. Would that experience make it more likely for Cornell to stay or to go? Rhys couldn't figure it out.

But as he thought about it, his mother's words rang in the back of his head, that dire warning that things could never work between them, that Cornell could never want him, that it was inappropriate. On impulse, he called his best friend, Raf.

The first thing he heard when Raf picked up was something Raf called out. "It's Rhys, Daddy. I'll keep it brief, okay?"

"Am I calling at an inappropriate time?" Rhys checked.

"Daddy is drawing me a bath, so I don't have long," Raf said. "But if you need me, I will tell him to wait," he added quickly, and how Rhys loved him for the concern he heard in his voice.

"Nah, this won't take long. Just wanted to vent about my mom being a total bitch to me again, sticking her nose in my business."

Raf sighed. "She complaining about Cornell being there again?"

Rhys had kept him up to date about her reaction from

the get-go. "Yeah, and she's alternating between he'll never want me and it's inappropriate."

"Don't let her get into your head, man," Raf said, his tone warm.

"I think we've passed that point," Rhys admitted. "We had a scene this morning, sort of, me and Cornell, I mean."

"Next time, lead with that, would you? Much more interesting than your mom, no offense," Raf said.

Rhys chuckled. "I know, right? It was nothing big, but it was the first time he acknowledged me as a Dom, and it went well, I think."

"Rhys, my friend, you've wanted this man for how long? Years. Don't let your mom ruin things for you. Keep her out of it. This is between you and Cornell, and if he's responding to you and seems open to it, then trust that. And your mom can go fuck herself."

"Raphael, language!" Rhys heard Brendan call out, his voice booming and stern. He could practically picture Raf cringing now, as this would mean a punishment for sure. His Daddy was strict on language, like he was on many things. That being said, Raf loved it, and he needed the structure Brendan brought.

"Yes, Daddy. Sorry, Daddy," Raf said, his tone definitely apologetic.

"You'd better suck him off good," Rhys told him, laughing. "Otherwise you can kiss that bath goodbye, and you'll be going to bed with a red ass."

"You think?" Raf said, the sarcasm strong. "I gotta go, dude. Remember what I said, okay? Don't let her ruin things for you. Trust your instincts."

And any doubts that remained were gone when he came home and found Cornell waiting for him. He quietly watched as Rhys unloaded the groceries and put everything away. Rhys didn't start a conversation either, sensing that Cornell had something on his mind.

"I want to stay," he said when Rhys was done.

Rhys swiveled around. He'd not seen that statement coming. His face broke open in a wide smile. "You do?"

Cornell slowly nodded. "Yes. Just...don't abuse my trust in you."

"Never," Rhys swore. "I promise."

He stepped closer and opened his arms, wanting to give Cornell the choice. He stepped into the embrace almost instantly, and Rhys hugged him with tenderness. "Thank you," he said softly.

Cornell put his head on Rhys's shoulder. "No," he whispered. "Thank you."

11

I t wasn't till the next day, when they were sharing lunch, that Rhys asked the question Cornell had been expecting. "What made you decide to stay? If I may ask," Rhys added.

Cornell studied him as he chewed on the delicious salad Rhys had prepared for them. He was an adequate cook himself, but what Rhys had been serving had been far beyond his own skill level. Today, he'd made them a hearty, filling bean soup for lunch, with a cucumber, peas, and mint salad on the side.

"This is delicious," he commented, pointing at his salad.

"Thank you."

"You're taking great care of me."

Rhys smiled at him. "Is that why you're staying?" he asked.

Cornell took his time to answer. He knew that if he didn't want to talk about it, Rhys would accept it. But he also knew that if they had any hope of moving past what had happened, open communication was key. Everything that had ever gone wrong in scenes between him and a

Dom had always been because of piss-poor communication.

"You're a caring Dom," he said. "Master Ford has taught you well."

Rhys's smile widened. "Or maybe he merely cultivated what was already in my character and instincts."

Cornell considered it. "Fair point. You're like your dad in that sense."

Rhys rolled his eyes, making Cornell chuckle. "Yeah, cause we both know my mom isn't the caring type."

Cornell held up his hands. "I'm not getting between you and your mom," he said. "I've borne the brunt of her displeasure enough times to know better."

Rhys's smile disappeared and he let out a long sigh. "I'm obviously an idiot for telling you this, but she's not a fan of you staying here."

"Color me surprised," Cornell said dryly. "No offense, but your mother has never been the kind-hearted type to take others in."

"No, that would be my dad. He never passed a donation bucket or sponsor table without donating. Hell, he even donated to the Salvation Army's Christmas kettle, even though he knew their position on gays."

Cornell nodded. "He and I have butted heads about that more than once. But he always believed that it was his job to be kind and the other person's job to handle the responsibility of receiving the money."

"Err on the side of kindness," Rhys quoted the same saying he'd thought of the day before.

"Is that why you invited me to stay?" Cornell asked. "Kindness?"

Rhys hesitated long enough for Cornell to realize he had other reasons as well. "Partly," Rhys said. "There was no doubt in my mind it was what my dad would have wanted me to do, let's be clear about that. But to be honest, I also did it because I was interested in you as a sub. I'd hoped that living together would be an opportunity to show you the other side of me."

"The Dom side," Cornell said, and Rhys nodded. "Why would you be interested in a sub like me? I have no doubt you could have your pick of subs, what with how young and..." He wanted to say *hot*, then thought better of it,"...attractive you are," he said. "I assume you're a member of the same club Ford frequents, and if I remember correctly, there is a wide assortment of available subs there."

"Have you been there recently?" Rhys asked. "I checked with Ford, wanting to make sure I wouldn't accidentally run into you and my dad, but he said you hadn't been in forever."

Cornell swallowed back the bitterness that rose in him. "Like I said, have you seen the subs that go to that club? Your dad and I couldn't compete with them. There's only so many times you can be ignored or rejected before it gets to you, you know."

Rhys's face tightened. "I'm sorry that happened to you. Some Doms are very limited in their tastes."

"But not you?" Cornell asked.

Rhys sent him a cheeky grin. "Maybe, but it so happens my tastes run a little more unconventional."

"So what am I to you, a challenge? Something different? You can't tell me you've already seen it all and are bored, not at your age."

Rhys shrugged. "To be honest, the endless lineup of sweet, twinky subs there never captured my attention. Even when I was still in training, my preference was for the outliers, the subs that were different."

"Much like Master Ford's," Cornell said.

"Have you ever played with him?" Rhys asked, and there was a question Cornell should've seen coming.

He let out a sigh. "I hate to say it, but at my age, you'll find that I've played with almost every Dom in the area. If that's an issue for you, you're shit out of luck."

"Not an issue, just curious. He's fiercely protective of his subs, you know. He never said a word about knowing you."

Somehow, that made Cornell feel better. He should have known after their conversation yesterday, when Master Ford had assured him as well that whatever they discussed would stay between them. Cornell was glad to see some Doms took the confidential part of their job seriously still.

"He's a great Dom," he offered. "I've only played with him twice, but very much worth it."

Rhys leaned forward, putting his utensils down as he stared at Cornell intently. "Do you usually have sex with your Doms?"

Cornell felt his cheeks heat up, much to his own irritation. This was nothing to be embarrassed about, so why did it feel like it? "Yes," he said, almost defiantly. "I never agree to it before I meet the Dom, but if it's someone I know and who I have played with before or someone with a good reputation, then yes. You'd be surprised how hard it is to score a good fuck, even without doing a scene. Most tops my age prefer younger bottoms."

Compassion bloomed in Rhys's eyes, and that was somewhat unexpected. Somehow, Cornell had thought he might get a little upset, jealous even, but he saw nothing but understanding.

"I'm sorry your needs haven't always been met," Rhys said. There was a polite wording if Cornell had ever heard one.

He wasn't sure where he got the courage to ask, since his self-confidence had taken hit after hit in recent years, but somehow, he found himself blurting out the words. "So, are you going to meet my needs?"

The air between them sizzled, Rhys's eyes so intense that Cornell couldn't look away if he wanted to. "Will you let me?" was Rhys's response.

"You really want to play with me?" Cornell asked.

"Very much so," Rhys said. "But do you trust me enough?"

Cornell considered the question. It was a good one, and yet one that was easy to answer now, after all the time he'd spent earlier thinking about his reasons to stay. "It's why I'm staying," he said softly. "I can think of many reasons to leave, some of them probably similar to your mother's objections. But at the end of the day, I came to the conclusion that I have one important reason to stay. You make me feel safe, and I do trust you."

Rhys's face lit up like he'd turned on a light. "Thank you. You have no idea how much it means to me to hear you say that, especially after I messed up so badly by not telling you."

"I mean it. And you know I made the decision before I was one hundred percent sure you wanted to play with me, though I'll admit that did factor into my decision. I could try to paint a more flattering picture, but as I said, the cold truth is that my options are very limited, so I really can't afford to turn down anyone willing to do a good scene with me."

Cornell wasn't sure how it was possible, but he saw his own pain reflected in Rhys's eyes. "I promise I will take good care of you," Rhys said, and Cornell believed him.

"Do you want a formal contract?" he asked Rhys. "Considering this won't be a one-time thing, at least, I assume."

Rhys almost looked offended. "Definitely not a one-time

thing. I'll leave that choice to you. I'm content with a verbal agreement, but if you prefer a formal one, I'm happy to oblige."

Cornell shrugged. "I think verbal will work for us, considering we know each other well."

"You already told me a little about your preferences, but what about your limits? Obviously, I won't go anywhere near them in the first few scenes, but I want to be aware of any triggers or soft or hard limits you have."

Cornell had done this spiel so many times that he knew it by heart. "Hard limits are water sports, scat play, and severe impact play. Because of my physical limitations, my pain tolerance level has gone down, so you'll find me safe wording relatively soon if it gets too intense. Kneeling is a soft limit, as is being restrained in a position that puts my weight on my knees."

He only realized who he was talking to when Rhys scoffed. "I hate to correct you, but kneeling is a hard limit for you."

Cornell smiled, strangely warmed by Rhys's genuine concern. "I'm sorry, I forgot that you know my physical limitations better than I do myself, probably."

Rhys nodded, a proud smile now adorning his face. "Other limits?" he asked.

"Aftercare is important to me, maybe as important as the scene. As you can hear, my preferences in combination with my limitations leave a very limited number of things to do," Cornell said, a wave of embarrassment and humiliation rolling through him. There were days when he longed to be twenty again, able to embrace whatever the Dom would throw at him. Then again, even at that age, he hadn't been extreme in his preferences.

"Bullshit," Rhys said firmly. "If you believe that, you've

never played with creative Doms, and if Doms ever told you that, they should definitely improve their skill level."

Sweet relief filled Cornell. "You think so?"

"Boy," Rhys said, and that word alone made Cornell's heart do funny things. "I can think of a million things I want to do with you."

RHYS WAS UNCHARACTERISTICALLY NERVOUS. He always had some sort of tension before a scene, but the sweaty palms he was experiencing now, combined with the floaters in his stomach and a heart that was racing, were of a whole different order. He'd prepared everything meticulously in the three days since Cornell had agreed to play with him. Hell, he'd even checked some things with Ford, wanting to make absolutely sure he had gotten everything right. There was little to no room for error here.

Maybe that's why he was so nervous, knowing how much was riding on this one scene. Oh, who was he kidding? Of course that's why he was nervous. He'd only been looking forward to this moment for what, years? He blew out a steadying breath as he waited for Cornell to show up.

His dad had created a playroom in his basement. It had been nothing elaborate or fancy, merely a private room away from curious eyes with some basic furniture that came in handy. Rhys had never known what had been in that mysterious room his dad had always kept locked until a few months ago, when he'd told him he'd been training as a Dom. Only then had his dad shown him around with a mix of embarrassment and pride.

Of course, the furniture had all been made by his dad.

There was a lovely St. Andrew's cross, a flogging bench, a sturdy table, and a few chairs with some handy features and embellishments. It would be the first time Rhys got to use the room, and maybe that, too, added to his nerves.

He felt his dad's presence in the entire house, but in this room? For some reason, it was even stronger here. It was funny, because aside from that one time he'd shown Rhys around, they'd never been in this room together. And yet, as he slowly walked around, his hand stroking the smooth surface of the furniture, he could almost feel his dad's presence.

He'd spent hours building this furniture, making sure it was able to withstand rough treatment. His hands had sanded the wood until it was soft as velvet to the touch, not a splinter anywhere. The kneeling bench had been padded with filling and fabric, probably to accommodate for the aging body of its owner. And for Cornell, Rhys knew. Cornell had played in this room with his dad many times, he guessed. How would he react to being back here? He would soon find out, as he heard his uneven steps on the stairs.

He was wearing a bathrobe with nothing underneath, and a wave of emotions rolled through Rhys as he saw the scars on his legs. He'd seen them plenty of times, but it was a painful reminder every single time how close he'd come to losing him as well.

Cornell slowly made his way over to him, sending him a tight smile. He was nervous too, Rhys realized. He wanted to reach out and hug him, but he held back, not sure that was what Cornell needed right now.

"How are you feeling?" he asked instead.

Cornell looked around the room, his eyes filling with sadness. "I haven't been down here since..."

He didn't need to finish that sentence, because they both knew what followed. Maybe it had been a bad idea to do the scene here. Maybe he would've been better off setting everything up upstairs, maybe even in the treatment room. After all, his massage table was plenty comfortable for Cornell. But it was too late now.

"We can do it upstairs," he heard himself say. "Not today, since I'd need some time to set it up there, but I'm happy to do it tomorrow if this room brings up too many painful memories for you."

Cornell met his eyes. "I gotta bite the bullet some time, don't I? I can't run away from the memories. He's everywhere in this house."

Objectively, he was right, but Rhys wondered if that really was the best headspace to start a scene in. Probably not, but what alternative did he have now? Should he cancel it? That didn't seem fair either when Cornell had told him he was okay to continue. God, he should've thought this through better, using this room.

"Are you sure you're good to go?" he checked again.

Cornell nodded. "Yes, Sir."

Rhys pushed his doubts down. If they were gonna do it, he couldn't second-guess himself. He needed to be confident. "Okay. Let's get started, then. Do you want to know what I have planned for you? Or would you like to be surprised?"

Cornell took a quick look around the room, then smiled. "I have a pretty good guess considering what I can see from your setup, but seeing as how this is our first scene together, I'd prefer to know."

"Were going to do some sensory play. It's low intensity, low impact, perfect to get to know each other a little bit."

"Sounds good, Sir."

Rhys kept marveling at how easy that word of respect came to Cornell, even when he took into consideration he'd been doing this for a long time. It felt as if Cornell could flip a switch as soon as they started playing and really saw Rhys as a Dom, not as his best friend's son.

"Do you want to use the color system or would you prefer to use specific safe words?"

Something flashed in Cornell's eyes, though his voice was level as he spoke. "I've been using the color system for years, because with a different Dom each time, I couldn't trust them to remember my safe words."

That simple statement held so much pain that Rhys felt it in his soul. "Let's start with the color system, then, and over time, you can decide whether you trust me to remember your safe words."

"Yes, Sir."

"Okay, I want you face up on the table. I'll make sure you're comfortable, so you don't have to worry about that."

This was the part where Rhys had expected Cornell to be uncomfortable, but the man calmly untied his bathrobe, carefully slid it off his shoulders, and neatly folded it. He put it down on a chair in the corner, then walked over to the table, which Rhys had outfitted with some extra cushions and rolled up towels to provide optimum support for Cornell.

Rhys took up position next to the table, holding out his hand to Cornell to help him up. He'd put at sturdy little footstool next to the table to make it easier for Cornell to climb on. The grateful look in Cornell's eyes meant everything to him.

Once Cornell was on his back, Rhys carefully put the cushions and rolled up towels in the right positions so his body was fully supported. "Are you comfortable?" he checked.

He loved that Cornell didn't answer right away but seemed to do a mental check of his body. "Yes, Sir. Thank you."

"I'm going to blindfold you now."

Cornell closed his eyes, and Rhys tied the black blindfold around his eyes, his hands shaking a little. Dammit, he had to get a grip on himself before Cornell picked up on his nerves. That wouldn't instill a helluva lot of confidence in his abilities as a Dom.

"You may make as many sounds as you want, but I would prefer for you not to speak unless you need to use your safe words," Rhys instructed him.

"Yes, Sir."

Rhys took a steadying breath, then reached for the first object he wanted to use. It was metal massage roller that you could heat up in hot water as well as cool off in the freezer. He'd warmed it enough so it was warm but not scorching hot. Rhys put it on Cornell's stomach. He jolted a little, so Rhys kept his hand still and allowed him to adjust. Then he started rolling it across his upper body with slow, light moves.

His goal was to get Cornell to relax, and that seemed to work as he heard him breathe out and saw the tension in his muscles lessen. When he was satisfied he'd reached his goal, he lifted the roller off his body and went for the next object. He'd cut a piece of the softest blanket he'd ever found and made a finger sleeve out of it, perfectly fitted to put one finger in. He started with Cornell's nipple, and again, his body jolted under the unexpected touch. Or maybe he had been expecting it, but it was hard to brace when you didn't know what was coming and where it would hit.

Rhys dragged soft circles around his right nipple, then did the same with the left. Cornell let out a little hum of appreciation, and Rhys trailed his finger down the man's sternum toward his bellybutton, and then even farther down. He bypassed his groin, of course. No need to rush things, now was there? Instead, he focused on his thighs, using the little piece of soft cloth to make random paths, working toward his groin area without ever touching it.

Next up was a feather, and he teased Cornell all over his body with it. He wasn't ticklish, Rhys discovered, not even under his feet, which was somewhat of a disappointment. Rhys had once observed a session where Ford had punished a sub by tickling him extensively, and it had been a lot of fun to watch.

So far, so good. Now it was time to mix things up. He'd only used comfortable elements, and now it was time to introduce something that was a little less comfortable. Ice came first, in the form of that same metal massage roller he'd used before, only this time one that came from the freezer.

He didn't warn Cornell before he put it on his nipples, and the man hissed in shock. Oh, but that had a lovely effect on him, his nipples turning in to gorgeous little buds. Someday, he would have to set up a session devoted to nipple play. He had a whole list of ideas for that.

The icy roller was also fun to use on Cornell's balls and dick, the first time he was touching him there. He'd been at half-mast before, but that quickly changed when he hit him with the cold. Rhys had to hold back a smile as Cornell instinctively tried to move his hips away from the freezing touch on his nuts and dick. No such luck, of course.

Rhys was also tempted to say something, but he knew from experience sensory play was so much better when you didn't say anything, when all the sub could do was feel. Ordinarily, he would put headphones on the sub as well, the noise-canceling ones, so he'd be unable to see or hear. But he had reckoned that was a bit too much for Cornell for the first scene.

After cold, it was time for sharp, and Rhys got out his Wartenberg wheel. A quick roll over both of his nipples had Cornell hissing all over again. Rhys frowned when Cornell's muscles tensed up. He wasn't moving, but trained as Rhys was to spot even minute muscle movements, he noticed that Cornell's body was not relaxed.

Should he ask if he was getting uncomfortable? As he kept moving the wheel across his chest, he quickly checked the man's positioning. It was almost impossible for him to be uncomfortable, what with how supported his body was. Maybe it was tension that came from expectation? The kind of anticipation that came from excitement? But if that was the case, why was he still completely soft?

His erection had gone down after Rhys had hit him with the cold, which was normal, but he should have recovered by now. Was it because he was older? Maybe his recovery time was different? But Rhys didn't trust that explanation. Something was off.

And with a sinking feeling in his stomach, he realized that he had no idea what was wrong.

12

Cornell wanted to soar, to fly. Hell, he wanted nothing more than to completely sink into the scene and get out of his head. But it wasn't working, and every second, he got more frustrated with himself. It wasn't anything Rhys was doing. No, this was all on him.

What the hell was wrong with him? So many times, he had complained to Jonas about not being able to fully sink into a scene because he'd been too uncomfortable, because the Dom had not taken his limitations into account, because he'd been playing with inexperienced Doms or with plain bad ones. And here he was, with a Dom who had taken more care than anyone else to make sure he was comfortable, who had clearly prepared this scene well, and yet Cornell couldn't do it.

For some reason, he was too much in his head, too aware of what was happening, of where he was, of who he was with. He couldn't stop thinking about the room he was in, the table he was on, which he had used so many times before with Jonas. And sometimes even without Jonas, as his friend had had no issue with Cornell setting up scenes with a Dom in his basement either, even if they didn't include him.

Was that it? Was his grief for Jonas, his lingering presence in this room, at fault? Or did he still have doubts about Rhys? Had he tried to convince himself he was okay with him as a Dom while his emotions hadn't caught up yet?

Rhys took the Wartenberg wheel away from his body, and Cornell forced himself not to tense up as he awaited the next step. It felt good, what Rhys was doing, so why couldn't he connect with it? It was like he was disconnected from his body, observing himself as if he wasn't in it. Objectively, he knew that whatever Rhys was doing should turn him on, and yet it didn't. And no matter how hard he willed himself to get hard, to get aroused, to get into the scene, dammit, he couldn't.

Something sharp pricked him, right below his left nipple. Needles? It had to be something similar. He was good with them, Cornell thought, pricking him in places he wasn't expecting. Suddenly, his left testicle was grabbed, and it was pinched together quickly. A clamp of some kind. Cornell usually loved that shit, as his balls were super sensitive, but even that didn't do anything for him.

God, he was such a failure. All he had wanted was to enjoy this scene, as much for himself as for Rhys. He'd wanted to prove to him he was good sub, an excellent sub, even with a Dom he never played with. And maybe, if he were honest, there had been a little hope involved as well. If he did well in their first scene together, surely Rhys would want to play with him again?

Fat chance of that happening now, with him failing so spectacularly. All he wanted was to please his Dom, and he wasn't delivering, not even close.

Maybe he'd been right all along. Maybe the accident had

damaged him, somehow, rendering him forever unsuitable as a sub. After all, he couldn't kneel, he couldn't perform a lot of activities that Doms expected from their subs. And even though he'd had erections, maybe things weren't working there as they had before either. Or it was a case of him getting older, which was a distinct possibility as well. Hadn't he read somewhere that erectile problems begin in your forties?

He hadn't even noticed Rhys had stopped until he suddenly heard him speak. "Red," Rhys said, his voice full of emotion. "I'm breaking off the scene. This is not right."

Something inside Cornell broke. He'd never had a Dom safe word out of the scene before because Cornell sucked at it. The clamp or whatever it had been was removed from his testicle, and seconds later, Rhys's hands untied his blindfold. Cornell kept his eyes closed, not wanting to see what had to be devastation in Rhys's eyes. Disappointment. Anger, maybe even.

"Cornell, will you please look at me?" Rhys asked.

He shook his head stubbornly. "No, I can't. Just... Leave me alone, please."

"You know I can't do that. That's not how this works. What happened?"

Rhys's voice was so full of hurt, of pain, that it sliced through Cornell's heart. He wanted to be honest with him more than anything, but if he did that, it would ruin any chance he had to ever play with him again. Plus, humiliation much?

"I don't know," he said instead.

"Oh, Cornell, please don't lie to me," Rhys said, and this time, the disappointment was clear.

"How's this? I don't want to talk about it," Cornell said, feeling himself getting more desperate. How could he tell

Rhys that despite everything he had planned and done, it still hadn't worked for him? He'd know instantly that Cornell was a failure as a sub, and that would be it.

"Tough shit," Rhys said, and there was the first spark of anger. "You know better than that. Something went wrong, and you and I are going to talk about it, whether you want to or not."

All Cornell wanted was to get the hell out of there, but with his aching body, even that dignity was out of the question. Finally, he opened his eyes, only to find Rhys staring at him. His eyes didn't hold the contempt or disappointment Cornell had expected, but rather sadness and a hint of anger. But there was something else there as well, something that was a little harder to pinpoint. It almost looked like...guilt?

Of course. He inwardly sighed as the realization hit him. "This wasn't your fault," he told Rhys.

Rather than responding, Rhys held out a hand to him to help him up. Cornell hesitated only briefly before he took it, knowing there was no way he could get up by himself, at least not gracefully. Rhys pulled him up by his good hand, while supporting his back with his other hand. As Cornell set up straight, waiting for his sense of equilibrium to return, Rhys walked over to the chair and grabbed his bathrobe.

He handed it to Cornell. "We're gonna go upstairs, where you will get dressed, and then we're gonna sit down in the living room, have a cup of tea, and talk about this. And whatever bullshit reasons you have or you think you have to try and get out of this, it's not gonna work."

And all Cornell could think about as Rhys looked at him that sternly was that he'd never seen him this dominant, and it was hot as fuck. Plus, impossible to resist, as he discovered. Because a few minutes later, he found himself exactly where Rhys had told him to be, awaiting what was bound to be one of the most uncomfortable conversations of his life.

He appreciated that Rhys gave him the time to settle down a bit. They set on the couch for a while, both sipping their tea, silence hanging in the room.

"It wasn't your fault," Cornell said. "You did nothing wrong."

Rhys gave him a sad smile. "It's hard for me to agree with your assessment when I don't have all the facts. So maybe you want to tell me what happened and I can decide for myself?"

He had a point there. Rhys would never accept he wasn't to blame unless Cornell gave him a more detailed explanation. And if he didn't, Rhys would blame himself. Cornell buried his head in his hands as he realized he was now caught in a catch-22. Either he kept this from Rhys, knowing that Rhys would blame himself, even though he hadn't been at fault. Or he would have to share the humiliating details, resulting in Rhys never wanting to play with him again. So which should he choose? His own humiliation or Rhys's?

Even before he fully formulated the question like that in his head, he already knew the answer. He would never deliberately hurt Rhys, and keeping the real reason why the scene had failed from him was exactly that.

"It was my failure," he said, keeping his head where it was so he wouldn't have to look at Rhys "I couldn't get into it, couldn't get out of my head."

"Do you know why? Were you physically uncomfortable? Was anything distracting you?"

Cornell shook his head. "I've never been more comfortable in a scene in my life. Like I said, it wasn't anything you did. This was all me. I just... I couldn't let go, couldn't get past all these thoughts that were running around in my brain."

"Maybe it wasn't intense enough for you to focus on," Rhys said. "Or maybe I should have put noise-canceling headphones on you after all, eliminating that distraction as well."

Cornell blew out a frustrated breath. "That wasn't it. I've done sensory play before, and I've always gotten into it, even when my hearing wasn't blocked."

"Do you think it would have helped if we'd done this upstairs, removed from the memories that room must have for you?" Rhys asked.

Something inside Cornell snapped, and his head shot up. "Are you not listening to a word I'm saying?" he bit out. "This was not your fault. This was me. This was me failing at being a sub and being good enough for you!"

His voice had risen to shouting level at those last words, and the room seemed to echo them around, throwing them right back into his face, adding to his humiliation. As if that wasn't enough, his eyes filled with tears. He'd cried more in the last months than he had in his whole life before, and he was sick and tired of it, sick and tired of feeling like this, of constantly hurting, inside and out.

"I wanted to be perfect for you, so you would want to play with me again. Clearly, I failed," he said, his voice much softer now, and breaking every few words. "You were perfect. The scene was perfect. It's me, and there is nothing you can do about it. I'm...broken."

His vision veiled by tears, he got up from the couch and walked out, unable to face the rejection he knew was coming after that emotional outburst. *Alone again*, was his first thought as he locked himself in his room, but then again, he and Rhys had never been together, now had they?

No, he'd been alone since the day Jonas had died, and fuck if that thought wasn't another crack in his already broken heart.

RHYS SAT for a long time after Cornell had stormed out, if you could call it storming out, considering how slow he'd walked. He'd been stunned by the man's outburst, blown away by the level of pain both in his words and on his face. How the hell had he missed that?

He'd been so focused on his own needs to perform, his own desire to be perfect, that he completely missed the fact that Cornell had felt the same. And no matter how much Cornell blamed himself, this was as much on Rhys. As a Dom, it was his responsibility to make sure he took care of his sub, and he had clearly failed here.

He should've known Cornell would raise the bar too high for himself. The man had always been a perfectionist, and Rhys knew that. Why had he not considered that would apply to subbing as well? Because he'd been too damn focused on himself, that's why. He'd concentrated on preparing the scene when he should have concentrated on preparing Cornell as well. If he had taken the time to assure him that there was no pressure, things could've worked out completely different.

With a deep sigh, he dug his phone from his pocket and called Ford. There was no way he was gonna try and muddle through this on his own. He needed advice, because as much as he realized Cornell was expecting him to walk away, there was no way in hell he was going to do that. No, he needed to fix this, and Ford needed to tell him how.

"Rhys, my young grasshopper, this is becoming quite the

habit," Ford said as a greeting, and Rhys couldn't help but smile.

"I need your advice," he said, getting straight to the point. "Is this a good time?"

He heard something rustle in the background, then a mumbled command he couldn't decipher. "I have a lovely sub on his knees right now, sucking me off, so as long as you don't mind me doing a little multitasking, I'm good."

Rhys grinned. "A little lesson in humiliation?" he asked.

Ford excelled at that, treating subs as if they were furniture. It was a jarring experience to see him do it, knowing how caring and empathetic he usually was. But Ford had explained that some subs needed it and others craved it, and after seeing it a few times, Rhys had been fully convinced. It wasn't his thing, but there was no doubt some people got off on it, Ford included.

"Oh, you betcha," Ford said. "I may have him on his knees all day, holding my dick in his mouth. Sounds like a perfect way to spend a day to me, right? But enough about me. Talk to me."

"We tried our first scene this morning," Rhys said. "It didn't go well."

He gave Ford a quick rundown of what had happened, including Cornell's explanation and emotional outburst.

"Damn," Ford said, that sexy teasing tone he'd used previously completely gone. "That's a lot of pain he showed you there."

"I missed it," Rhys said, feeling miserable all over again. "I had no idea he had put so much pressure on himself to be perfect. I think he believed that if he failed at this, for lack of a better word, that I would never want to play with him again."

Ford let out a short laugh, but it was not a happy one.

"The man has no idea of the depths of your feelings, does he?"

"No. But to be fair, I had no idea he felt like a failure, so clearly, we need to work on our communication."

"That's a given," Ford said. "But frankly, I think you need a little more than that. He's got a lot more going on than can be fixed with an open talk with his Dom."

Rhys considered that. "You're talking about his perception of failing at being a sub."

"I'm talking about all of it. Rhys, I know you lost your dad, but he lost his best friend, and from what I understand from your stories, they were a hell of a lot more than that. Who does he have left? Does he have a support system in place? Who is he talking to about this? You have me to talk to, and I know you talk to Raf as well, maybe not as specific about the D/s part, but you can certainly emotionally unload on him. But what about Cornell? Who can he talk to?"

Rhys leaned back on the couch, stunned by Ford's question. "I don't think he has anyone," he said slowly. "He has a sister, and they talk on the phone every now and then, but not long, and from what I can tell, not about personal stuff. He's been with me for ten days now, and I haven't heard him talk to any friends at all."

He shook his head as he realized this was something else he should have noticed.

"Don't blame yourself for this," Ford said, his voice warm and understanding. "This is not a lack of care or lack of interest. This is simply a lack of experience. Plus, it's often easier for an outsider to see things like this than it is for those who are involved in the situation directly."

"I think he needs grief counseling," Rhys said. "I have the feeling he thinks he needs to move on already from grieving, but I don't think he's ready yet. I talked to him about it back when he was still in the rehabilitation center, and he talked to a grief counselor there, but I don't think he had much of a connection with her."

"That sounds like a good step," Ford said. "But I also think you'll need to figure out how to connect him with more people, preferably people who are in the scene as well, so they have something in common. Bluntly put, he needs new friends. No one can ever take the place of your dad in your life or in his, but both of you will need to try."

That was actually an excellent idea, Rhys thought. He needed to find friends for Cornell, or at least a friend. Someone who could, even if it was just a little, be a sounding board for him. "How do I find friends for him?" he said out loud. "Most of my friends are my age, and I think he needs to have someone his own age as well."

"I agree. I'd be happy to come over and talk to him some-time, but I don't think I'm what he needs, considering I'm too close to you. Maybe you could ask Brendan and Raphael over for dinner? You and Raphael are already friends, so maybe he and Brendan could connect?"

Rhys frowned. "That kind of sounds like a double date."

Ford chuckled. "Why does it need to have a name? It's two couples getting together for a relaxing evening. If they don't click, no harm done."

"We're not a couple," Rhys said.

Ford's reaction was to chuckle again. "You keep telling yourself that, sweet summer child. But I gotta go. I have an urge to come, and I can't do that, because this naughty sub hasn't earned my seed yet. I think I need to fuck this obsti-nate streak out of him first. I'll talk to you later, Rhys."

13

Cornell had been nothing but confused in the two days that had passed since their aborted scene. He'd expected Rhys to be upset with him, angry, disappointed, even. But instead, Rhys had acted like he had before. He hadn't brought up the incident again, but he hadn't treated Cornell any differently either. Maybe this was his way of showing pity? Like, he wasn't actually going to come out and say they weren't going to play anymore, but he assumed Cornell would just understand that?

For a fleeting moment, Cornell had considered leaving again, but he'd shoved that thought deep down. He couldn't even deal with the other people that would bring right now, not when his mind was already in such turmoil. Instead, he had followed Rhys's lead and had pretended everything was okay.

And it had been, strangely enough. Rhys had run his daily exercises with him, even doing a quick massage on his shoulder this morning. He hadn't followed it up with a sensual one like before, but Cornell had been grateful to get his attention and care.

And today, Rhys was having friends over for dinner, and he had explicitly invited Cornell to join them. That made zero sense to Cornell, but he decided to go along with it anyway. He felt adrift at sea, and anything that Rhys could do to give him at least a little sense of direction, he'd embrace.

He'd swapped his usual sweatpants for something he hadn't worn in months—a pair of dark-blue slacks. They were a little loose on him, he'd realized when he'd put them on. Apparently, he'd lost weight. Still, he looked a hell of a lot more presentable in that, combined with the pink and light-blue checkered shirt that he'd barely worn.

"It's good to see you in clothes like that," Rhys commented when Cornell walked into the living room. "How does it feel?"

"It feels good," Cornell admitted. "I've gotten used to wearing the sweat pants and everything, but I have to admit, I feel different when I wear this. Maybe a classic case of clothes make the man and all that?"

Rhys smiled. "Well, it's nice to see you like this."

"I wouldn't welcome guests dressed in that ratty outfit I've been wearing for months now," Cornell said, almost shocked Rhys would even consider that. Then he realized it had been exactly what Rhys had watched him wear the whole time he'd been staying here, and he blushed a little. Should he have made more of an effort for him? That was a weird consideration for sure.

The doorbell rang, and Rhys got up to answer it. Cornell was strangely nervous now, his hands even growing a little sweaty, though he had no earthly idea why. Was it because these were friends of Rhys and he wanted to make a good impression? Or rather, he wanted not to embarrass Rhys. How was that for setting a standard?

The couple was not what he had expected at all. The first to walk in was a slim guy who looked familiar. He was practically bouncing with energy, his brown curls dancing on his head as he hurried over to Cornell to shake his hand.

"It's so good to see you again," the guy said, and as soon as he heard his voice, Cornell remembered. This was Raf, who had been Rhys's best friend since high school. He'd met him a few times when Rhys had still been a teen, but it had been a while since he'd seen him.

"Raphael," Cornell said warmly, then added, "though if I remember correctly, you prefer to be called Raf, no?"

He was rewarded with a happy smile. "Right. The only one who calls me Raphael is my Daddy when he's upset with me," Raf said, beaming an excited look at the muscular bear of a man behind him.

Ah, Cornell thought, that type of Daddy. He extended his hand to the man, who had to be close to him in age, judging by the silver that was popping up at his temples. "Cornell," he introduced himself. "Very happy to meet you."

The funny thing was that he really was looking forward to this evening, though he couldn't explain why. He'd always liked Raf, so maybe that was it. He'd been a happy kid, bouncy, full of energy, and a little mischievous. But he had the biggest heart you could ever find, and he and Rhys had been joined at the hip.

"Brendan. Thanks so much for having us over," Raf's Daddy said. For a second, Cornell wondered why the man would thank him when it was Rhys's house he was invited to, but then he mentally shrugged. It was a polite expression, nothing more.

They settled in the living room, and Rhys said, "Can I get you guys some drinks to start with?"

Raf immediately looked at Brendan. "Can I please have a glass of wine, Daddy?"

Cornell admired him for being so secure and confident in his relationship both with his Daddy and with Rhys that he trusted to be himself like that.

His Daddy's answer was swift. "Absolutely not. You remember what happened the last time you had alcohol?"

Raf's cute mouth pulled together into a pout. "Please, Daddy?"

Brendan's eyebrows drew together. "I said no, baby boy. Now stop whining, or you lose your bath privileges."

The look Raf sent Rhys told Cornell this was not something to joke about, and he wasn't surprised when Raf said, "Apple juice, please."

And as if it was the most normal thing in the world, Rhys asked, "Do you want a regular glass or a sippy cup?"

"The sippy cup, please, and thank you," Raf said, and his happy smile melted Cornell's heart a little.

Rhys took the rest of the drink orders, and when he had disappeared to the kitchen to fill them, Raf looked at Cornell. "Did Rhys tell you anything about me? About the relationship I have?"

If there had ever been a time where Cornell was grateful for his experience and exposure to all kinds of kinks, it was now. "No, because he takes confidentiality seriously, but I kind of got the gist of it."

He didn't say anything more, wanting to leave it to Brendan and Raf how much they were willing to share.

"We usually check with people to make sure it doesn't make them uncomfortable," Brendan said, half apologetic. "Raf tends to drop into little-mode when he's around people he trusts, like Rhys, but if you object to that in any way, we'll make sure to keep it limited."

Cornell chuckled. "Vanilla is boring," he said. "Please, be yourself. I've seen pretty much everything there is to see, so not only won't it shock me, it doesn't bother me in the least. I'm always happy to see people expressing their true selves."

"See, Daddy?" Raf said, his clear voice ringing through the room. "I told you Cornell was cool."

Brendan smiled at his boy, the love radiating from his eyes. "Yes, you did, baby boy. But you know I'm always careful. I don't want you to get hurt."

Without any embarrassment, Raf climbed on his Daddy's lap and snuggled against him. "That's why you are the best Daddy in the whole world."

Rhys came back carrying a tray with the drinks, which he handed out one by one. "Does he want to play for a little bit?" he asked Brendan, and Cornell realized he was talking about Raf.

It warmed his heart, this complete acceptance Rhys had of his friend. He wasn't merely tolerating his relationship with Brendan, he was completely embracing it, facilitating it even.

"He had a rough day at work," Brendan said quietly, and he held Raf a little tighter. "If it wasn't for the fact that we knew you'd be okay with it, we would've canceled tonight, because he really needs some time to relax."

Rhys nodded. "I figured as much. I'll get out some toys for him."

Cornell watched in amazement as Rhys brought out a special playing rug, then put down a box of cars on the floor for Raf. "Here you go, buddy," he said. "Have fun."

The smile on Raf's face was blinding, and he immediately slid off his Daddy's lap and crawled onto the playing rug on the floor, reaching for the cars. It did something to Cornell, watching the genuine care Rhys had for his friend.

When he looked up from studying Raf for a bit, he found
Rhys's eyes locking with his. Something burned in them,
something he hadn't seen there before. Whatever it was, it
was mesmerizing, and he couldn't look away. Their eyes
stayed locked, until Rhys finally smiled at him before
looking away. What had that been about?

Conversation flowed easily, and Cornell discovered he
and Brendan had a lot in common. Brendan worked as a
real estate agent, and he and Cornell both shared some
amusing incidents with completely oblivious clients. All
that time, Raf was happy playing with his cars, taking a sip
from his apple juice whenever his Daddy handed it to him.

"Dinner will be ready in five minutes," Rhys said after
coming back from checking on the lasagna in the oven.

That seemed to be some kind of signal, because Brendan
got up from his seat and crouched down next to Raf. His
hand found a spot on his head, caressing his curls. "I'm sure
you can play some more after dinner, but we need to get
ready first."

Raf let out a little sigh, but then leaned into Brendan's
touch. "Yes, Daddy."

Brendan helped him up, and the two of them disappeared into the guest bathroom. Before Cornell could even
say anything, Rhys said, "He's deep into little mode tonight."

It only took a second for Cornell to decipher the
meaning of that. "He's wearing a diaper," he concluded.

Rhys nodded. "I noticed when they came in. He doesn't
usually wear them during the week, but as Brendan said, he
had a rough day at work, and he needs it then. It's his safety
net."

"You're a wonderful friend to him," Cornell said. "Not
many people would have as much understanding as you do.
He's lucky to have you."

"I'm just as lucky to have him," Rhys said, his voice breaking a little. Cornell didn't understand why, until he saw the look in his eyes. The sadness wasn't for himself—it was for Cornell, for losing Jonas.

It hit him out of nowhere, this horrible cloud of dark grief that descended on him. His throat clenched up, his breaths painful as he had to force them out, his eyes filling with tears so fast they were already spilling down his cheeks. A sound erupted from his mouth, inhuman. He hardly recognized his own voice as he made another sound, something that sounded an awful lot like a wail.

Rhys held him, a strong wall around him, and Cornell gave in to the grief that battered him, wave after wave after wave. And then he did wail, loudly, crying and yelling over and over and over again, until his voice gave out and he had no more words.

"I miss him. I miss him so much."

NEEDLESS TO SAY, this was not how Rhys had planned for things to go. Out of all the things he had anticipated, Cornell breaking down like this had not been one of them. And yet, somehow, it seemed inevitable at the same time, as if it had been coming for a long time. Rhys held him, first loosely, but as Cornell crawled into his arms, as tight as he could manage on the couch.

When it became clear that this was not a simple crying fit, but something much deeper, Brendan signaled him that he'd taken the lasagna out of the oven. Rhys nodded, sending him a grateful look as his two friends quietly left. He didn't even feel guilty, knowing that as much as he and Cornell needed privacy right now, Raf could use it as well.

Cornell never even seemed to notice them leaving, his face buried against Rhys's chest. Did he even realize he was completely on top of Rhys, their bodies pressing against each other everywhere? It wasn't even sexual. Sure, it excited Rhys, but the emotional impact far outweighed that.

When Cornell finally calmed down, it was almost half an hour later. His body had gone slack on top of Rhys's, his breathing slowed down to a soft trickle now, no longer the desperate sobs. Rhys had held him, alternating between holding him tight and softly rubbing his back, his head, even his ass. He wanted him to feel his touch, to let Cornell know he was not alone.

He could pinpoint the exact moment Cornell became aware of what had happened. One second, his body had been completely relaxed, the next, tension filled it, and he shifted. Rhys heard him take a breath. "If the next words out of your mouth are in any way an apology, I don't want to hear them," he told Cornell softly but firmly.

As he had expected, Cornell closed his mouth again.

"You have absolutely nothing to apologize for, and if you try to anyway, I will find a way to punish you that you will find distinctly unpleasant."

He wasn't even sure why he took this approach with Cornell, this firm tone. Call it instincts, but something told him this was what he needed to hear right now.

Cornell's quiet "Yes, Sir" told him he'd done the right thing.

"Did they leave?" Cornell asked maybe a minute later.

"Yes. But again, not something to feel guilty about. My guess is that if the dinner hadn't been set up to meet you, they would've canceled, what with how Raf was feeling."

"I didn't notice anything off with him," Cornell said. "Is he okay?"

"Like you, he's good at pretending. Good thing he has a Daddy who sees straight through his bullshit."

Cornell was quiet at that for a bit. "I wasn't aware I was pretending," he said finally. "I really thought I was past this stage of grief."

Rhys held him tight, his fingers slipping under Cornell's button-down and finding some tense points in his muscles to knead. "It's not a linear process, grief. Everyone is different. And if you don't allow yourself to feel the pain, it will sneak up on you later."

Cornell let out a soft moan as Rhys massaged a tender spot on his back. "How did you get so wise?"

Rhys let out a short laugh. "I'm not wise. I'm winging it, as much as you are. I just happened to have read a few books on grief recently."

"You always were a bookworm," Cornell said. "Like me."

"Not so much a bookworm as someone who prefers theoretical knowledge before trying something out. Whenever we got some new tool or appliance, Dad would start flipping buttons and turning knobs, whereas I would read the manual first."

"And what does the manual on grief say?"

"That it takes time and that you have to allow yourself to feel whatever it is you're feeling. There's no timetable here, no pressure to move through this process in a certain way or at a certain speed."

Cornell breathed in deeply. "I felt like I should've moved on by now, like it wasn't normal for me to still be at this stage of such intense pain."

"Oh sweetheart," Rhys said, the term of endearment slipping out of his mouth all by itself. "It's okay for you to miss him as long as you need to. No one is telling you you need to move on."

"I don't understand how it's so different for you. He was your dad. I know how much you loved him. Why aren't you suffering in the same way?"

It wasn't an unreasonable question, and Rhys had thought about it as he'd held Cornell during his breakdown. "First of all, like I said, everyone is different, and everyone grieves differently. There is no worse or better way, no right way. And second, I had a fantastic support system from day one. Say what you want about my mom, but she was there for me those first weeks. And so were Raf and Brendan, as well as Ford."

Cornell's exhale sounded a little shaky. "I never realized how small my world had become until this happened. I have a shit ton of acquaintances, people I have gotten to know over the years, that I've worked with or played with. But no one was as close as your dad, and losing him robbed me of the one person who understood me."

How accurate had Ford's analysis been, Rhys realized all over again. "I know, sweetheart," he said, this time deliberately using that term to see how Cornell would react.

Other than a quick intake of breath, he didn't react at all, but he stayed in Rhys's arms, and that spoke volumes.

"I'm exhausted," Cornell said after a while.

"I can imagine. Do you want anything to eat before you go to bed?"

"A light snack, I think. Something to tide me over."

"Okay, why don't you go take a nice, hot shower to help you relax a little? When you're done, I'll help you get into bed and bring you a snack."

Rhys wanted so much for Cornell to accept his care, but he couldn't force it on him. It had to be his choice to submit to it. And so Rhys waited, with bated breath.

"I'd love that," Cornell whispered, and Rhys's heart did a happy little dance.

He helped Cornell get up, and when the man studiously avoided looking him in the eye, he grabbed his chin and forced it. "Don't you dare feel ashamed or any of that crap," he told him sternly. "You needed this."

Cornell's face softened. "Thank you."

Rhys didn't trust him to be steady enough, so he held him as they shuffled to his bedroom, Cornell a good deal slower than usual. The lines on his face were deep, showing how tired he was. Of course, his swollen, red eyes didn't exactly improve his look either.

Rhys didn't let him go until Cornell had lowered himself on the bed, and then he walked into the bathroom to start the shower. It was one of the few disadvantages of the house; it took forever for the warm water to reach the showers, so you had to run the water for at least a minute before it had the right temperature.

When he walked back into the room, Cornell was sitting exactly as he'd left him. "Let's get you undressed," Rhys said calmly, taking charge.

Cornell let it happen, another clear indication he was beyond exhausted. Rhys took off his shoes and socks, then gestured for him to stand up so he could unbutton his shirt and drag down his pants and underwear. Cornell didn't react to standing naked in front of him, and Rhys wanted to hug him something badly. Instead, he gently steered him toward the shower.

"Take a brief shower. Relax a little. I'll be right back."

He prepared an apple for him, one of the slightly sour Granny Smith ones that Cornell loved so much, then added some almonds and a few cubes of cheese to it. That would have to do, combined with a glass of milk.

When he walked back into Cornell's bedroom, the shower was still running. He put the tray with the food down and went into the bathroom, where he found Cornell standing under the hot water like a zombie. His heart clenched painfully in his chest, then filled with compassion.

He switched off the shower. "Come on, sweetheart, time for bed."

Cornell allowed Rhys to dry him off with a towel, something that would be unthinkable under normal circumstances. Rhys found him a clean pair of boxers, then wanted to put his pajama pants on, but Cornell shook his head. "Too warm. Just the boxers."

Rhys helped him into bed, where Cornell almost immediately closed his eyes. "Don't fall asleep yet," Rhys told him. "You have to eat a little."

"Too tired," Cornell protested, then yawned loudly as if to underscore his point.

"If you don't eat a little something now, you'll wake up in the middle of the night because you're hungry," Rhys pointed out.

"Yes, Sir," Cornell said, then opened his mouth like a little bird, his eyes still closed.

Rhys smiled as he popped a bit of cheese into his mouth and watched him chew it, never opening his eyes. As soon as his mouth was empty, he opened it again, and Rhys fed him another bit of cheese. It took a few minutes before he'd cleared his plate.

"Good boy," Rhys said, unable to hold back the praise that he had earned.

That made Cornell open his eyes, and the look he shot Rhys was a mix of shock and pride. He opened his mouth as if he wanted to say something, but then closed it again. Rhys tucked the covers under his chin, then couldn't resist the urge to caress his hair.

"What did you want to say?" he asked him softly.

"I don't want to be alone right now," Cornell said, his voice barely audible.

Rhys's insides fired up with a deep sense of victory. This was the first time Cornell had admitted his needs so clearly. He didn't hesitate, but stripped down to his own underwear within seconds, carelessly throwing his clothes on the floor. Then he switched off the light and climbed into bed next to Cornell.

Before he had even positioned himself completely, Cornell rolled against him. Well, half on top of him, more correctly. He moved around until he found a comfortable position, it seemed. His head was on Rhys's shoulder, his arm wrapped tightly around his stomach, while his one leg had found a spot between Rhys's legs. Rhys was effectively trapped by Cornell's body, but hell if he cared.

Within seconds, Cornell was asleep, and much to his own surprise, it didn't take Rhys long to follow him.

14

Cornell woke up disoriented, his throat parched and his head throbbing behind his eyes and temples. Where was he? What the hell had happened? Then he became aware of the warm body he was draped all over, and his priorities shifted. For one glorious second, he thought he was with Jonas again, but then reality came crashing in on him.

Breathe, he told himself. It's okay. Slowly, his heart rate came down and as a result, so did his breathing. No, it wasn't Jonas, and it would never be again. But he'd bawled his eyes out over that yesterday, hence the dry throat and the slight headache. Shame bubbled up inside of him, but Rhys's words echoed through his mind. *You needed that*, he'd said, and how right he had been.

He'd always thought that when you were in your forties, you'd completely know yourself to the point where you couldn't be surprised by your own feelings or emotions anymore. Ha! How wrong he had been. That outburst yesterday? He'd never seen that coming.

He'd thought the grieving over Jonas had been coming

along. Sure, it had been hard to think about it, much less talk about him without finding it hard to breathe, but that seemed to be consistent with mourning, with grieving. But he hadn't been aware that he hadn't let his feelings out, not until they had forced themselves out.

And when he'd finally come down and Rhys had held him, he'd been struck by the inevitability of that breakdown. As if finally his mind allowed him to see what had been building up all that time. He'd cried, and he'd been sad over Jonas plenty of times, but never with the full force of his emotions. He'd always held back, maybe because he'd been scared of them.

Now he knew. Now he knew that as horrible as that sensation of being swallowed whole by the grief had been, he'd survived it. That meant he could do it again if he had to. There was no reason to be scared anymore. He'd hit rock bottom, it felt like, and he'd found his way back up.

Not by yourself, his mind whispered at him, and he only had to feel the warm body underneath him to know the truth of that thought. He hadn't done it by himself, because he hadn't needed to. Rhys had been there, like a rock, his anchor, holding him for as long as he had needed. Cornell had clung to him as if he'd been the only thing keeping him afloat in that ocean of grief. Maybe he had been.

One thing he did know: their relationship would never be the same. Then again, they kept shifting their definitions, their boundaries, anyway. The massages, Rhys watching him come, then that aborted scene, and now this outburst. Hell, they were in bed together now, having spent the night together. To Cornell, that was far more intimate than sex, than playing together.

So maybe in light of the realization that he clearly hadn't been honest with himself about his emotions, maybe it was time for a long, hard look at how he felt about all of this. About him and Rhys, and if someone had told him a year ago there would be a him and Rhys, he would've laughed them out of the room.

The expected rejection after their aborted scene hadn't come. They hadn't really talked about it after the initial conversation, but Rhys's behavior toward him hadn't changed from before, much to Cornell's surprise. If anything, he'd been even more caring and attentive. Cornell wasn't sure how Rhys felt about that scene, but clearly, he didn't full-on blame Cornell. Or if he did, he seemed to have moved past it. Had he moved past it to the point where he was willing to play with him again? Cornell wasn't a hundred percent sure, but the signs indicated he might.

Before, his own biggest issue had been whether or not he could trust Rhys, fueled by the fact that he'd conveniently forgot to tell him he was a Dom at first. As big as that breach of trust had seemed in the beginning, it now felt more like a misunderstanding, a blip on the radar. Rhys had shown such care of him since, such trustworthy behavior, that he couldn't find a single reason not to trust him. And boy, was it easy to obey him. That, more than anything, surprised Cornell.

There were differences in obedience. There was the outward obedience he gave a Dom he didn't know well but who said the right things. That was obedience out of routine, if you could call it that, years of experience in doing and saying the right thing. As long as a Dom wouldn't go too far or ask him to do something he really didn't want to, that obedience came easy.

Then there was the real obedience, the kind that seemed to come from his soul, the type of obedience that brought him pleasure. That one wasn't routine by any standard, but came out of an innate desire to obey. That's exactly what he felt with Rhys. When Rhys told him to do something, he *wanted* to obey. He wanted to please him, to make him happy, to serve him.

The question was, what did that mean? And more importantly, where did they go from here? If Rhys wanted to play with him again, should he say yes? Never mind, that was a stupid question. Of course he should say yes. There was no way he'd be able to say no. But where would that lead?

"I can almost hear you thinking," Rhys mumbled. His hands found Cornell's head, softly caressing his hair. "How did you sleep?"

Cornell leaned into his touch, resisting the urge to purr like a kitten. "Really well. I have a bit of a headache now and my throat is parched, but other than that, good."

"Mmmm, glad to hear it," Rhys said, still sounding a bit sleepy.

"And you?" Cornell asked.

A soft chuckle reverberated through the chest his cheek was resting on. "The best night's sleep I've had in a long time."

"I wasn't too clingy for you? Invading your personal space?" Cornell checked.

That resulted in another chuckle, and Rhys scratched his neck a little. "In case the signals weren't clear, I don't mind at all. Quite the opposite, in fact."

Cornell's heart did a happy little skip when he heard that. He wanted to say how much he loved waking up like this, then decided against it. He'd better not move too fast.

"So, I was thinking," Rhys said, and Cornell chuckled.

"Wasn't that what you accused me of doing? Isn't it a little early for thinking?"

Rhys's hand dropped to Cornell's ass and gave it a quick slap. "Don't you get mouthy with me now," he said, his voice light but with that wonderful undertone of dominance that Cornell loved so much.

"Yes, Sir," he said, barely able to keep the happiness out of his voice.

"That's better," Rhys said, and the hand on his ass started rubbing him. Cornell had to resist the impulse to move against it, knowing that would not have the desired effect. "As I was saying," Rhys continued. "I was thinking that you might benefit from another scene today."

Well, that wiped the smile right off Cornell's face. Sure, he'd hoped to play with Rhys again, but today? When he was still so fragile and vulnerable? That was a disaster waiting to happen.

"Don't you get all stressed now," Rhys said softly, his hand now rubbing in big circles over Cornell's ass, then traveling up his back and down again. "I know you're scared after what happened last time, but that wasn't your fault."

"It wasn't your fault either," Cornell felt obliged to say.

Rhys let out a little sigh. "It was, a little, but I've stopped beating myself up over it. And so should you. Look, we both know that these things happen, especially when a Dom and a sub don't know each other very well."

"But we do know each other, better than anyone I've ever played with," Cornell brought up.

"I know, but in this case, I think that was exactly what caused the frustration. Both of us wanted it to be perfect right out of the gate, because we know each other and wanted to please the other. I think our expectations of ourselves were a little unrealistic. So we'll try again, but this time, we'll lower expectations."

"I don't know how to do that," Cornell said, feeling he

should be honest to avoid any miscommunication. "I want to be perfect."

"Why?" Rhys asked, and it didn't sound like an accusation at all. More like genuine interest, someone trying to understand.

And with his head on Rhys's chest, the man's left arm wrapped around him while his right was still caressing him, Cornell felt safe enough to confess the truth. "I'm scared that if I fail, you won't want to play with me anymore."

He heard Rhys's sharp intake of breath, and his hand stopped for a second before it resumed. "I'm sorry I gave you that impression," he said, and Cornell was blown away at how he took responsibility even for that. "I should've made clear that your performance, for lack of a better word, has no bearings whatsoever on my desire to play with you. I will do scenes with you for as long as you want me to, regardless of how things go. The only reason that would make me stop is if both of us agreed that we're not a good fit."

Something happened inside Cornell. Something broke free he hadn't realized was bound. It was a strange feeling, the liberation of something so deep inside you, you were barely aware it existed. To say it was his soul sounded overdramatic, but it had to be pretty close to it. This quiet assurance that Rhys wanted him as a sub no matter what happened, that created such freedom inside him.

He struggled to find the words to express himself, so in the end, he settled on, "Thank you."

"So when we play again today, what is the only thing that you have to focus on?"

With the long breath Cornell expelled, the last tension released from his body. "On obeying you, Sir."

"That's right, boy. All you have to do is do as I tell you. That's it."

Cornell's heart soared. *Boy.* Had there ever been a more precious word?

DESPITE THEIR TALK this morning in bed—and there was a situation Rhys had been dreaming about for years—Rhys knew Cornell was still nervous. They both were. But he wouldn't make the same mistake as last time by pretending they weren't.

He'd debated whether or not he should use the basement, and in the end, he'd decided not to. He wasn't sure what role the lingering memories of his dad had played in what had happened in the previous scene, but it couldn't hurt to take precautions and avoid a repeat. Even more because of how emotional Cornell had been the day before, grieving so deeply.

Doing a scene upstairs meant he had more limited options, but then the perfect idea had come to him. Maybe he'd wanted to do something way too elaborate for their first scene, he analyzed in hindsight. He'd wanted to impress Cornell, apparently as much as Cornell had wanted to impress him, but it had been too complicated to start with. So he'd learn from his mistake and keep it simple this time. Simple, but perfectly tailored toward Cornell.

He asked him to report to the living room an hour after lunch, so Cornell's food would've had time to settle. Cornell stepped into the room at exactly the agreed time, dressed in the slacks and button-down shirt Rhys had asked him to wear. Cornell had looked at him quizzically when he'd asked, but he hadn't asked any questions, and Rhys had been pleased with that. It was another sign of the growing trust between them.

Rhys rose up from the couch to greet him. "I want you to stand straight for me, your feet about twenty inches apart, your hands clasped behind your back. Don't pull on them, so you don't put pressure on your shoulder. Now, keep your back straight and bow your head."

Cornell allowed Rhys to help him find the correct position, and then he stood still, perfectly displaying himself.

"Ah, that looks beautiful. Please hold that position for now," Rhys said.

He walked around Cornell, wanting to make sure the position wasn't aggravating his injuries in any way. He did a quick check of his shoulder to make sure Cornell had obeyed him and wasn't putting a strain on the muscles, but they felt relaxed. He caught a slight tremble in his left leg, the one that had been shattered, but that was simply because he wasn't used to standing yet. That would get better over time. They had to build it up.

"From now on, when you present yourself to me at the beginning of a scene, I want you to take this position to show me respect," Rhys said.

"Yes, Sir," Cornell said, and Rhys could hear the joy in his voice that he'd been able to please his Dom.

On impulse, he rubbed his head. "Such a good boy."

He swore Cornell's face started glowing.

He walked around him one more time, pleased that this part was working out, then took position behind him. They were close in height, but he had maybe an inch on Cornell, and he loved that, petty as it was. It allowed him to step close to him, pressing his body against him from the back and lower his mouth to Cornell's ear.

"This time, I'm not going to tell you what we're going to do. That way, you won't have anything else to focus on but what I ask you to do. And you are going to do what I tell you, aren't you?"

"Yes, Sir."

Oh, the perfection of those two words coming out of Cornell's mouth. Rhys was dizzy with it all over again. "So if I told you it would please me to see you do a striptease for me, what would you do?"

He let his teeth graze Cornell's ear lobe, and the man shivered. "I would do it, Sir."

"And if I told you I wanted you to walk around naked for the rest of the day, so I could fill my need to see you, would you do it?"

"Yes, Sir," Cornell said, sounding breathy.

"Would you let me play with your beautifully responsive nipples for a few hours? Find out how close to insanity I can bring you with that?"

He'd switched to Cornell's other ear, blowing hot breaths over it, then put his teeth into the shell lightly. Cornell trembled against him.

"Yes, Sir. Whatever you want, Sir."

"Whatever I want? That's a dangerous thing to promise to your Dom, boy," Rhys said, oh so pleased with Cornell's answers.

"I trust you, Sir."

Rhys felt like he'd been shocked with electricity, not the bad kind that only hurt, but the good kind that give you a rush like nothing else. "Ah, what a perfect answer," he praised him.

He was still standing behind him, but Cornell hadn't broken his posture even once. Rhys ground his hips, slowly circling them so his now iron hard cock rubbed against Cornell's hand. Such a perfect boy, standing still for his master to use him. Someday he would, but today, he had different plans.

With regret, he stepped back, then walked in front of Cornell, who kept his head bowed. "Arms to your side and raise your head."

Cornell's eyes were on fire, burning with whatever it was that crackled between them. Rhys reached for the top button of the man's shirt. "Someday, I will let you do a little striptease for me." He flicked open the first button, quickly followed by the second. "And in the summer, when it's hot, I will definitely have you walk around the house naked for a whole day. Or maybe for a whole week, because I like looking at you."

He opened button after button while talking, revealing Cornell's chest. The man had neatly trimmed chest hair, dark with some gray sprinkled in. Rhys slid his hand over Cornell's chest, pleased when Cornell didn't react other than with a quick intake of breath. He flicked one nipple, then the other, which made Cornell gasp even more.

"You like that, don't you?"

"Yes, Sir," Cornell said, his voice thick.

"Mmm, I'll have to remember that. You know how most Doms tell their subs not to touch their balls or their cock? Maybe I should add your sweet little nipples to the list. What do you think?"

He saw Cornell swallow before he answered. "If that would please you, Sir."

Rhys smiled at the perfection of that answer as he gave one last, loving caress over Cornell's chest, then pulled his shirt tails out of his slacks. With his shirt hanging off his shoulders, Cornell looked like he was about to have sex, which was a good look on him, Rhys decided.

"You look sexy," he told Cornell, slipping his index finger

behind his waistband and teasing his sensitive skin there a little. Goosebumps broke out all over Cornell's chest, and his nipples hardened all over again.

"Thank you, Sir."

"You know, when you walked into the room, immaculately dressed in that nice shirt and those neat pants, you looked perfectly respectable. Like a serious businessman, a moral cornerstone of society."

He flicked the clasp of his slacks open with one hand, then roughly shoved his hand down his pants, grabbing Cornell's cock and balls in one bold move. The sound Cornell made was delicious, a mix between a grunt and a squeal. He jerked his hips back for a second, but he could be forgiven for that, as there was not a man on earth who wouldn't have the same reaction.

"But you're not so moral on the inside, are you? You're quite the dirty boy."

"Yes, Sir," Cornell breathed.

Rhys's smile widened as he intensified his grip on Cornell's junk a little. "You like it when another man holds you like this, don't you?"

Cornell's cheeks were fiery red now, his eyes blazing with need. "Yes, Sir," he managed, but it was clear that it cost him to talk right now.

He almost had him where he wanted him, which was to be so overcome by all the sensations that he would forget to think. He took a step back, then pulled Cornell forward by his cock. He sought Rhys's eyes to make sure he was allowed to move, and Rhys nodded at him ever so slightly to indicate permission. Another step back, and Cornell followed again. He allowed Rhys to lead him forward by his dick, not once protesting.

Rhys walked backward until he felt the couch behind

him, then sat down. Without saying a word, he unzipped Cornell's pants, shoving them down in one move with his underwear. Cornell's cock slapped against his stomach with a wet sound.

"No one who sees you like this would still believe you were so respectable, now would they?"

Cornell bit his lip before answering. "No, Sir."

"What would they think if they saw you like this, with your pants shoved down and your junk hanging out?"

"They'd think I was dirty, Sir," Cornell said, his voice dropping to a whisper. But oh, he liked it. If the fire in his eyes and the blush on his cheeks hadn't been enough of an indication, his cock was leaking, so hard it almost quivered.

Rhys grabbed his cock, spreading the precum with his thumb. That resulted in a deep moan from Cornell. Good, the man had remembered Rhys like to hear his sounds. "Dirty? Or naughty?"

He fisted Cornell a few times, lightning fast, making him gasp. "Both, Sir. Both!"

"Perfect answer," Rhys said.

He let go of his cock and reached for his wrists, pulling him in the right position. With any other sub, he would've yanked them over his lap, but Cornell's body couldn't take that. He needed more support than Rhys's knee as well, since he couldn't put any weight on his knees. This was the perfect solution.

He pulled him until Cornell got the cue, and he went willingly, lowering himself as Rhys supported his weight until he was settled across his lap, but both his upper body and his legs and feet were resting on the couch.

"Dirty, naughty boys deserve a spanking, don't they?"

15

For a few seconds, Cornell forgot to breathe. *A spanking?* He almost came at the thought. The fact that he was still half-dressed only contributed to his arousal. There was something inherently dirty about wearing such nice clothes, only to have them shoved aside and be planted face down on a man's lap. And if that wasn't hot enough, the fact that Rhys had thought it through and made sure the position was comfortable for Cornell physically only made it more perfect.

He drew in a shuddering breath that almost got stuck in his lungs when Rhys's hand boldly squeezed his ass cheeks, as if he'd done it a thousand times before. He loved it. Rhys had found the perfect mix of dirty talk with an edge of humiliation thrown in, and Cornell sucked it up like a sponge.

"I really like your ass," Rhys said conversationally. "It has the perfect amount of jiggle when I do this."

He merely tapped it with a light touch that, yes, did make his ass jiggle a bit. If Cornell could've somehow magically increased his body's response, he would've, because right now, he wanted nothing more than to please his Dom.

"But a dirty, naughty boy like you shouldn't have such a pristine ass, don't you think? I think you deserve a well-spanked ass, brightly red and glowing."

If Cornell would've been able to bring out words, he would've, but by now, he was too far gone to even speak. All he could do was lie there, fully surrendering to whatever Rhys would do. And please, let him do it fast, because Cornell's patience was running out. He needed him, needed that touch, that firm hand that Rhys had promised him.

"Are you ready?" Rhys asked.

He gently swatted Cornell's ass again, one little slap on each cheek. It was almost cruel, this sample of what he wanted so much. Oh, wait, Rhys had asked a question, right? That meant Cornell was supposed to answer. He wanted to say yes, but his mind had trouble connecting to his mouth, and in the end, all that came out was, "Please, Sir."

"How lovely to hear you beg for my touch, boy. You are perfect for me," Rhys said, and Cornell soaked it up, his soul rejoicing in the simple praise.

"Now, soar for me, my boy. Let it go," Rhys said, his voice warm and firm at the same time.

Before Cornell could even process what that meant, Rhys's hand came down on his ass with a firm slap. This time it wasn't a sample, a tease, but the start of a solid rhythm of slaps. He built up fast, five slaps on one cheek, five on the other, then going back and forth until Cornell lost count. His ass warmed up instantly, his skin protesting the sting that increased and increased until it took over everything else.

He was already so close, so hard, what if he...? *Soar for me*, Sir had said. He had permission to fly. He felt it, the moment his brain decided that this pain was good pain, that it loved this pain, that it wasn't pain, but pleasure. It exploded in his brain first, then radiated outward through his body, this zing, this burst of pure pleasure.

He made sounds, unintelligible sounds. Groans, moans, keens and whimpers that sounded like somebody else made them. But it was him, rising higher and higher until he could touch the clouds, then even higher until he felt the sun on his face. His eyes pinched shut, he surrendered completely, and then he reached heaven.

He lost all track of time as the spanking lessened in intensity, then transitioned into tender caressing of his flaming ass. He sought friction with his cock, only to discover he was rubbing against something wet, so he must've come already. But a strong hand wrapped around his cock, and he rose high again, chasing another orgasm until he exploded among the stars, tears streaming down his face.

He was held, cuddled, felt a warm, wet cloth cleaning him. Someone carried him, then put him on his stomach on a bed. Cool lotion was gently applied to his ass. It smelled like cucumber, like summer, and he smiled. He felt drunk, high, detached from the world yet deeply connected to it.

Sir talked to him, praised him for being such a good boy, and he soaked it all up. When he found himself alone in bed, he cried out, and Sir shushed him immediately, assuring him he was still there. He crawled in bed next to Cornell and held him, whispering the most beautiful words that made Cornell drift gently through the clouds.

He had no idea how much time had passed when he returned to earth, finding himself in bed, still in Rhys's arms. He blinked a few times, assessing the state of his body. His ass would hurt something fierce tomorrow, but other than that, he felt good. Groggy, still tired, but oh, so fucking good.

Rhys moved every so many seconds, tiny moves that indicated he was doing something. The room was dark, but there was a glow. Rhys was reading on his Kindle, Cornell realized. Rather than leaving him alone for however long he had slept—and judging by the fact it was now dark outside, it had been at least a few hours—he'd chosen to stay in bed with him and read. It almost made his eyes tear up again.

He shifted, wanting Rhys to know he was awake. The man moved instantly, and the glow lessened as he put his Kindle down. "Hey, sweetheart, are you awake?" he said softly, and Cornell wanted to stay there and never leave again.

"Yeah," he said, his voice a croak.

"Can you sit up so you can drink a little water?"

He carefully rolled off Rhys, and with his help, managed to get into a sitting position. His ass didn't like that, but strangely enough, the pain was comforting. He often felt that way after a good scene, the pain reminding him how high he'd flown, and god, he had reached the stars this time.

Rhys held out a water bottle, and Cornell drank greedily, his throat already feeling better after the first few gulps of cold water. He drank half the bottle before he gave it back to Rhys. "Thank you."

"How do you feel?" Rhys asked. He switched on the soft lights on both nightstands, and Cornell blinked a few times to let his eyes adjust.

"Good. Tired and sore, but really good."

Rhys stretched out next to him on the bed, his head resting on his hand as he studied Cornell. "I'm really glad to hear that."

"I hit subspace," Cornell said, even though there was no way Rhys would've missed that.

"I know. I'm so happy for you, and so damn proud of you," Rhys said, and there was a wonderfully rich intensity in his voice. Cornell could feel he meant it, that it wasn't some polite statement.

"Thank you for staying with me as I came down from my high," Cornell said. "I hate waking up alone after an experience like that."

Something flashed over Rhys's face, before he sent Cornell a warm smile. "You're welcome, though it's not something I deserve thanks for. As far as I'm concerned, that's both my job and my privilege as a Dom. I would never let you wake up alone."

A wave of emotion rolled through Cornell at that statement, and to prevent himself from making an utter fool of himself by blurting out something mushy, Cornell rolled on his side and cuddled close again with Rhys. "I need more cuddles," he whispered.

Rhys's arms came around him instantly. "As many as you want and need."

He slept in Rhys's bed that night, and he never wanted to leave. Somewhere in the back of his mind was a small voice telling him this was something to worry about, but he felt way too good to care.

THE NEXT DAY, Cornell was still drifting a little, Rhys noticed. He was mellow, more relaxed than he'd been since he'd moved in with Rhys, and snuggly too. Rhys rubbed lotion on his ass twice more, the skin fiery red and warm, but already starting to heal. He didn't get any work done, as Cornell was like a puppy that didn't want to leave his side.

And when night fell, he didn't need to say anything, didn't even need to ask. Cornell followed him wordlessly into his bedroom and installed himself in Rhys's bed. Rhys knew it wouldn't last—it couldn't, not this fast and this easy —but how he cherished sleeping with Cornell nestled against him. God, he loved it, this needy Cornell who soaked up everything Rhys gave him and still wanted more.

But he also worried. It worked out now, since he still had one more day off, but after that, he would have to get back to work. And leaving Cornell on his own, Rhys didn't like the idea of that one bit. The man wasn't ready yet, and if he were honest, neither was Rhys. Still, he'd tackle that problem when the time was there. His first priority was something else.

After a high that intense, Cornell would have to come down, and that wouldn't be pretty. So when he woke Cornell the next day—Rhys had gotten up early to get a workout in —he was ready for it. Breakfast was still okay, but after Cornell's shower, reality hit hard. One minute, Cornell had been lounging on the couch on his stomach, reading a book, and the next, he started crying.

"What's wrong, sweetheart?" Rhys asked. He'd been using that word more and more, and since Cornell hadn't objected even once, he kept doing it. Cornell might not realize it yet, but Rhys had zero intention of letting him go anytime soon, so the man had better get used to his affection.

"I don't know," Cornell said, tears streaming down his face. "I just feel...sad."

Rhys plopped down on the couch next to him and pulled him close, positioning him so Cornell's head rested on his lap. "Talk to me," he said softly. "What's going through your mind?"

He had a pretty good guess what the issue was, but first of all, he couldn't be a hundred percent sure, and second, even if something else was troubling him, in both cases, talking would help.

Cornell let out a sigh that sounded so sad, Rhys wanted to hug him and take his pain away. "You don't want to know," he said. "It's all equally bleak and depressing."

Rhys's left hand started gently rubbing Cornell's head and his right slipped under the man's sweater to caress his back. "If I didn't want to know, I wouldn't ask. Just tell me. I promise I won't judge or get upset with you."

Cornell was quiet for a long time, maybe a minute or two, but Rhys waited patiently. "I'm scared of being alone most of the day when you go back to work. I know that's selfish, considering you already took off two weeks, but—"

"It's not selfish," Rhys interrupted him. "The same thing went through my head. I'm not looking forward to going back to work either."

He kept rubbing him, touching him, and the first bit of tension was already seeping out of the man's body.

"What if I'll never fly that high again?" Cornell whispered.

"You will, sweetheart. I promise," Rhys said. "That was only the beginning. You and I, we're gonna make beautiful music together."

Cornell turned his head to meet his eyes. "I'm experiencing sub drop, aren't I?"

Rhys smiled at him, proud of him for recognizing it. "That would be my guess, yes. It's okay. I was kind of expecting it, considering how deep into subspace you went."

Cornell rolled his head back, snuggling against Rhys's

thigh. "I haven't flown that high in years," he confessed, and damn if that didn't make Rhys's heart sing with pride.

"You were beautiful," Rhys praised him. "Absolutely stunning."

In response, Cornell made a sound like that of a purring kitten, and Rhys's heart got all soft and fluffy. "How's your butt feeling?" he asked.

"It's still warm, and when I looked in the mirror this morning, it was still red as well. But I don't mind. The pain centers me."

Rhys could understand that. People outside of the scene often thought that pain was pain, but they couldn't be more wrong. Pain like that, the good kind of pain, it could distract you from all the other pain, physical and emotional. Unfortunately, you always had to come down to earth at some point.

"I feel better when you hold me," Cornell said a while later, after they'd snuggled in silence for a few minutes.

Rhys smiled at him, even though his head was turned the other way. "I know you do. I like holding you."

"You're a good Dom," Cornell said, and he couldn't have paid Rhys a bigger complement.

"Thank you. You tend to bring out the best in me."

Another purr–like sound. "Will you lie down with me?" Cornell whispered. "I love it when I can wrap myself around you."

How could Rhys say no to a request like that? Especially when it was exactly what he longed to do himself. He stretched out on the couch—grateful his dad had bought such a deep one—and Cornell immediately pressed himself against him, his face buried in Rhys's neck.

Rhys's hands touched Cornell wherever he could find bare skin, and after a short hesitation, Cornell did the same with him. His hands found their way under Rhys's long-sleeve shirt, and he broke out in goosebumps at the first touch.

"You're so perfect," Cornell said, and even though Rhys knew part of that was endorphins, it still got to him.

He leaned his head back so he could look at Cornell, meeting the man's blue eyes. Cornell looked at him as if he was starving and Rhys was a delicious dinner. He retrieved his hands from Cornell's back, then brushed his lower lip with his thumb. "I would really like to kiss you. Would that be okay?"

Cornell's reaction was instant. "God, yes, please," he said, nodding at the same time, as if to leave no room for misunderstanding.

"You understand this changes things?" Rhys asked him. "This is not a scene. This is not a Dom asking for your obedience. This is me, wanting to kiss you."

"Rhys," Cornell breathed, his scent dancing on Rhys's lips. "Please."

He closed the distance between them, capturing that soft mouth with his. The first touch was tentative, yet electrifying, tiny sparks shooting between them. Cornell moaned a little, and Rhys traced the outline of his lips with his tongue, then gently pressed against the seam. Cornell opened for him, letting him in. He was shy at first, allowing Rhys to swipe his mouth before letting him catch his tongue.

Their tongues met, danced, as their bodies pressed closer together. Rhys's hand grabbed Cornell's head, pulling him even closer. He explored his mouth, his taste, his tongue. They found a rhythm, giving and taking, chasing and catching, the heat rising quickly. The hand on Cornell's head became a fist as the kiss intensified, grew bolder and rougher.

Rhys took and Cornell gave, allowing Rhys free roam of his mouth, of his body. One hand was fisted in Cornell's hair, but the other one found a spot on his ass, which he pressed. He knew it hurt, but he didn't care, and neither did Cornell, who moaned into his mouth. It spurred Rhys on, the sounds, the sighs, the way Cornell started moving against him.

His heart rate sped up, tripled, and sweat started breaking out all over his body as it anticipated more. He kissed Cornell until the man's lips were swollen, and then he nicked them with his teeth until he had him squirming beneath him with pleasure. Cornell was on his back now, Rhys stretched out on top of him, completely in control.

Cornell had spread his legs as far as he could, which allowed Rhys to position himself between them, bringing their groins in full alignment. Cornell was as hard as he was, the only thing separating them the thin layers of clothing. God, he wanted inside him something fierce, the need thundering through his veins.

He broke off the kiss, watching with satisfaction as it left Cornell panting, a glassy look in his eyes. His cheeks were red, his lips swollen from their kiss, and his body was trembling underneath Rhys's. He wanted to say something, needed to express this kiss had been everything, but for once in his life, he couldn't find the words. The emotions inside him were so overwhelming that he didn't know where to start.

"Rhys," Cornell said, his tone bordering on whining. "Please, please."

Rhys took his mouth again, simply because he had to. He couldn't resist tasting him again, and he boldly swept his tongue in that sweet mouth all over again, licking and tasting and nibbling until he ran out of breath.

"Fuck me," Cornell whispered. "I want you inside me."

Rhys clenched his fists, because this was sheer torture. He wanted to take Cornell up on his invitation more than anything, but he couldn't. Not today. Not like this.

He let his forehead rest against Cornell's for a bit, then kissed his nose, his mouth. A sweet kiss, this time. "I want to, so badly, but I can't. Not when you're experiencing sub drop. You're too vulnerable, and it would make me uncomfortable. When we do that, I want you to fully experience it if that makes sense."

Cornell groaned in protest. "I want this. I wanted this before, and it's not because of how I'm feeling right now."

Rhys wiped a wet strand of hair from Cornell's forehead. "I believe you, but I can't. Not today, not like this. When you feel the same way tomorrow, the day after, I will be so deep inside you, you'll be writhing on my cock. But not today, baby."

A flash of anger crossed Cornell's face before Rhys saw acceptance. He never acknowledged Rhys was right, but he saw it in his eyes. At the same time, he understood it was hard for him to say the words when he wanted this so badly.

"If you want to, I can still make us come," he said softly. "We can take our time and do the steps before we get to penetrative sex."

Cornell nodded, his eyes radiating gratitude.

Rhys lowered his head, claiming that warm, wet mouth again. The kiss was sweeter now, slower, but at the same time deeper and more intense. He found a rhythm with his tongue as well as his hips, fucking Cornell's mouth with deep strokes in the same pace as he rutted against him.

Cornell moaned, canting his hips so the friction between their groins was optimal. Rhys would've loved to be able to reach his nipples and play with those a little, but in his current position, that was hard. So instead, he focused on his mouth, kissing him until they were completely in sync, almost one person.

The tempo increased, his mouth and his hips, as the tension in his balls built up. A little tremor went through Cornell's body, indicating he, too, was close to his release. On the next downward move, Rhys put his weight into it, and Cornell grunted as he tensed up, the shiver wrecking his body. He cried out, and Rhys felt him jerk against him with the uncontrolled effects of his orgasm.

He was so close himself, only needing a little more. On impulse, he pushed himself off Cornell into a sitting position, and within seconds, yanked open his pants to whip his cock out. It was leaking in his hand, and he fisted it with a tight grip, moaning with anticipation.

Three hard strokes and he exploded, shooting his cum all over Cornell. He painted his face, Cornell instinctively opening his mouth to catch some of it, the rest landing on his chest. Seeing that only intensified Rhys's orgasm, and he had to steady himself with his left hand against the couch to avoid dropping on top of Cornell, who now looked thoroughly debauched.

"Ungh," he cried out, followed by another low moan as his cock spurted out the last bits of his release.

It was a mess, considering they were both still wearing clothes, but this was one mess that would totally be worth the effort of doing laundry. And that was before Cornell licked off his lips, looked at Rhys with eyes that were still dark with desire, and said, "That was seriously hot."

16

It had definitely been sub drop, Cornell recognized the day after. It was funny how even after so many years, it was still hard for him to recognize it when he was in the midst of it. It always felt like an oncoming depression. You'd think that by now, he would've learned to recognize the signs, but it was so overwhelming, so sudden, that it always seemed to swallow him whole.

Good thing Rhys had recognized that. The way he'd taken care of him. Cornell closed his eyes, thinking about the tender way Rhys had held him, the way they'd cuddled on the couch, the way he had brought Cornell to that roaring climax. It had been everything he needed, and then some.

Rhys was the perfect Dom for him, and if someone had told him that a few years ago, he would've never believed them. How the hell was it possible that the last man he should've ever played with turned out to be the one who could read him like a fucking book? It wasn't fair. Then again, if Jonas's death had taught him anything, it was that life wasn't fair.

It wasn't fair that yesterday evening, he'd wanted nothing more than to return to Rhys's bed, but he hadn't been able to come up with the words to make it happen. The day before, when he'd still been high from that scene, he hadn't even needed words. Hell, he'd not even considered his own room. But yesterday, even after that spectacular orgasm, he hadn't found a way to casually mention how much he wanted to be in Rhys's bed. In Rhys's arms. It wasn't fair that he was starting to feel so much more than he should for a man who could never want him in the long term.

His feelings about Rhys returning to work weren't fair either, considering how much time the man had already taken off to take care of him. Two whole weeks. Two whole weeks Rhys had spent at home to make sure Cornell was taken care of, and Cornell had soaked it all in, reveling in the extraordinary feeling like he was at the center of Rhys's universe. And yet, now that he had to go back to work, Cornell resented it somehow. None of that was fair, and yet the feelings were strong.

"I'm leaving," Rhys said, and Cornell looked up from the breakfast he was eating in his room. That would be the last time, too, that Rhys would have time to make him breakfast. He'd warned Cornell that he was starting a little later today, but after this, he would have to get out the door earlier to be at work on time. Another thing that wasn't fair to resent, and yet there they were.

It was ridiculous, being so upset about being on his own, when he'd been alone for such a long time. Hell, his relationship with Arnold—Asshole Arnold, as Jonas had consistently referred to him—had ended six years ago, so it wasn't like he was used to having someone around him. And yet, over the last two weeks, he had grown used to it. God, he craved it now, feeling like he mattered, like someone *saw* him. He'd attached way more meaning to what Rhys had done for him than he should have. He'd have done the same for any of his subs, probably.

"Okay," he said, determined not to show Rhys any of what he was feeling. It wouldn't be fair to him, to make him feel even remotely guilty. There was that word again, *fair*. "Have a good day at work."

He couldn't quite look Rhys in the eyes, and the man studied him for a few seconds before he gave a slow nod. "I should be home around five thirty or so. Take good care of yourself, okay?"

And then Rhys left, and Cornell sat there, all by himself in the house he knew so well, feeling desperately alone. It was ridiculous, and more than a little pathetic. As if someone like Rhys could ever want him for real.

He finished breakfast, rinsing out his bowl and putting it in the dishwasher. He'd been reading a book the day before, and finishing that took care of the first hour. Then he went through the exercises Rhys made him do daily, as much because they benefitted him as because he didn't want to disappoint Rhys when he came home and asked about it.

Another cup of coffee. It was only ten. How the hell was he supposed to get through the rest of the day?

He decided to run a load of laundry, something he could do with his still limited physical abilities. He'd just turned the machine on when his sister called. He sighed. This was not a conversation he was looking forward to, especially considering the mood he was in.

"Hey Sarah, how are you?" he answered.

They chatted for a bit about her kids, the dogs, the rabbit that someone had dumped on her front step, knowing she would take it in.

"How are you?" she asked. "How's the physical therapy going?"

Cornell almost laughed. *Physical therapy*, there was a euphemism for what he and Rhys had been doing. But he was pretty sure his sister didn't want to know about that, even if he were willing to talk about it. "It's going slow, but well. With every session, I can feel improvement afterward. My shoulder especially is still getting better daily."

"So you're ready to move back into your own house?" Sarah asked.

A wave of emotions rolled over Cornell. What the hell was she talking about? Of course he wasn't ready. "I'm not there yet," he said. "There's still a lot I can't do by myself, and my physical endurance is still low."

"So you hire someone to do your household work for you or a nurse or something to check in on you daily," she said.

There, in a nutshell, was Cornell's problem with his sister. She meant well, he knew she did, and she loved him, but she had the annoying habit of always trying to fix things for him, even things that he didn't feel needed fixing.

"For now, I'm happy to stay here," he said.

He could almost hear the wheels turn in her head. "But surely Jonas's son must be tired of having you around by now. You've been there for two weeks. Isn't it time to get out of his hair?"

"His name is Rhys, and he said I'm welcome to stay as long as I want to," Cornell said, feeling himself getting defensive.

Sarah chuckled. "Cornell, I hate to say this to you, but you can be a little naïve sometimes. Are you sure he didn't say that out of politeness? It's the socially acceptable thing to say, you know."

It was funny how he had every patience in the world as a sub, waiting for his Dom to give instructions, but zero when it came to his sister. "Considering you've never even met him, I'd say I'm probably better at gauging whether or not he means something, don't you think?"

"It feels to me like you're taking advantage of his hospitality," Sarah said, and now *she* sounded defensive. "Besides, your own house is sitting there empty, which is kind of a waste as well."

He rolled his eyes, glad she couldn't see it. "What the hell difference does that make? It's not like I'm paying rent here."

"I wish you would set yourself some deadlines," Sarah said. "To help you get motivated to move on."

Ah, *moving on*. There was Sarah's catchphrase. She'd been on his case about moving on since a week after Jonas had died. For some reason, she'd never been a fan of him, even though his parents had loved Jonas and had always welcomed him with open arms. Then again, the whole relationship between him and Sarah had changed irrevocably since their parents had passed away.

"How about you let me decide when I'm ready to move on," he said, forcing to keep his tone friendly.

"I feel like you've been stuck ever since Jonas died," Sarah said. "You're not working, you're not moving back into your house, you're not doing anything."

"I'm recovering, for fuck's sake!" he snapped at her. "I'm trying to get my body back to a place where I can live rather than exist. I'm trying to process the fact that my best friend is gone. I'm trying to imagine a life after what I've been through. I'm trying, okay?"

"I hope you realize how privileged you are," Sarah said, her tone ice cold. "There are few people would be able to *try* as long as you have. Must be nice, having a financial cushion like that."

And there they were again, the real reason why Sarah had started to resent him. No matter what, it always came back to the money. "That's a funny definition of privilege to have, considering I not only lost my best friend but am permanently injured myself."

Sarah was quiet for a few beats before she responded, her tone slightly more mellow. "You know what I mean."

"Yes, I do. And just so you know, I would give away all the money in a heartbeat if I could have Jonas back. Think about that next time before you call me privileged, would you?"

He ended the call after that, not willing to entertain her bitterness anymore. She'd already managed to get way more of a rise out of him than he wanted. Jonas had warned him to stop giving her so much power over him. Cornell had cracked up with laughter about Jonas's dry explanation of a fuck budget, meaning the amount of fucks you had to give in any given day, and how he should stop giving fucks about Sarah, since he'd run out of them for the things that really mattered. God, he'd been so right.

Cornell and Sarah had never been particularly close, which he'd always attributed to the six-year age difference between them, with Sarah being older. But they'd at least been friendly, even if Sarah had disapproved of a lot of the life choices he made. That had all changed after their parents had died within months of each other, his mom taken by breast cancer after a four-year battle, his dad succumbing to liver cancer months later.

It wasn't their deaths that had made Sarah angry, although she had taken it hard. It was that they left most of their money to him, something he hadn't known until their lawyer had read their will. How he wished they would've told him so he would have at least been prepared or could've told them he didn't want it, didn't want the drama that came with it. Their reasoning had been that he was alone, whereas Sarah had a husband with a good job and with siblings who did well in life too. In short: she had a support system, he didn't—at least, that had been their reasoning.

Sarah had been furious when she'd learned about it, accusing Cornell of influencing their parents. Hell, she'd even gone as far as suggesting he'd set it up, considering he was an estate lawyer. But apparently, their parents had expected that, and their will had contained an irrefutable passage in direct, crystal clear language about Cornell not knowing anything about it, and their lawyer had confirmed that. None of that had mattered to Sarah, who'd turned bitter, resenting Cornell.

He'd hoped it would get better over time, but here they were, three years later, and she still held a grudge. He really should stop giving a fuck.

He got the laundry out of the washer and put it in the dryer. A few more exercises, another cup of coffee he really shouldn't allow himself but did because he felt sorry for himself, and by then it was only eleven.

He didn't want to think about it, but it slowly dawned on him that maybe Sarah had been right about one thing. Her casual mention of work left him feeling slightly guilty. Shortly after the accident, he'd checked in regularly with his firm, but he hadn't done that in days now. With reluctance, he pulled up his phone again and called his secretary, a brilliant, type A-organized guy called Roan.

"Hey, Cornell, it's so good to hear from you," Roan said. "How are you?"

Cornell gave him the short spiel, surprised when Roan

asked more questions. "So, how have things been there?" he asked.

"Good. I handed off all new cases to Mr. Pike, as you requested. There have been a number of calls from clients, and the ones that I couldn't answer, I asked for advice from Mr. Pike, and he helped me. I've sent you a few emails that you can look over at your convenience."

"I'll have a look at them later," Cornell said, surprising himself by how little he cared. "It sounds like you've got a good handle on things."

"I've got everything covered," Roan said.

They chatted a bit more, with Roan asking him some quick questions about practical stuff, and then they ended the call. Cornell knew he should look at those emails, should look at his email in general, but he really didn't want to. It felt like a different life, a different person, like that hadn't even been him. And in a sense, it hadn't been, not the person he was today. He'd changed irrevocably because of the accident, both physically and emotionally, and he'd never ever be the old Cornell again.

It was a disorienting realization, almost like looking at a stranger. No, not a stranger, because he was still intimately familiar with that person. A friend. He could look at himself, at the old Cornell, like a dear friend, but it wasn't him. And it never would be him again.

Because that Cornell had held a full-time job. That Cornell had had a soulmate. That Cornell had struggled with getting older, but had still been healthy. That Cornell hadn't been checking the clock every ten minutes, awaiting the return of a man he should've never gotten involved with in the first place.

～

EVEN BEFORE HIS father had passed away, Rhys had known that his job at the large physical therapy practice wasn't one he wanted to stay in for the long term. He loved working with the broad range of patients from all walks of life he encountered there, but he didn't have much tolerance for the level of politics and lack of flexibility that came with working in a practice that size. But when he'd graduated with his bachelor's in physical therapy, he'd needed the experience, and that place had been a wonderful start for his career.

Of course, with the passing of his father and the money he'd inherited, things had changed. In the last two months, he'd made great progress on his plans to open up his own practice, but in the back of his mind, he'd still known that it would take a little while longer. After all, he would lose benefits, the backup of more experienced colleagues, and the ability to participate in a lot of free training his current employer offered.

The plan had never been to quit so soon, yet halfway through the day, Rhys knew that he would have to. No matter what Cornell decided in the long term, whether there was even a chance of the man staying with him beyond a few weeks more, Rhys wanted to spend every moment he could together. His heart ached from being away from him, and his mind had trouble focusing on his patients because it wanted to make sure Cornell was okay.

And as arrogant as it sounded, Rhys knew Cornell wanted his presence as well. Or maybe he needed it, more accurately. It was a strange experience, to be so closely connected to someone that you could read their needs without them having to say anything.

Cornell's body language this morning had been clear as day, and while Rhys respected him for not saying anything, he'd picked up on it nonetheless. Cornell had not been happy Rhys had been leaving for work, and that was putting it mildly. Sure, that was a compliment, but Rhys understood it to be much more than that. Cornell *needed* him, and that was a heady feeling unlike anything else.

It only took a few hours of being at work for Rhys to realize it was what he wanted as well, to be with Cornell. Even though it was only a forty-minute drive home, it felt like too great a distance to keep an eye on him, to check in on him, to take care of him. He felt like he was failing him, somehow, by not being home. Rationally, he knew that was ridiculous, but he couldn't shake a deep sense of unease for being away from his sub.

He checked in with him a few times during the day, texting him and calling him twice. He was glad to hear Cornell had done his exercises, had eaten his lunch, had even done some household work Rhys hadn't ask him to do, and yet, Rhys could hear the quiet undertone of boredom, of need, of desperation.

Ford texted him sometime during the day, wanting to talk to him, so Rhys told him to call him on his drive home. He was barely in his car when the Dom was already on the phone.

"How are things going?" Ford asked, and Rhys had rarely appreciated the man's genuine concern more.

"Really good. We've had a few breakthroughs since the last time we talked."

He caught Ford up on what had happened during the dinner with Brendan and Raf and the second session they'd had. Ford listened quietly, indicating his approval more than once with appreciative hums. When Rhys got to the part where Cornell had asked him for sex and he turned him down, Ford whistled between his teeth.

"Can I say this without sounding condescending in any way?" Ford said. "I'm so, so proud of you. Saying no under those circumstances, it was absolutely the right call, but it also wasn't easy for you, and I recognize that. I'm so proud of you for doing the right thing, because it wouldn't have been good for either of you."

Rhys's heart warmed at the Dom's rich praise. "Thank you, but to be honest, as much as I wanted him, it wasn't that hard to say no. I knew he meant it in that moment, but I also knew he wasn't in his right state of mind, and there was no way in hell I was going to take advantage of that."

"Still, for you to recognize that, that's a sign of a good Dom," Ford said. "And I'm so glad to hear things are going well between you two. The fact that you managed to get him into subspace, that's amazing."

"You should've seen him," Rhys said, hearing his own voice go a little dreamy. "He was so beautiful, the way he sank deeper and deeper. He had this glow about him, this radiance that transformed his face into that of an angel."

Ford chuckled. "Listen to you, waxing all poetic. You're like a regular Lord Byron, man. But I'm proud of you."

Rhys smiled at the Dom's joke. "I'm proud of him," he said. "The fact that he managed to get past his own emotions and find freedom in that scene, that's a big accomplishment."

"So, what's next for you two?" Ford asked. "Is he still going to stay with you for a while?"

Rhys took a deep breath. "I quit my job today," he said.

It was quiet on the other end of the line for so long that he checked to make sure he hadn't lost the connection. But no, Ford was still there. "You did what now?" Ford finally asked.

"You know I've been talking about starting my own practice ever since I graduated," Rhys said.

"I know, and with the money your dad left you, you thought you might be able to make that reality in a year or so."

"Exactly, except it's not gonna be in a year or so. It's gonna be right now. I gave notice today."

"If I may ask the obvious question, why? I thought you wanted to wait," Ford asked.

"I did, until I discovered what it was like to be away from Cornell."

"Rhys," Ford said, and Rhys had no trouble picking up on the warning in that tone.

"I know. Everything you want to say to me, I know. Trust me, I told myself as well. It's too fast, it's too much, I don't even know if he's going to stay with me. I *know*."

Ford hummed in approval. "Well, in that case, I'm not going to repeat those arguments. Clearly, you've considered it and made your decision. If you feel this is what you should do, then I have no doubt it's the right call."

For some reason, that almost brought tears to Rhys's eyes, this easy acceptance of his decision. "Thank you," he said quietly. "It means a lot to me to have your support in this."

Ford chuckled. "With anyone else, I would've pushed back much harder, but I've never known you to make a truly impulsive decision in your life. Clearly, you've thought about this, whether it was in your subconscious or in your conscious mind. So yes, I trust you're making the right call."

"But it *is* really fast, right?" Rhys said, trying to look at it from Ford's point of view.

"That depends on when you start counting," Ford said rather cryptically.

Rhys frowned, trying to follow his line of reasoning. "What do you mean?"

"Well, clearly this thing with Cornell, however you want to define it, didn't start two weeks ago. If you'd met him two weeks ago, I would've said you're absolutely batshit crazy for quitting your job, but the fact that you've known him for years, that you've been fascinated with him for years, that makes it completely different. This is not a two-week thing. This is a two-year thing, maybe even more."

Rhys had to swallow embarrassment for a second that the Dom knew about his fascination, as he called it, with Cornell.

"Yeah," he said softly. "This has been way more than two years in the making."

17

By the time Rhys got home, Cornell was near tears. As much as he told himself it was pathetic and he should get a grip, he couldn't help the growing sense of desperation as the day progressed. How had he gotten attached to this man this fast?

He'd made the decision a few hours before Rhys was due home. They hadn't talked about this, hadn't mentioned any plans for the future, but Cornell had to do *something*. He needed to show Rhys he was all-in with this thing between them, whatever *this* was.

And so he'd made preparations, not even knowing if Rhys would want to take him up on his offer. He'd declined the day before, though in hindsight, Cornell not only understood, but respected him for that. He didn't think he would've regretted it afterward, had they gone through with it, but it had solidified his trust in Rhys, knowing that the Dom would never take advantage of him, not even when he was in a vulnerable state.

This time, he wanted to offer and let Rhys decide whether he thought it would be a good time. He showered again, thoroughly cleaning himself. It took effort to shave himself down there, what with his limited mobility and painful shoulder, but he managed it without nicking himself —always a bonus.

Holding a hand mirror, he checked to make sure he looked presentable. He wasn't as tight and taut as he'd been twenty years ago, but at least he looked like the best version of himself he could manage right now.

He walked down buck naked, and in the basement, retrieved one of his own butt plugs, still neatly marked in Jonas's handwriting. Memories threatened to assault him as soon as he entered the playroom, but he pushed them back. There was a time to grieve, and right now wasn't it. He had to stay in the present and maybe even allow himself to look at the future again and dream about what could be.

Back in his bedroom, he liberally lubed up and took his time loosening himself with a dildo, then inserted the butt plug. Again, he checked in the mirror to see if it looked good.

Ugh, who was he kidding? Just one glance downward revealed the plethora of scars on his body, especially his legs, but there was nothing he could do about those. He would never be sexy again, but last time, Rhys hadn't seemed to mind much. It would have to do.

As the time neared that Rhys would come home, Cornell's nerves intensified, a twisted pretzel in his stomach. He took position in the hallway where he knew Rhys would enter, his hands clammy and his body slightly shivering. The emotions inside him swelled up into a crescendo, making tears threaten behind his eyelids. He was feeling too much, hoping too much, maybe even assuming too much. But there was no turning back now.

He heard the garage door open, then the car drive in.

The engine shut off. The garage door closed. Then the car door opening, closing, and finally, the hallway door opening. He kept his head bowed, standing in the exact position Rhys had shown him.

He heard him gasp softly, then a soft thud as Rhys dropped his bag on the floor. Wrestling sounds followed, Rhys taking off his jacket, then kicking off his boots. All Cornell could do was interpret the sounds, as he couldn't see him with his head bowed. He walked over to Cornell, entering his line of vision. The appreciative low hum he let out was music to Cornell's ears.

"Look at you," Rhys said, his voice like honey. "Perfect position, all ready for me to come home."

His hand, so soft and yet so strong at the same time, caressed his head, then his neck, his shoulder, trailing down his back. Cornell loved how possessively Rhys grabbed his ass, a tingle shooting through him when his fingers brushed the butt plug.

"Oh," Rhys said, his voice changing in tone, dropping lower and getting a seductive edge. "I see you got *all* ready for me."

"Yes, Sir," Cornell said.

Rhys stepped closer, lifting Cornell's chin up with his index finger. Cornell met his eyes, burning with something he couldn't even try to define. Then Rhys took his mouth in a scorching kiss, and he couldn't think at all anymore.

He held position, as much because Rhys hadn't told him he could move as because he was unable to, what with his mind going to absolute mush at the onslaught on his mouth, his lips, his tongue. Rhys didn't just kiss him—he claimed him, possessed him with a bold confidence that was intoxicating.

Then Rhys started to move, walking them backward

until Cornell had his back against the wall. The cold wall hit his ass cheeks, but that shock was quickly forgotten when Rhys pressed his own body against Cornell's. Oh, that tongue, that devious, slick tongue that stroked in and out of his mouth, fucking it the way he dreamed of Rhys fucking him. His cock, so unreliable in its reactions lately, was rock hard, caught between Rhys's body and his own.

"You're so perfect," Rhys whispered against his swollen lips that were slightly throbbing with the force of the kiss.

At first, Cornell wanted to protest the gross inaccuracy of that statement, but then he looked into Rhys's eyes, and saw the truth there. With all his imperfections, Rhys saw something else. Rhys had called him perfect, and he had meant it.

"Thank you, Sir," he said.

Rhys's face broke open in a broad smile. "You really are perfect for me," he said, and then they both stilled as they looked at each other, the heaviness of that statement hanging in the air.

Again, Cornell wanted to deny it, but he couldn't. Not when Rhys looked at him like that. Instead, he whispered, "Will you please fuck me?"

His heart dropped when Rhys didn't respond immediately, but instead, kept looking at Cornell with a far more serious look than was befitting a question like that. Was he about to get rejected again?

Rhys cupped both his cheeks, pressing a soft, sweet kiss to Cornell's lips. It didn't do much to stop the sinking feeling in his stomach.

And then Rhys uttered the one sentence that had never been good news in any relationship. "We need to talk."

Cornell felt himself recoil, but Rhys felt it too. He must have, considering he tightened his grip on Cornell while at the same time reacting with visible shock. "No, not like that.

That came out all wrong. There's nothing for you to worry about, I promise."

Cornell had to swallow a few times before he trusted himself to speak. "Then why do we need to talk before you can answer my question?"

The way Rhys caressed his cheek with one finger caused butterflies to swarm in Cornell's stomach. It took away some of his fear, because surely, no man would be so cruel to gesture that sweetly and then follow it up with a rejection. But still, he wasn't convinced the talk Rhys had proposed would be good news for him.

Rhys leaned in for another slow, soft kiss. "I promise you, sweetheart, everything is fine. I just want to talk about our mutual expectations, and I know this sounds boring and heavy, but indulge me, please."

The fact that he called him *sweetheart* again relieved some of Cornell's worries. How he loved the careful way Rhys always said it, never routine or thoughtless, but always with the power of intention behind it.

Cornell allowed himself to pout. "You know, when your sub awaits you naked, prepped and all, a boring talk is not the desired outcome."

Rhys smiled at him, then winked. "I promise you that you'll love the outcome of this talk."

Somewhat ameliorated, Cornell smiled back at him. "Does this talk require me to wear clothes?"

Rhys's smile widened. "No, absolutely not. In fact, I much prefer having you naked."

Minutes later, they were on the couch together. At first, Cornell had thought Rhys had been kidding about wanting him to stay naked, but it seemed he was serious about that. As soon as Cornell had indicated he wanted to go to his bedroom to put on some clothes, Rhys had shot him a dark look that made it crystal clear how he felt about that. Then he'd cranked up the heat and pointed toward the couch.

So there they were, Rhys still fully clothed and Cornell butt naked, that stupid plug still in his ass. He didn't mind it so much, but it was more the slight humiliation of it, knowing that he'd gone through all the trouble, only to be... Well, he had been rejected, right?

"So, what was so important that you prioritized it over my offer?" he asked, unable to keep his disappointment out of his voice.

"I'm sorry," Rhys said, and the gravity of his tone indicated he meant it. "I wasn't expecting this when I came home, obviously, and I made some big decisions myself today that I wanted to share with you first. These are good things, but we do need to make some decisions together before we can move on."

Cornell's eyes darkened. "I'm getting a bit tired of people telling me to move on. I like where I am right now just fine."

"I get that you are disappointed, but if you insist on being bratty, we can also postpone this talk to later, and you can parade around all night butt naked for my enjoyment. How does that sound?"

Oh god, the way Rhys's voice dropped when he got all stern with him. It did funny things to Cornell's stomach, to the butterflies that seemed to have taken up permanent residence there. And the funny thing was that his threat was as scary as it was exciting, fucked up as it was.

"I'm sorry, Sir," he said.

Rhys pressed a soft kiss on his forehead, signaling his forgiveness, and Cornell let out a relieved breath.

"I want to talk to you about the future," Rhys said, and Cornell's stomach dropped all over again.

RHYS REMEMBERED a few important conversations in his life. The one where he'd told his parents he was gay came to mind—not that he expected much of a reaction from that. The talk he'd had with Raf about him becoming a Dom. Raf telling him about his Daddy and being a little. Then there were job interviews, the talk with his dad's lawyer after the accident, and he could think of a few more. But none of them had been as important as this one. He could not fuck this up.

As soon as he mentioned the word *future*, he could see the expression on Cornell's face change. It was clear the man wasn't expecting anything good to come from this. He had to manage his expectations, lead the conversation the way he wanted to go.

"I want to talk about if we have a future together," he said softly.

Cornell's eyes widened in surprise before he caught himself. "What do you mean?" he asked, and Rhys couldn't fault him for being careful.

"Look, we've moved from doing scenes together into what seems to be a more romantic relationship. Kissing, me pleasuring you, now you offering sex outside of the scene, that's not part of the D/s dynamic that we have."

"Are you saying you don't want that?" Cornell asked, and the pain on his face was so stark it cut through Rhys's heart like a knife.

"No! God, no, that's not what I'm saying at all," he said as quickly as he could, almost tripping over his own words. "I want that, but I want to make sure you're aware of what it means."

"I don't understand," Cornell said. "You're not making any sense. What are you talking about, what it means?"

Rhys was not sure if Cornell really didn't follow him or if he needed him to say the words. Whichever it was, he was fine with it. If they were to be in a relationship together, he would have to be the dominant partner. That much had always been clear.

"Okay, I'll put my cards on the table. I want to be more than just your Dom in a few scenes here and there. I want to be your boyfriend. Because that's what we would be, if we keep going along this path. The kissing, having sex, that's a romantic relationship, which means we would be boyfriends. I need to know you understand that."

Well, that answered his question whether or not Cornell had truly not followed, because the man's eyes grew big as saucers in his mouth dropped slightly open. "B-boyfriends?" he stammered.

"Yes, boyfriends. You know, the common term used for two men in a romantic relationship."

"But... But you're twenty years younger than I am," Cornell brought up, and Rhys couldn't help but laugh.

"If you're only realizing that now, we *really* need to have a talk."

Cornell softly shook his head, as if to shake off something. "Of course I realized that. I just... When you said a romantic relationship..."

He gave another helpless shrug. "I guess you hadn't put two and two together yet," Rhys said, his voice kind. "But the question is, do you have a problem with me as your boyfriend?"

"Of course I don't," Cornell said immediately, and that was a sweet relief for Rhys. "I know this is going to sound incredibly stupid, but what we did so far, I thought it was more out of pity. Like, you did it because you felt sorry for me. That doesn't seem like a good start to more serious relationship... And it sounds like that's what you want?"

Rhys took a deep breath. It was time to get a little more honest with Cornell. "Do you know when the first time was that I started to look at you differently?" he asked softly.

Cornell shook his head.

"It was when I was sixteen. You and Dad already knew I was gay, and I loved how you made me feel like that was completely normal. And then Mom and Dad went away on that last-ditch effort to save their marriage, which I didn't realize at the time, and I stayed with you for the weekend."

Cornell's face lit up with recognition. "We went to the movies," he said. "I remember that."

"You took me to a rom-com, because I told you I wanted to see it. And you weren't embarrassed about the fact that we were the only single men watching it, the only ones without a woman by our side. You showed me not to be scared of what other people thought, and I admired you for that."

Cornell shrugged. "That's no big deal," he said. "You talked about wanting to see that movie for weeks, so I took you."

"Did you know that during the romantic scenes, all I could think about was how good it would feel to hold your hand?" Rhys said. Cornell's eyes met his, and Rhys saw the confusion, followed by something else. "It was the first time I saw you as a man and not as my dad's best friend or some kind of uncle or something."

"Rhys, that was years ago," Cornell whispered.

Rhys smiled at him. "You're telling me. I've been intrigued by you for a long time now, and that has only grown more and deeper. I like you, Cornell. I like you far more than I can express. Trust me when I say that what I feel for you doesn't have anything to do with pity, not even remotely. And yes, I do want something more serious with you, but I'm willing to wait until you're ready for that."

Cornell opened his mouth as if to say something, then closed it. It took almost a full minute before he spoke again, his face deadly serious. "I never thought someone like you could be interested in someone like me," he finally said.

Rhys shrugged. "You were wrong."

Cornell blinked a few times. "You've liked me for years?" he asked, the disbelief heavy in his voice.

The man had no idea. Even now, Rhys was still holding back, not showing Cornell the full depth of his feelings. He wasn't ready for that, and if he were honest, neither was Rhys. Those feelings were so big, so scary, that he needed more time before facing them.

"Yes," he said simply. "I've seen you as a man since I was sixteen, and that has never gone away. This, what we're doing now? I've dreamed of this."

Cornell studied him. "People will have an opinion on this, considering the age difference."

Rhys waved with his hand. "I don't care much what people think, but yes, they will. And anyone who doesn't know us will assume you're my silver daddy or something. Let them think whatever the hell they want. It doesn't bother me."

"Your mother? Doesn't that bother you either?" Cornell asked.

Rhys let out a long sigh. "As much as I would love to say it doesn't, we both know I would be lying. But she'll have to get over herself, because her opinion doesn't mean enough to me to value it over what we have."

Cornell looked at him, his eyes narrowing. "You're really serious about this."

"Yes," Rhys said calmly. "Which is why I'm willing to have this somewhat awkward conversation, because it matters too much to me to jump into it blindly and run the risk of us hurting each other. I've been dreaming of having sex with you for years, but damn if I'm going to jump the gun and hurt you because we haven't thought things through."

"I feel like I'm back in high school, having a conversation with a guy about whether or not I want to be his boyfriend," Cornell said. "Not because of your age, but I have that same formal feeling, like you have to define something before you even know what it is."

Rhys could understand where he was coming from, considering he had the same mix of trepidation and anxiety sitting in the pit of his stomach. "Maybe the question isn't what this between us *is*, but what we want it to be. That's why I started with asking you how you see the future between us. So let me ask you again, what do you want this thing between us to be? Are you content with only the D/s relationship, or do you want more?"

Did Cornell realize he hadn't said anything about his feelings for Rhys yet? Rhys hadn't exactly given him a declaration of love, but at least he'd admitted to having liked him for years and being interested in him. Cornell hadn't said anything similar, so now Rhys was left to wonder if maybe he'd misinterpreted things. Maybe Cornell was looking for something short-term and would never consider anything serious with someone so much younger.

"I missed you today," Cornell said, and Rhys had to shift gears to follow where he was going. "I never expected that after having spent two weeks with you."

"I missed you too," Rhys confessed. "I hated leaving you on your own today."

"I hated being on my own. And that's coming from a man who has basically been by himself for years. And even before that, when I was still with Arnold, I was alone half the time, considering how much he traveled."

Rhys had strong opinions about Asshole Arnold, but this was neither the time nor the place to share them. "I'm glad to hear you missed me too," he said softly. "That means you'll be happy to hear that I've given my notice."

"You did?" Cornell asked, his voice full of shock. "But...why?"

Rhys leaned forward and took both of Cornell's hands, kissing first the left, then the right. He looked him straight into his eyes as he spoke. "Cornell, sweetheart, I know you've been hurt and rejected before, and I get that. But this dance you're doing right now, avoiding answering me directly, this needs to stop. I need to know where you stand. I've told you how I feel about you and where I want this to go, but now it's your turn."

Cornell bit his lip, his eyes never leaving Rhys's as he saw him gather courage. "I have a hard time believing you want to be with me, but I know you wouldn't be so cruel as to lie to me about that. So I'm going to try my hardest to accept that you see something in me that I don't see myself. My feelings right now are a hot mess, what with grief and anger and frustration still mixed in. But I do know that you make me feel safe, you make me feel at home, you make me feel special and protected, and I want that. I want how you make me feel, and I want how I feel about you, which is so complex I can't even find the words. So I guess this is my convoluted, long-winded way of saying that yes, I want to be your boyfriend, as stupid as that word sounds at my age."

Joy surged up in Rhys. He leaned in and kissed Cornell, a soft kiss at first, but one that quickly grew deeper. As always, one taste of that man wasn't enough.

"I quit my job because I want to be home with you," he said when he knew he had to break off the kiss before it would lead to things they still weren't ready for. "And I know it's fast and it may scare you because of how big this gesture is, that I need to be there for you. So I'm starting my own practice right now."

He watched as Cornell's eyes filled with tears. "I can't believe you did that for me," the man whispered.

Rhys wiped them gently away with his thumb. "You may not believe it yet, sweetheart, but I would climb mountains for you, cross deserts, and fight dragons."

More tears escaped as Cornell looked at him with pure devotion. Rhys smiled. The man might not realize it yet, but Rhys could see it in his eyes. It was already there, the same love that Rhys felt for him. All he had to do was be patient.

"Now that we've had your talk," Cornell said, his voice breaking a little as he looked at Rhys with tear-stricken eyes. "Will you please fuck me?"

18

Wasn't it interesting how you could be nervous for something, even when you knew you had nothing to be nervous about? Cornell hadn't even realized he'd been tapping his right foot while waiting for the doctor to finally call them in until Rhys put calming a hand on his knee to stop him. He didn't even need to say anything, the message loud and clear.

Cornell shot him an apologetic look from between his lashes, grateful when Rhys merely smiled at him. "I'm nervous," he said, as if that hadn't been clear already.

Rhys's smile turned into a bit of cheeky grin. "No kidding," he said dryly.

"Not because I have reason to be nervous," Cornell hastened to add.

Rhys took his hand, lacing those strong fingers through his. "I know. Now stop worrying."

Funny how that tone was enough to make Cornell's mind at peace. How he wanted to put his head against Rhys's shoulder and give in to this deep need to touch him, feel him near, know that Rhys was taking care of him. At least he'd slept in Rhys's bed again last night, snuggled up against him. The joy that brought was ridiculous, considering his age, but he couldn't help feeling so safe in his arms, so...*loved*. Was it love? That was way too fast, wasn't it? Deep affection, then, because after everything, Cornell couldn't deny how much Rhys cared for him. And how much he...*liked* Rhys.

Minutes later, they were called into the doctor's office. "I see you're here for some rapid testing?" she said, getting right to business.

She addressed Cornell, and he realized this was what they could expect from now on. People would automatically assume that he was the dominant partner, considering the age difference. He wasn't sure how to respond, but Rhys was ahead of him.

"We are," he said calmly. "You can start with me."

Her eyes widened for a second before she caught herself. "Okay. Is it okay if I call you Rhys?"

Rhys nodded, and she grabbed an iPad and started firing questions at him about his sexual history. Cornell wasn't surprised to hear he'd never tested positive for anything. He hadn't expected anything else, not from someone with experience in the scene.

"When was your last oral or penetrative sexual contact?" the doctor asked.

"Four months ago," Rhys answered calmly.

Cornell's mouth dropped a little open. Four months ago? That meant he hadn't had sex since the accident. Why? He could've easily done a scene or scored some ass before Cornell had moved in with him.

The doctor ran through a few more questions, then repeated the whole spiel with Cornell.

"Four months ago," was his answer when she asked him when he'd had his last sexual contact.

He and Rhys shared a look, and before he could even say anything, Rhys took his hand and squeezed it softly. He knew Cornell and his dad had been coming back from a scene at the club when they'd gotten into the accident, so Cornell didn't need to say anything else. It had been bad sex, but it had still been sex.

"The assistant will be right in to draw some blood, but everything looks normal, and there's no reason for concern," the doctor said after she was done with the questions and a brief physical examination. "You will have the results within an hour."

Cornell wasn't worried at all, knowing that he'd always played safe, and he expected Rhys to have done the same. It was a precaution, and more importantly, something Rhys had asked them to do. Cornell hadn't liked being rejected again when he'd asked Rhys to finally take him up on his offer, but when Rhys had explained why, he was okay with waiting a little longer.

"I want to claim you," Rhys had said in that low, deep tone of his that reached places inside Cornell he didn't even know existed. "But I want to do it bare. I've waited for you for so long that I want to share with you what neither of us has shared with anyone else ever before. I want to claim you, own you, explore every bit there is of you, until you're drenched in my smell, dripping with my essence."

Was it cheeky and corny? Hell yes. But it was also intoxicating, the way Rhys looked at him, talked about him, devoured him with his eyes. Any doubt Cornell had had whether Rhys really wanted him had vanished right then and there. Rhys had painted such a vivid picture that Cornell had been shivering with want. So when Rhys had proposed they'd book a rapid testing appointment at the clinic the next day, he'd instantly agreed.

The assistant walked in only minutes later, and she only needed drops of blood from their fingertips, so they were done within minutes. Spring had started, the last snow melting from the sidewalks and the huge piles in the parking lots. The sun was still a little watery, but it teased the still bare landscape into the first promise of warmer weather.

"Do you want to go somewhere for lunch?" Rhys asked.

Cornell instantly nodded.

"Any preference for a place?"

"Not really. You can decide," Cornell said. He'd always been easy that way, whether it was choosing which movie to watch, which music to listen to, or which restaurant to eat at. He genuinely didn't have preferences, and he hated the decision stress it gave him. There was always the fear of making the wrong choice and displeasing the person he was with.

"Why don't we go for the sandwich shop?" Rhys said. "That way, you can have one of those roast beef sandwiches you love so much."

Cornell's heart swelled. Rhys took such good care of him, in big things as much as little things. "That sounds delicious."

"Another plus is that we can walk over there and leave the car here," Rhys said, holding out his hand to Cornell.

He took it instantly, reveling in the way his hand fit in Rhys's. It wasn't till they walked for a minute or so when he realized they were out in public. Holding hands. "What if someone sees us?" he asked.

Rhys shot him a quick look sideways. "Would it bother you if someone you knew saw us?"

Cornell thought about it. This wasn't the town where he lived or worked, but it was the next town over. The chances of him running into people he knew were not insignificant, considering how many people he'd met professionally over the years. Would it bother him if they saw him with Rhys? They'd instantly jump to conclusions, that much he did know. An old man with a younger one, they'd draw all the wrong conclusions. Did that bother him? That was the question.

"I don't know," he said honestly. "Not because I'm embarrassed to be seen with you, but because people will get the wrong impression."

Rhys hummed in agreement. "Yes, they will. They'll think you're the dominant one in the relationship."

"That's what bothers me," Cornell admitted. "Because I'm not, and it almost feels unfair to you if it comes across that way."

Rhys pulled on his hands to bring them to a stop, then faced him. "You don't need to worry about my feelings," he said softly. "I can take it."

"I know," Cornell said. "But it's as much about your feelings as about my own. I hate that people always assume that because I'm older, I am dominant in a relationship. I'm proud to be myself, and I hate that I have such a hard time convincing people that it's okay to be submissive."

Rhys's smile was a reward in and of itself, but the soft kiss he pressed on Cornell's lips was the icing on the cake. "I love that you are so comfortable in your identity as a submissive."

They started walking again, Rhys accommodating his tempo to Cornell's much slower one. "People so often think there's shame in submitting to someone else, but there's not. When you do it to the right person, there's freedom and peace of mind," Cornell said. "It's hard to convince people because society teaches us being dominant, being in charge, is good."

"And the fact that I'm so much younger doesn't change that for you?" Rhys asked. "Because it's even more frowned upon when the person you submit to is twenty years younger."

Cornell shrugged, wincing when that gesture sent a hot stab of pain through his shoulder. "I think I have more of an issue with you being Jonas's son than with the age difference between us, to be honest."

Lunch was comfortable, relaxed. Cornell enjoyed his sandwich as they chatted about everything and anything, conversation flowing easily between them. He couldn't believe Rhys had taken another day off when he'd only been back at work one day. He'd explained to Cornell that he still had accrued leave and that he'd rather take his leave than having it paid out, which apparently, his practice had been reluctant to do anyway.

They took their time for lunch, and they'd just gotten back to the car when Rhys's phone rang. "The doctor's office," he told Cornell.

He took the call, and Cornell could hear the assistant rattle off their results through the phone. He'd given permission for them to release his results to Rhys as well, since it seemed easiest to do it in one phone call rather than have them call both of them consecutively.

Rhys ended the call, then looked at Cornell with eyes that darkened. "Let's go home. I have plans for you."

~

THEY DIDN'T SAY anything else on the ride home. Rhys shot a

look sideways every now and then to make sure Cornell wasn't choking on his nerves. Because the man was nervous, that was clear from his slightly trembling hands, the way he kept wiping his palms on his pants, how his eyes kept shifting to Rhys and back.

It was a weird position they were in, Rhys realized. Sex between a Dom and a sub was often planned, since scenes usually required some advance preparations. But sex between boyfriends was supposed to be spontaneous. So which one of the two was it? Was he acting as a Dom here or as a boyfriend? Could he be both at the same time when their relationship was still so fresh, when they hadn't even entered into this territory of having sex yet?

He tried not to let Cornell show his own nerves. Because he *was* nervous, he could admit to himself, his stomach twisting and twirling. He wanted to get this right, more for Cornell than for himself. But damn, this was hard to navigate. Cornell wanted him to take the lead, that much he could surmise, but did he want him to approach it as if it were a scene? That was the question.

He could ask him, but somehow, that didn't feel right either. He noticed time and again how happy it made Cornell when he didn't have to make the decisions, when Rhys made them for him. Like choosing where to eat for lunch or even what to eat. Others might find it overbearing, but Cornell craved it, ate it up, and reveled in the sensation of it.

By the time they arrived home, Rhys hadn't found a solution in his head for his Dom versus boyfriends conundrum. So he decided to go with his gut. As soon as he'd closed the garage behind them, he shut the engine off and turned toward Cornell.

"I want to see you in my bedroom in half an hour, naked, prepared, and ready for me. Is that clear?"

The gratitude that flowed from Cornell's eyes confirmed he'd made the right call by taking more of Dom than a boyfriend approach. In the end, Rhys had decided that Cornell would probably like the structure it provided, the clear expectations, where he knew nothing else was expected of him than to obey. That didn't leave a lot of room for nerves or for fuck ups on his part, which should bring him relief.

Cornell hurried into the house as fast as he could, and it pleased Rhys to see how much his mobility was still improving. He followed at a slower pace, mentally going over how he could make this work for Cornell. He wasn't planning on doing a full-on scene, but he could incorporate a little of what he had learned about his preferences to help him center and make it so he could relax.

Because if he were honest, as much as he wanted Cornell, this wasn't about sex for him. This was about intimacy, about him wanting to give Cornell a wonderful experience. The man had been rejected too many times, even by him, though he'd had good reasons. He needed to feel wanted, desired, loved. And because it was Cornell, maybe also a little used.

He quickly got changed, then left his bedroom to give Cornell time to prepare and present himself for when Rhys walked back in. As cliché as it was, there was something very erotic about wearing leather pants. He didn't wear them often, because they could easily come across as over the top, but if there'd ever been an occasion worthy of wearing them, it was now. He wasn't wearing a shirt, comfortable showing up bare chested with bare feet, letting the pants hug his legs and ass, which he'd always felt were his best features anyway.

When he walked into the room, Cornell was positioned perfectly, his body tight, his head bowed respectfully. No kneeling sub had ever showed him more deference, and Rhys felt his heart swell up with pride.

"You're so beautiful," he told Cornell, who reacted with a smile, keeping his eyes down.

He walked around him, inspecting him from every angle. He knew Cornell looked at himself with frustration about his scars, but to Rhys, they showed the man's strength, his story. He didn't mind them at all—quite the opposite, in fact.

Cornell shivered when Rhys touched his neck, scratching it a little in a comforting gesture, before he let his finger trail down his spine. Goosebumps popped up on his skin, and Rhys smiled a little. He'd never met anyone who was as sensitive to touch as Cornell was. He was like an expensive instrument, responding to every touch, every minute movement, begging to be played by a master.

He tapped the flared end of the plug that stuck out between Cornell's ass cheeks. "Are you ready for me?" he asked, bringing his mouth close to Cornell's ear.

"Yes, Sir," Cornell said.

He said it with a lot of warmth and affection, and yet it suddenly sounded off to Rhys, as if something was missing. He frowned as he tried to pinpoint what it was, then shook it off.

"So if I wanted to sink balls deep inside you right now, I could?"

"Yes, Sir."

"Do you want me to?"

To his credit, all that time, Cornell had kept his gaze low. "I'll do whatever pleases you, Sir."

There was that strange feeling again. It wasn't unease, nor the sense that something was wrong. It was more that it felt like it wasn't enough, *Sir*, as if it didn't cover the dynamic they had. It puzzled him enough to distract him for a few seconds while he tried to work it out in his head. Luckily, Cornell didn't seem to notice.

"I'm so lucky with you, boy," he told him, and funny enough, that word *did* feel right. Calling Cornell his boy wasn't about age difference. It was about acknowledging that he wanted Rhys's care, needed it. It was about assuring both of them what the rules were in their relationship, with Cornell as the submissive partner.

"Thank you, Sir," Cornell said, and that emotion in his voice was easy to spot.

"What if it pleases me to use you a little?" Rhys asked, even though he already knew the answer. Cornell was a verbal guy, enjoying the words almost as much as the actual actions.

"You can do whatever you want, Sir."

He meant it, there was no denying the deep desire to please that was clear in his voice. Rhys caressed his cheek in approval before raising up his chin with his index finger. "You're perfect," he said again, feeling this deep need inside him to get that message across.

"So are you," Cornell whispered, and then he took in Rhys's outfit and let out a little gasp. The sound shot straight to Rhys's balls, already heavy and full. He loved feeling like this, the anticipation building in his body for what was about to come.

"I want you on the bed on your back, your head hanging

over the edge. I've dreamed about your mouth, so it's time to see if my dream matches the reality."

Cornell's cheeks flushed as he hurried over to the bed to obey Rhys, telling him it was something he looked forward to. Within seconds, he had positioned himself on the bed, his head hanging over the edge, his body fully supported by the mattress, and his mouth already dropping wide in anticipation of what was about to come.

"Hands to your side, and don't move them."

He walked closer, only shoving his pants down far enough to take out his cock and balls. He loved how dirty that felt, letting them hang out while he was still wearing those sinfully tight leather pants. Cornell studied him upside down, his mouth opening even wider.

"Stick your tongue out," Rhys told him. "And don't move or do anything until I tell you to."

He grabbed his cock in a firm grip, then slowly brought it toward Cornell's mouth. He caressed his lips first, basically tracing his mouth with the fat head of his cock. Cornell moaned, but like the good, obedient sub he was, he didn't move. Rhys dragged the tip of his cock along Cornell's wet tongue. As much as he loved blow jobs, there was something much more intimate and tantalizing about this stage. He appreciated taking it slow, teasing and enjoying the first contact.

He loved how Cornell's slightly coarse tongue felt against the tender head of his dick as he dragged it from the back of his tongue all the way to the tip. He repeated the move, loving the soft moan Cornell made. His cock grew heavy in his hand, the first pearl of moisture beading at the tip.

Cornell waited patiently when he withdrew, and Rhys

rewarded him by swiping that first drop on the tip of his tongue. "Taste me," he said, his voice slightly hoarse.

Cornell pulled his tongue in, smacking a little before licking his lips. "Can I please have more?" he asked, and it didn't sound like a cheesy line at all.

"You can have whatever you want, sweetheart," Rhys said, and he'd never meant a statement more.

He sank his cock into his throat slowly, feeling Cornell open up around him. "Mmmm," he sighed as he slid in all the way.

The angle was perfect, and that wet mouth was so hot and tight around his cock. He rocked back and forth, his balls slapping gently against Cornell's face. His eyes were watering, but Rhys didn't pull back yet. He wasn't much of a sadist, didn't really get off on pain or subs struggling, but the sound of someone choking on his cock was one of the sexiest, most intoxicating sounds ever.

Ah, there it was, the slight gurgle, Cornell's nostrils flaring as his eyes watered more. "Such a good boy," Rhys said, "letting me use your mouth."

He slid a finger over Cornell's throat where he could feel his cock lodged deep inside him. What a feeling that was, knowing you were inside another man, controlling his breath. It was a responsibility that never failed to arouse him. And Cornell's face, growing red now, showed nothing but submission and joy at serving Rhys.

With regret, he pulled back to allow Cornell a few gulps of breath. Saliva pooled around his mouth, and Rhys smiled. "I like seeing you like this," he said. "You're usually so composed, so put together. I like making you lose that composure, love making you look used... Because that's what you are, isn't it? My cock-hungry boy?"

Cornell made a sound that was close to a keen, opening his mouth again for more. How had Rhys gotten this lucky? He didn't hesitate but sank back inside his throat, fucking his mouth with deep, languid strokes until Cornell gagged again. He held his dick as deep inside him as he could for just two seconds more, reveling in the sounds, before pulling back.

Cornell gasped for breath, tears meandering down his cheeks, but any question Rhys might have had of whether he was reaching his limits evaporated when Cornell opened wide again. "You like choking on my cock, don't you?" Rhys said, deeply pleased. "Such a good boy for your Sir."

There was that hesitation again, as if he should say something else. But what? Your boyfriend? Your Master? Neither seemed to fit. He'd have to ask Ford, maybe, because it bugged him.

Cornell let out a little moan of pleasure, and Rhys refocused on him. "I'm gonna reward you for being so good for me."

Even upside down, with watery eyes, Cornell's face lit up. How deep was his need for praise, for reward, Rhys realized all over again.

"Oh sweetheart, you're so perfect... Look at you, taking my cock like such an obedient boy. Yes, sweetheart, swallow good and tight now. I'm gonna come down your throat, let you taste all of me," Rhys babbled, his body tensing in anticipation.

Both his hands grabbed Cornell's head, fisting his hair as he rammed his cock in deep now, not being gentle either. But Cornell took it, his face growing red, but his eyes, oh, god, his eyes... They were on fire, burning gemstones of want, of desire. There was not a sliver of doubt he not only allowed this, but wanted it. Needed it.

Rhys allowed him one more respite to draw in a few

gasping breaths, and then he sped up again, fucking his mouth with the desperation of someone chasing an orgasm that was within reach, so close he could taste it. One last shove, so hard his balls made that filthy slapping sound, and then he pulled back enough so his cum would flood Cornell's mouth and not be wasted straight down his throat.

"Every drop, my boy," he said, his voice raw. "Take every drop."

And Cornell did, sucking and swallowing, his cheeks hollowing as his throat and tongue worked overtime to keep up. He sucked him dry, even cleaning him off afterward, until they were both panting.

Rhys steadied himself against the bed, his chest heaving. "Look at you," he whispered. "You look like you've been thoroughly fucked, your lips all swollen and red, your eyes on fire for me... Your whole body is flushed and your cock is so gorgeous, leaking and desperate for more. And we've only just started. I'm gonna use every inch of your body, my boy, make you pleasure me in every way I can imagine...and you'll love it, won't you?"

19

Cornell had always been good at multitasking, but right now, his brain was failing him. Or maybe it was his body. Both? All he knew was that Rhys had asked him a question, and for the life of him, Cornell couldn't form words. He didn't even have them in his brain, too overwhelmed with the sensory overload.

The sound of his rasping breaths as he tried to get oxygen back into his system. The thick taste of Rhys's cum that lingered on his tongue. The way his skin felt too tight, too hot, and yet perfectly right. Rhys's leather pants that smelled so good and that caressed his skin every now and then as he brushed against him. His balls, throbbing with indignity that they hadn't been allowed to unload. His cock, so full and desperate for attention. Rhys's eyes on him, looking at him as if he was perfect. The smell of sex that hung heavy in the air. His ass, clenching around the plug inside him, eager for more.

He wanted to answer, needed to, but the words wouldn't come. Instead, he rolled on his stomach, then carefully edged off the bed until he could take up position against it.

He bent over, finding good footing and letting his upper body rest on the mattress. With his legs spread wide, this was as clear an invitation as he could extend in lieu of those pesky words.

"Oh, Cornell," Rhys said, his voice filled with awe and sweetness. He'd *pleased* him, Cornell felt, and his brain found peace in that. "Look at you, presenting yourself to me like that. Are you desperate for more, sweetheart? Do you need me?"

He understood, Cornell thought. Rhys *got* him. Others might've thought that he did this to please them, but that was only part of the equation. The other part was that it brought him so much pleasure. He needed to be filled, craved that hard fuck Rhys would deliver. Hell, he'd been desperate for it for months, even before...

Before Rhys, before the accident, before everything had changed. But this, this hadn't changed. The way his body needed it, wanted it, craved it. Shamelessly. And Rhys understood. He didn't judge, didn't think Cornell was a slut for craving cock. Or maybe he did think him a slut, but in a good way. The kind that turned him on because he wanted to use him, wanted to be the person to give him what he needed.

And then finally, he found the words. "I need you," he managed, his voice sounding awfully close to a sob. "Please, Rhys... Please, Sir. Please."

His dignity was gone and so was his pride. He had nothing left, not when his body was screaming to be taken.

"Hush now, sweetheart. I've got you," Rhys said in that wonderful deep tone, and Cornell's brain let go. He had him. He had nothing to worry about, because Rhys would deliver.

He moaned when Rhys yanked the plug out of him. No

finesse there, no slow and careful steps. It wasn't even two seconds later that he felt it, the unique feeling of a fat cock head pressing against his hole. His eyes teared up as he bore down and let him in. Rhys knew what he needed.

His body relaxed as Rhys surged in, confidently and deep, bottoming out after seconds. Cornell's skin tightened with the burn, the tension, the way he had to overrule his body's instinct to fight this intruder.

He hadn't fully adjusted when Rhys's hands came around him, finding his right nipple. A hard pinch that made him gasp, and then a clamp set firmly, causing him to hiss. He didn't even have time to react before the other one received the same treatment.

"That's gonna hurt when I fuck you into the mattress," Rhys said, and Cornell wanted to cry at how perfect it all was. That deep tone, with enough care to know one word would be enough to stop this while at the same time an edge of glee that told him Rhys would love to see him squirm and suffer a little.

He didn't make Cornell wait either, bending him down with a firm hand on his neck while sliding back out and surging in deep. Cornell closed his eyes and opened his mouth, letting out the sounds he knew Rhys would want to hear. As if he could hold them back, the moans, the grunts, the gasps, and hisses. He was an instrument, being played by a master.

His nipples pressed against the sheets as Rhys took him in a steady rhythm, making the clamps rub even deeper against his flesh. God, that would hurt like a motherfucker when those came off. He'd worry about that later. Right now, he had to focus on not seeking friction with his dick, because fuck, he wanted too. He wanted to rub it against the sheets, knowing he wouldn't need much to fly over the edge.

But Rhys hadn't given him permission, and he wouldn't disobey him, not the first time they had sex. He pinched his eyes shut. Rhys was fucking him. That perfect cock that claimed his ass like he belonged there was Rhys's. Gorgeous, sexy, caring Rhys. His boyfriend. His Sir. His... His everything. He shouldn't be, he couldn't be, but he was.

Cornell moaned when Rhys pegged his prostate dead on, unable to resist the urge to rub his leaking cock against the soft sheets. All he needed was a few more strokes, and then...

"You'd better not be coming, boy," Rhys said, and Cornell stopped.

Rhys had to come first, maybe twice more. Rhys had to give him permission. And so he fought against himself, against his own body that wanted to come so bad. He'd always been good at edging, had been complimented more than once on his ability to stave off his orgasm. Why was he having such a hard time now?

"Oh, my sweet boy, you feel so good. You fit so perfectly around me, and you're so willing, so eager... God, what a turn on you are, so hungry."

"For you," Cornell said. "Hungry for you."

That was the difference. It wasn't some random Dom fucking him, some hookup he'd scored. It was Rhys. Perfect Rhys who made him feel all the things, and not just in his body. He fought with himself, his need to please Rhys battling with his need to come.

In the end, Rhys won, and Cornell found himself entering that state where he could take anything. It wasn't subspace because he was too aware, too present, but it was close, like balancing on the edge of a ravine. One small push and he would fall. Or fly, depending on how you looked at it.

He'd never gotten this close by mere fucking, but he

sensed himself creeping near that ledge. Rhys's cock was perfect, splitting him wide open, invading and occupying his body and his mind. There was so much pleasure, especially when he hit his prostate dead on, but there was still that discomfort, that fight his body put up with the force of Rhys's thrusts.

He didn't hold back, owning Cornell like he'd promised him. Not like a fragile old man, like someone who couldn't take a hard fuck, but like a boy who was being used to pleasure his Sir, his Master, his... And the word escaped Cornell again. It was more. Rhys was more, but he couldn't pinpoint it.

Rhys sped up, his thrusts growing faster and harder, slapping against Cornell now. His body started to ache, yearn for the release. Or for the last shove before it would fly.

Then Rhys's hands sneaked around his chest and before he realized it, removed the nipple clamps. The blood rushed back into his buds with a vengeance, and he howled, his vision going black for a second. His balls, completely confused, decided they *liked* this, and as Rhys grunted with a low, animal-like satisfaction and spasmed deep inside Cornell, he teetered over the edge and fell.

He never reached the ground, his body swooped up in the ecstasy that barreled through him—pain and pleasure in perfect synergy, reinforcing each other until they were undistinguishable, one sensation. He flew. God, he flew.

~

ONE DAY, he would film Cornell, Rhys decided. He would capture that enraptured look on his face as he found the stars, that blissed out expression that made Rhys want to do all the things to him and then some more. But right now, he would drink it in, drink *him* in, because he couldn't get enough of him.

Cornell hadn't even reacted when Rhys had changed positions, concerned that the prolonged bending over would get too hard on Cornell's body. Sure, he could've stopped, could've gathered him in his arms and cuddled, but where was the fun in that? He wasn't done yet, emotionally or physically. That was one of the advantages of being his age, he supposed. His recovery time was short.

And so he'd lifted him up and had found a comfortable position on a sofa chair, Cornell straddling him in the reverse cowboy position with his back toward Rhys, his head resting against his shoulder. He held him close, but he'd damn well sunk his cock right back inside him with zero intention of leaving. It was deliciously dirty, slowly fucking his own cum out of Cornell's hole while the man rocked himself on Rhys's cock as if it was a mechanical bull.

Someday, he'd stay inside him all night, filling him over and over and over again until he was overflowing with his seed. He might have to check with Ford how much fucking someone could take, though. That man had done some intense shit with some of his subs, so if anyone would know, it would be him.

Cornell moaned softly, the sound making Rhys smile. His left hand kept steadying Cornell, who had trouble controlling his muscles, fucked into complete surrender, but his right hand started exploring. He traced Cornell's lips with his finger, his smile widening as Cornell opened up immediately and sucked his fingers in.

"Mmm, my perfect boy," he said. "You haven't had enough either, have you?"

When his fingers were wet, he took them out, and

Cornell's mouth made a plopping sound as he let them go. He found his right nipple, still hot and tender from the clamps. He rubbed it gently, and Cornell whimpered. He shrank back, only to lean back into Rhys's touch almost instantly. He was at that point where it hurt, but it hurt so good that he wasn't sure if he wanted more or wanted to stop. And so Rhys rubbed his nipples softly, playing with them until Cornell squirmed on his lap, rocking in uncoordinated moves on his dick.

Rhys was hard, but nowhere near coming, and he could keep this up for a while. He moved his attention to Cornell's abdomen, caressing and stroking him, finding every dip, every plane of muscle, every soft spot where he wasn't all that tight anymore. Rhys marveled in the strength of the body that was pressed against his, still so deep inside him that they were basically one.

He found the scars, the old ones and the newer ones, the ones that reminded him of the loss they had endured. It still hurt, even in the midst of this bliss, but it felt sweet too, as if the accident had brought pleasure as well as pain. Maybe, someday, they'd be able to see the good that had come out of it.

He explored farther, lower. Cornell's balls were hot in his hands, tightening at his touch. He'd look good with a cage, Rhys decided, that beautiful cock locked up for his pleasure, at his mercy. He liked that idea, and Cornell would too, he knew. Not constantly, not all the time, but every now and then when he wanted to drive him crazy, when he needed to hear him beg again. Because he begged so beautifully, and there was such power in that.

Cornell rolled his head, letting out another one of those soft keening sounds. "Rhys..." he pleaded, and Rhys discovered he didn't mind Cornell hadn't called him Sir.

"One more time, sweetheart," he told him, his mouth close to Cornell's ear. He nibbled on his ear shell, making Cornell shiver. "Are you gonna be a good boy for me?"

"Always," Cornell whispered. "I want be good for you."

"You are," Rhys assured him. "You're the best boy I've ever had."

Cornell turned his face toward him and his dreamy smile was a bigger turn on than anything else. "I love your cock," he said, his smile like that of a cat who had just discovered someone had left a juicy salmon steak unattended on the counter.

Rhys grinned. "I love your ass, so I'd say we're pretty even."

He wrapped his hand around Cornell's cock. It was about the same length as his own, but not as fat, and it fit in his hand perfectly. "I really like the idea of locking your cock up," he said as he stroked him, too soft and too slow to do more than tease him. Cornell leaned into his touch, arching his back. "Don't you think it would look pretty in a cage?"

"Yes, Sir," Cornell said with a sigh, subtly pushing his hips forward.

"Mmm, you don't sound very excited," Rhys teased him. "I think you need to show the proper enthusiasm for this idea before I let you come again."

"Sir..." Cornell grunted in protest, and Rhys could hear he was becoming more alert.

"Don't you think it would be perfect if I could fuck you for days without you having to worry about accidentally coming? You'd be able to enjoy it so much more if that stress were gone."

Another grunt. "I'm not so sure about that, Sir."

"Oh, but there are other benefits too," Rhys said conversationally, his hand only tightening slightly, with nowhere near the grip or speed that Cornell had to want. "I'd get you one of those cages where you could still do everything else, like bathe or pee."

It was tiny, the way Cornell's body jerked at that last word, but Rhys was paying close attention.

"I figured that would get your attention, sweetheart. You like that idea, don't you? Having to pee through a cage, knowing that I own your cock…"

Another involuntary shiver, and Rhys decided to push still a little further to see what got Cornell excited. The man had a penchant for a little humiliation, he already knew that.

"I think I'd like to see that," he said, and there it was, the second Cornell's body froze in response before he controlled himself again. Rhys smiled. He had his answer. "I think someone likes the idea of me watching him pee, don't you, sweetheart?"

Cornell didn't answer him, and that wouldn't do, so he tightened his grip around his dick enough to get his attention. He got a hiss in response, and then Cornell said, "Yes, Sir. I'd hate it, but I'd love it."

God, he really was perfect, Rhys decided, and as a reward, he started jerking him off for real while increasing he deep thrusts as well. He still took his time until Cornell was pleading with him again, and when he'd begged enough, Rhys finished the job and allowed them both to come again.

As they fell asleep later that night in his bed, an exhausted Cornell already on the cusp of that cute little snoring he did when he slept, Rhys wondered how he would ever be able to top what he had with Cornell. This was everything he'd hoped for, everything he'd wanted, everything he'd dreamed of, wrapped into the one man he'd yearned for for years. There was no one else for him, and there never would be. Now all he needed to do was make Cornell feel the same way.

20

Rhys woke up the next morning with Cornell in his arms, and it was the most magical feeling in the world. Cornell was wrapped around him, like he'd done before, touching Rhys wherever he could. A strong sense of contentment filled Rhys that hit him deep in his soul, his heart as much at peace as his body.

He turned his head to look at the clock, blinking a few times when he realized how late they'd slept in. Good thing he didn't have to go into work today since it was Saturday. He had a few more days next week to wrap up some patients, and that was it. His supervisor hadn't been happy that he'd quit, but he didn't care. The day he'd spent with Cornell yesterday had proven how right his decision to walk away had been.

He couldn't see Cornell's face since it was hidden against his shoulder, but he felt his breath dance across his skin. The deep rhythmic sounds indicated he was still asleep, and Rhys had no intention of waking him. It had been late by the time they finally got to sleep yesterday, so Cornell deserved to sleep in today.

Rhys managed to angle for his Kindle and grab it without disturbing Cornell, then settled in to read. He had no idea how much time had passed when the front door bell rang. He frowned. Who the hell could be there at this ungodly hour? They'd have to come back another time, since he had zero intention of leaving his bed.

The doorbell rang again, and Cornell's breathing pattern changed, becoming a little faster and more superficial. Dammit, the doorbell had woken him up. Rhys was not amused. He was about to put a calming hand on Cornell's head, hopefully lulling him back to sleep, when he heard a key turn in the front door.

Oh, no. Fucking hell to the no. There was only one person who could walk in like that, and shit was about to go down. He didn't have time to wake Cornell up but instead gently rolled his body off him. He threw on the first clothes he could find, then hurried out of his bedroom, remembering to close the door behind him.

He ran into her in the hallway. "What the hell are you doing?" he asked her, not even bothering to keep his tone civil.

His mother gave him a quick look up and down, her eyes narrowing. "Why weren't you answering the doorbell?"

He crossed his arms, meeting her gaze head-on. "Because it's Saturday morning and I'm sleeping in?"

"You never sleep in," she pointed out.

"Still not a good reason to come barging in when I don't answer the door," he said, unable to keep the anger from his voice.

"I could see you're home, and I got worried when you didn't answer," she said.

It sounded reasonable, and yet Rhys didn't trust her explanation. She'd never done this before, not even when he'd been a student and had been hungover, lounging in his home till way past noon.

"What do you want?" he asked her. He knew it was rude, but he couldn't seem to find the patience to stay friendly right now, not after the way she'd interrupted him and Cornell. Besides, he was still salty about their previous conversation when she'd called him while he was driving, and he hadn't talked to her since.

She was spared having to answer when the door behind them opened and Cornell walked into the hallway, dressed in his boxers and one of Rhys's T-shirts. He looked all kinds of adorable and sleepy, dragging a slow hand through his bed hair. Then he looked up, and he froze as soon as he saw Rhys's mom.

"Cassie," he said, and that one word held the knowledge that he realized she'd seen which room he'd come from. As if his attire hadn't given it all away.

More than anything else, Rhys wanted him to know it wasn't his fault. Things were about to get ugly, but it wasn't on Cornell, so he held out his hand to him. "Good morning, sweetheart," he said, deciding to make clear where they stood right away.

Cornell sent him a hesitant smile, but he did take Rhys's hand and allowed him to pull him close. Rhys didn't care that his mom was watching, or maybe he cared a great deal and that was the reason he did it, but he grabbed Cornell's neck, pulled him in, and kissed him firmly.

"Did you sleep well?" he asked.

Cornell's eyes softened, and for a few seconds, his focus was on Rhys alone. "Like a baby."

He gave him another kiss, then turned his attention back to his mother, keeping Cornell close to his side. Her eyes were spewing fire, so he merely raised his chin. "Got something to say?"

"This," she spat out, and Rhys could practically see the spit flying as she gestured wildly to them. "This is ridiculous. This needs to stop."

Rhys squeezed Cornell's arm, which he was holding onto. "Why?" he asked. "What is your problem?"

"My problem? What do you mean, what is my problem? Do I need to spell it out for you?"

Rhys shrugged. "Apparently, because I don't see why you have an issue with this."

Her face grew red as she kept gesturing with agitated moves that made him almost fear she was going to give herself a heart attack. "He's twenty years younger than you are," she snapped at Cornell. "You're sleeping with your godson, your best friend's son. Have you no shame?"

Rhys felt his anger bubble up inside him. His mother raging against him? That he could take. He didn't like it, but he could see where she was coming from, and he could handle it. His mother flying off the handle against Cornell, going full-on Domme on him? That was unacceptable.

"If you have a problem with our relationship, you talk to me, not to him," he told her, forcing himself to keep his voice ice cold.

"No, my problem is with him," his mother all but shouted. "He's the one who should know better. Hooking up with someone half his age."

Rhys clung to the last thin strands of his patience, digging deep to force himself to ignore the sting of the *hooking up* part of her comment. "If I remember correctly, your last sub was fifteen years younger than you," he pointed out.

"But he wasn't related to me," she said, venom dripping from her voice.

"Cornell isn't related to me," Rhys said. When she opened her mouth to speak again, he held up his hand. "And don't you sprout that bullshit about him being my godparent, because we both know that's a formality that has zero legal status. We're not related in any way, not even emotionally. And you've never had an issue with age differences, so I don't see how all of a sudden it's a problem now."

"It's a problem because this is *you*," she said. "You're my son, my baby, and I'm trying to look out for you. Don't you see that? This isn't a relationship that's good for you in the long run. I know you've had this unhealthy obsession with him for a long time, but you need to open your eyes. Anything between you doesn't stand a chance of lasting, not when all you feel when you look at him is pity. I know you feel sorry for him, Rhys, but that's no way to start anything. It isn't fair to him either."

That was it. Rhys had had it. She could sprout shit all she wanted, but when she started feeding insecurities that were already running rampant in Cornell, he had to stop her.

"You have no idea what you're talking about, and I mean that literally. The contradiction in what you say is so fucking obvious that I can't believe you don't hear yourself talking. How could all I feel for him is pity when I've had that obsession for him, as you call it, for years? It sounds to me like you are trying to come up with as many arguments as you can possibly think of, not even caring that they contradict each other. But no matter what you say, it's not gonna make a difference. Cornell and I, we are serious. This is not some hookup, some phase, or whatever you wanna call it. And it's not going to go away just because you want it to."

For maybe ten seconds, she stood there, her chest heaving with the deep breaths she was taking. Her eyes were still showing the rage she felt inside, but her gaze switched once again to Cornell. "You're going to regret this. He'll grow tired of you, tired of being with someone who can't keep up with him, and then he'll trade you for a younger model."

"Mom!" Rhys said, raising his voice to levels that would've gotten him grounded back when he was still a teenager. "You need to stop right now, before I ask you to leave."

"You would choose him over your own mother?" she asked, and it was such a ridiculous, pathetic attempt at manipulating him that he almost had to laugh.

"Yes, any day, any time. I love you, Mom, but you've been acting crazy since Dad passed away. I don't know what the fuck is going on with you, but you need to get your shit together. This demanding, judgmental attitude of yours toward me, and now toward me and Cornell, it's gotta stop. I'm not a child anymore, and you need to stop thinking that you can tell me what to do and run my life."

Suddenly, the fight left her, and her shoulders dropped low as her eyes filled with tears. "You're all I have left of him," she said, her voice much softer now. "You know how they say you don't know what you have until it's gone? I didn't know how much I still loved your father until he died."

Rhys let out a rather audible sigh. He wasn't sure if what she was saying was the truth, and at this point, he didn't even care anymore.

"Mom, I've reached the point where nothing you say right now is going to make things better, so I suggest you leave. You've already done more damage than you realize, so

I think it's better if you take some time to reflect on how hurtful your words were."

He let go of Cornell and walked right past her, opening the front door behind her to underscore his words. Much to his horror, there were tears streaming down her face when she turned toward him. "You're kicking me out?"

God, she could be such a drama queen. On a good day, Rhys had little patience for it, but today, he had zero. "That's what happens when you don't respect people's boundaries. I love you, Mom, but right now, you need to leave."

She sputtered a bit more, then finally left. When he closed the door behind her and turned around, he expected to see dejection on Cornell's face, maybe even sadness or whatever someone looked like who had been dealt a blow. Instead, he found Cornell's eyes radiating with what looked a hell of a lot like love.

IT HAD BEEN the strangest experience of Cornell's life. You'd think that at his age, with how many years he'd been submissive, he knew himself. How was it possible that you could have this epiphany out of the blue, this experience of things clicking into place that had been there forever, and yet somehow, you had never connected them, never labeled them, never allowed them to fully surface? He felt like he'd been struck by lightning, but in the best way possible.

"Sweetheart?" Rhys asked, and Cornell could see the confusion on his face.

"Give me a sec," he said, his brain still trying to process the magnitude of what he'd realized. "I just had a *moment*."

"A good moment or a bad moment?" Rhys asked.

Cornell cocked his head, studying him. As if having a

relationship with a man twenty years his junior who was his dominant wasn't special enough in itself, this realization would take it to a whole new level. *If* Rhys was on board with it, but despite all his insecurities, Cornell somehow knew he would be. And wasn't that the strangest thing of all? As insecure as he'd been about this thing between him and Rhys, this brought no doubts whatsoever, but more like a calm realization that this was what they were supposed to be. *Who* they were supposed to be.

"A good moment," he said. "A very good moment."

But should he tell him now, right after this horrible confrontation with Cassie? Rhys might not be in the right frame of mind to be open to it right now. Then again, keeping things from your Dom was never a good idea, that he did know. Even more when he wasn't just your Dom, but your boyfriend as well, and much more than that.

Rhys walked up to him and cupped his cheeks with both his hands, looking deep into his eyes. Cornell's heart did that funny little jumping thing again it always seem to do when Rhys looked at him like that. "What's going through your mind, sweetheart?" Rhys asked softly. "I can see your brain working at full power, but I have no idea what's happening."

And as he stood there in his boxers and a T-shirt that smelled of Rhys, his knee especially painful this morning and his shoulder still stiff from sleeping so long, Cornell took the jump, knowing that after he'd said this, things would never be the same again. He looked at the man who'd become his everything: his anchor, his safe place, his Dom, his boyfriend, and now...

"I want you to be my Daddy."

He watched as Rhys's mouth dropped open in shock, his eyes widening. He still had his hands on Cornell's face, and they now dropped to his side, while Rhys stared at him in disbelief. It didn't scare Cornell, funny enough. He didn't know why, but he had no fear this would go wrong. All he had to do was wait till Rhys figured out that all that would change was the both of them embracing what was already there.

"You've been taking care of me from the moment you asked me to move in with you," he said softly. "You feed me, make sure I take my meds, you take care of my body, help me to improve. You make sure I get enough sleep, you help me find sexual release, and when you realized I needed a scene, you gave me one that made me fly higher than I've ever flown before. You quit your job so you could be with me, and one day without you assured that I didn't even feel guilty for that, because I missed you way too much. You're happiest when you get to make the decisions for me, and I'm happiest when all I need to do is obey you and follow your lead."

Rhys had looked at him all that time, his eyes growing a little misty as Cornell finished by saying, "You're not my Dom or just my boyfriend. You're my Daddy."

Rhys blinked a few times, then swallowed. "I don't know what to say," he said. "How did we not see this before? How did we not recognize this?"

Cornell smiled, those two questions confirming what he'd known to be true, that Rhys would recognize the truth when he pointed it out. He didn't say anything yet, not wanting to give Rhys the chance to catch up on his thought process.

"The last few days, when you called me *Sir*, it felt slightly wrong somehow," Rhys said. "Not wrong like you weren't showing me respect, but wrong as if it didn't cover everything between us. I thought it was because we were moving from Dominant and sub into boyfriend territory, but I wasn't sure what else you could call me either. I thought myself silly for even thinking about this, as if it matters what you call me. But it does, doesn't it?"

And Cornell took a deep breath and let the word roll off his tongue. "Yes, Daddy."

Much to his own surprise, he teared up. It was ridiculous to be this emotional about a mere word, but all he had to do was look at Rhys to see his own emotions reflected on his face.

"Say it again," Rhys whispered.

"Anything you want, Daddy," Cornell said, his voice breaking a little.

"God, it's perfect," Rhys said, his voice filled with awe and wonder. "How does it feel for you?"

Cornell knew why he was asking. Acknowledging someone so much younger than you as your dominant was one thing, but calling him Daddy? To others, it would make no sense at all, and yet it felt perfectly right to Cornell.

"It feels like coming home," he said, not caring that he might be revealing way too much. "I don't know if I never realized this was what I needed or if I wasn't looking for it until I met you, but I love the way you take care of me. I don't care that you're younger or that others might think it's ridiculous we have this dynamic."

"I have to wonder how Dad would have felt about this," Rhys said softly.

"I have to believe he would've been happy for us," Cornell said. "Your father was one of the most open-minded people I've ever known. His only rule was consent. Whatever people did, as long as it was between two consenting adults, he was fine with it. I have to believe he would've felt the same about you and me."

He teared up, thinking about how often he and Jonas had talked about this deep longing to be taken care of. Cornell wasn't sure if Jonas had wanted to take it quite as far as he was now doing, but he would've understood. He did understand, he always had.

"I think your dad would've been happy for me," he said, having to swallow in between words. "Even if he might've struggled a bit with the idea that it was with his son, he would've been happy for me that I had found what I've been looking for for so long. He would've been happy for me that I was taken care of, because in the end, that's what we both wanted more than anything."

He was barely finished when Rhys's strong arms wrapped around him, pulling him close. "I don't ever want us to feel like we can't talk about him because it might be awkward," Rhys said, holding him tightly. "I know there's the potential, considering he's been intimate with you as well, but you have so much history with him, and I'd love to hear about everything, even if it means getting over some awkwardness when I learn more about my dad's intimate business then I might have wanted to."

"He wouldn't mind me sharing with you," Cornell said, allowing the tears to stream down his face freely. It felt different this time, the grief over Jonas. A little softer, a little less raw and desperate, as if his mind and body knew how to do this now. "He loved you more than anything, I hope you know that. He was so very, very proud of you."

Rhys let go of him enough to lean back and meet his eyes. His cheeks were wet with tears as well, and Cornell could taste the salt on his lips when he softly kissed him. "Thank you," he whispered against Cornell's lips. "It makes me happy that between you and me, we'll keep his memory alive."

It was bittersweet, the way they clung to each other as they both allowed their emotions to come down. Maybe there would be a time when the grief they shared wouldn't be part of their daily lives, but for now, Cornell was nothing but grateful that he could share that burden with Rhys, making it a little lighter.

No, not Rhys. With *Daddy*.

21

"I feel like we need to talk more about this," Rhys said later that day.

They'd had a lazy breakfast, followed by a cuddle session on the couch, where they'd both been reading. Rhys loved the casual intimacy between them, but now that the high emotions of that morning had sunk down a bit, his brain started firing off all these questions that needed answers.

"And by *this*, I assume you refer to the daddy dynamic?" Cornell asked, sending him a bit of a cheeky smile.

"Yes, smartass," Rhys said.

"Not yet, but I wouldn't object to that," Cornell quipped, and much to Rhys's chagrin, it took him a few seconds to work out that pun.

Then he couldn't help but chuckle. "I've been your Daddy for only a few hours, and you're already soliciting a spanking? Not quite sure this is how it works."

"I'm pretty sure that's exactly how it works," Cornell fired back, and Rhys had to give him that.

"You do realize that being a brat will result in consequences, right?"

Cornell's face lit up with something that made it shine like a beacon. "There's freedom in knowing that, if that makes sense. If I'm being disrespectful in a scene, I run the risk of you being displeased, having to punish me, or even stopping the scene. In this, knowing it's a twenty-four seven dynamic, it's different. I feel like I have more latitude to have moods or be a little bratty every now and then, knowing that you will discipline me, but not punish me, if that makes sense."

Huh, that was interesting, Rhys thought. He'd never looked at it like that. "This is definitely something you want to do as a lifestyle, then. Not something for the bedroom or just scenes?" he checked.

Some of the glow on Cornell's face disappeared as he hesitated briefly before saying, "If you feel the same way, that would definitely be my preference."

It was funny how Cornell tended to hide behind more formal language when he was insecure. This was a prime example. Apparently, he hadn't even considered that Rhys might not embrace the daddy dynamic full time, that he could've only wanted to use this in their sexual dynamic.

"Sweetheart, I'm already taking care of you full time. I don't want it to just be in the bedroom. I want to be your Daddy all day, every day. I just wanted to make sure we understood each other."

"Thank you, Daddy," Cornell said, relief painting his face.

Rhys still got a shock every time that word fell from his lips. It was so perfect, so beautiful, so befitting their relationship. It made his heart swell in a way that was hard to describe, like it was somehow his true name, his true identity.

"Let's talk a little more about expectations. Now that we've decided to do this, is there anything you want to add to what we're already doing?"

Cornell looked at him, and Rhys could see the wheels in his head turning. There was something he wanted to bring up, Rhys was sure of it, but would he feel secure enough yet? He waited patiently, hoping Cornell would find the courage to say it. He could coax it out of him, no doubt, but he hoped he wouldn't have to.

"I would love it if you gave me rules," Cornell finally said, his voice soft. "A daily structure, for example, where you tell me what time to get up or what to eat for lunch. Maybe even add things you want me to do."

"You want to have consequences when you don't do it," Rhys said, understanding what he was trying to say. "It sounds like you would like to add a solid dose of domestic discipline to it."

Cornell nodded instantly, and Rhys was happy he'd hit the nail on the head. "This is why it's so important we talk about it, because that would not have been my first instinct. Well, it maybe would've been my first instinct for myself, but I would've held back, fearing it would be too much for you. I don't know if you realize it, but if you give me free hand, I can be quite overbearing and dominant, even in little details."

Cornell smiled. "Yes, please."

That made Rhys chuckle. "Okay, then. Let's make sure we keep checking in on this, so I don't overstep your boundaries. What else? How do you feel about orgasm control?"

The soft blush that appeared instantly on Cornell's

cheeks endeared him. How was it possible the man could still blush after so many years?

"I see somebody is excited about that idea?" he teased him, which, as he had hoped, intensified the color on Cornell's cheeks.

"Yes," Cornell admitted. "I really like that idea."

"And what if I would want to use some tools? A cock cage, for example, like I mentioned yesterday?"

Cornell's cheeks grew so red it almost made Rhys feel sorry for him. Almost, because it was such a wonderful feeling to play with him like this, to embarrass and humiliate him a little.

"I'm gonna need your verbal consent, sweetheart," he teased him when Cornell merely nodded.

"You already know the answer, but yes, I would like that. I'm fine with plugs as well," Cornell said, finally meeting Rhys's eyes again. "In fact, I'm more than okay with you making the sexual decisions for us."

"You're giving me a lot of power," Rhys said, letting go of the teasing tone. "Allowing me to tell you what to do in so many aspects of your life, including your daily life, your sexual life, that's a lot of power you're giving me."

"I'm tired," Cornell said quietly. "I think I may have been on the verge of burnout before the accident, but after everything that happened, I'm so fucking tired. I didn't realize how much I wanted someone else to make decisions for me until that's exactly what you started to do. There is a peace in my head now that wasn't there before, and I don't want to lose that. I know I'm basically handing you the reins of my life, and if you don't want that responsibility, I totally understand. But I would love for you to take over."

"Maybe at some point you'll want to scale back," Rhys said.

Cornell shrugged with his good shoulder. "Maybe. The future will tell. But right now, I'm happy to hand you over everything. I trust you, Rhys. I really do."

The magnitude of that statement didn't escape Rhys. They had come far in such a short time. "I promise I won't abuse your trust," he said.

"But are you sure it's something you are comfortable with?" Cornell asked, and Rhys loved that he wanted to make sure. "It's a big responsibility."

"It is, to a degree that surprises me, to be honest. I have a friend—well, like an acquaintance, really—who's in a domestic servitude relationship with his sub. I've always looked at that as something I wouldn't be interested in, and in the same way, total power exchange relationships didn't appeal to me either. But what we're describing now, as close as it is to either of those, it does hit all my buttons. I don't know if it's because of you, because of how well we know each other already, because we've taken some components from both dynamics, added the Daddy stuff into the mix, and created something tailored to our needs, but I can't wait to do this with you. I have this deep need, this deep urge to take care of you, and the fact that you not only let me but that you crave it as much as I do, that's a turn on unlike anything I've ever experienced."

As soon as the alarm went off, Cornell's eyes flew open. Whereas usually he needed a few minutes to wake up, he was now instantly awake, fueled by eager anticipation. Today was the first day of their new dynamic, and he couldn't wait to see what Rhys had in store for him. It was enough to make him jump out of their bed and instantly head for the shower, as Rhys had told him to do.

As *Daddy* had told him to do, he corrected himself in his head. That would take some getting used to, calling him Daddy in his head as well. It rolled out of his mouth so easily, as if he'd done it for years, but because he'd known Rhys for so long, the mental shift inside his head was a different matter. Still, he didn't think Rhys would get upset with him if he got it wrong. The *Daddy* wasn't a requirement. It was an honorific, something that came from his heart. It couldn't be forced or demanded.

They'd talked all day yesterday, agreeing on rules and boundaries, things they were comfortable with and others where they drew the line. It had helped that they were both familiar with the terms, with the concept of soft and hard limits, and after he'd gotten over his initial embarrassment, Cornell had loved Rhys's openness to whatever he suggested.

And god, the list of things Rhys was willing to try with him, the things he wanted to experiment with, as relatively mild and innocent as they might be, Cornell couldn't be more excited. It was funny how, for example, the idea that Rhys would lube him up and plug him to be used at his convenience made him harder than any promise of flogging, edging, even fucking in a scene had ever done.

Cornell got half hard thinking about it as he soaped himself, but he knew better than to violate Daddy's rules on the first day. And he had communicated in no uncertain terms that Cornell was not to touch himself beyond what was necessary to get clean. He made it quick, then used the little shower implement to clean himself on the inside as well.

Rhys had made it crystal clear that at the core of their

relationship was his genuine desire to take care of Cornell and to do whatever would be best for him. At first glance, others might interpret that as that everything Rhys did was centered on Cornell's pleasure, but it wasn't.

That was because Rhys understood that part of what brought Cornell pleasure was to serve Rhys. That was the deep submissive side of him. He loved being used for Rhys's pleasure, so the idea of being all prepped and ready for him to take at any time he wanted, that was a huge turn on. And the funny thing was that even knowing Rhys might not allow him to come didn't diminish the anticipation in the least.

He turned off the shower, his cock still half hard, and toweled off quickly. Rhys had told him to be in position at eight-thirty, so he'd better make sure he was. He took a quick comb through his hair, then made the bed as Daddy had asked, and got ready for him.

When Daddy walked in two minutes later, Cornell was in position, waiting for him. Even though his cock had grown even harder from anticipation, his mind was at peace.

"Good morning, sweetheart," Daddy said, and Cornell's heart swelled at those simple words. "Did you sleep well?"

"Yes, Daddy. Very well."

Rhys ruffled his hair a little, then let out an appreciative hum as he inspected him. "Raise your chin for me, sweetheart, so I can see your gorgeous eyes." Cornell obeyed immediately. "Ah, that's better. I want to see your eyes when I inspect you. Did you clean yourself for Daddy?"

There it was, the reason he'd been so excited to get up instantly. It was so subtle, this hint of humiliation in this exchange. Knowing that he stood there completely naked while Rhys was fully dressed, inspecting him everywhere, it brought color to his cheeks in a way that he loved, even if he was embarrassed. And moreover, Rhys knew it, and the little smile that played on his lips said he enjoyed this as much as Cornell. And so Cornell surrendered to it, this almost confusing mix of stress and excitement, anticipation and embarrassment.

"Yes, Daddy, just like you told me."

Daddy's hands roamed his body as if it was his, which was true, to a certain extent. He flicked Cornell's nipple, chuckling when it reacted instantly, then gave the other one the same treatment.

"I really do want to try to make you come from just playing with your nipples one day," he said with a smile. "Pretty sure I could make that work, even if it would take me a few hours."

A little shiver trickled down Cornell's spine at the idea of Daddy playing with his sensitive nipples for hours while he wasn't allowed to touch himself. It would be torture of the sweetest kind, something to fear as much as to look forward to.

He gave the only acceptable answer. "Yes, Daddy."

Daddy squeezed his ass cheeks possessively. "Did you clean yourself inside as well, boy?"

"Yes, Daddy," Cornell said, forcing himself to keep breathing.

Wordlessly, Rhys held out his middle finger to Cornell, and he sucked it into his mouth greedily, thoroughly wetting it. Rhys smiled as he pulled his finger out with a plop, then brought it instantly between Cornell's ass cheeks and pushed slightly. He didn't have to think about it, but spread his legs a little more, canted his hips, and pushed back to let him in.

"That's a good boy," Rhys said, and Cornell's insides went all warm and fuzzy.

Rhys moved his finger slightly, bringing it inside to the first knuckle, and Cornell instinctively pushed his ass farther back. "Such a greedy boy you are," Rhys said. "So eager for your Daddy's finger... Or did you have something else in mind?"

Cornell's brain was about to shut off from overload, but he still had enough wits about him to answer. "Whatever you want, Daddy."

Rhys's smile widened. "I had hoped you would say that. Turn around, hands on the bed, and bend over."

Cornell's heart jumped, and he couldn't keep himself from shivering as he did as Daddy had asked him to. He spread his legs, pushed his ass backward and leaned on the bed. The telltale sound of a cap opening made his cock twitch. Oh god, Daddy was really going to do this. Would he use his fingers? Plug him? Or did he have something else in mind?

He had barely formed that thought when he felt two slick fingers pressing against his hole. They entered him as if they had every right to, which he guessed was true, but it was a heady feeling. He let them in, and they surged in boldly, creating that sting in his ass that made him want more, so much more.

In less than a minute, Rhys was fucking him steadily with two fingers, and he wasn't too gentle or careful about it. Cornell loved it, loved how even that choice was taken away from him, while at the same time knowing that one word would be enough to make it stop. He hadn't lied when he said there was incredible freedom in that. He wouldn't have to worry if it was too much, if Rhys thought it would be too much, if he would go too far. All he had to do was let it happen and remind himself that any given time, he had the power to stop it.

His cock was already leaking when Rhys pulled his fingers out, and Cornell was fully expecting a plug to be shoved in. Instead, he had one second to register the sound of a zipper being tracked down, then that fat head of Rhys's cock pushed inside him. God, it was such a tight fit with so little preparation, but he fucking loved it.

Goosebumps broke out all over his skin as Rhys breached him confidently, sliding in without ever stopping until he was balls deep inside him. Rhys bent over him, the coarse hairs of his chest rubbing against Cornell's back.

"Now this is how I like to start my day, by getting rid of my morning wood in the best way possible," Rhys said as he started sliding in and out of him with deep strokes. "You know, usually I rub one out in the morning in the shower, but I think starting now, this will be your job. I think your first job every morning should be to make your Daddy happy, what do you say?"

"Yes, Daddy," Cornell said, his brain about to short circuit from the incredible sensation of being split open by that fat cock.

"I may have you suck me off, use you as a little cum hole, make you jerk me off, or I could even make you lie on the bed and jack off myself, spraying my seed all over you. I'm sure I can find a million ways, all equally satisfying. What do you say?"

What do you say? He was supposed to talk? Cornell couldn't even form words, struggling to keep himself from touching his dick as Rhys fucked him so perfectly. And god, those words, those perfectly filthy words coming from his mouth. They only fueled his arousal, aided by the images the words conjured up. His Daddy using him like this every morning? God, yes, please.

Rhys chuckled. "I don't know what's going through your

mind, my perfect boy, but you'd better not be coming. That wasn't on the agenda this morning."

That shouldn't make it even more sexy, but it so did. Cornell fisted the sheets with both his hands, as much to steady himself as to have something to focus on. Rhys was close, he guessed, judging by the fact that he was speeding up, Cornell closed his eyes, letting the sensations roll over him.

The slapping sounds as Rhys surged deep inside him, his balls smacking against Cornell's skin. The unmistakable smell of sex that now hung heavy in the air. The way Daddy's fingers dug into his hips, the bruising grip centering Cornell. The tightness in his balls as they ached for release. The licks of flames burning under his skin, teasing, dancing, wanting to become a roaring fire.

And yet, even as he stood there, almost passively taking what his Daddy dished out, he still felt like he was the center of his universe, and his heart soared as high as his body did. Daddy came with a low grunt, his body jerking a few times as he unloaded deep inside Cornell. God, he was so glad they'd gone there. There was nothing like the sensation of feeling that hot liquid inside you.

"That was perfect," Rhys let out with a contented sigh.

He pulled out, and before Cornell could even mourn the loss, the dick in his ass was replaced by a thick plug that slid in easily. Rhys let go, slapping his ass playfully. He then gently pulled Cornell up, holding him until he'd found his footing.

Cornell was rock hard, of course, and the smirk on Daddy's face told him that hadn't gone unnoticed. "Did I ever tell you about my fetish?" he asked, and Cornell slowly shook his head. "I love the sight of cum dripping from a man's ass. Never had much opportunity to indulge in it personally, considering I've always played with condoms, so it's been mostly a thing I love watching in porn. But today, I've decided to finally take the opportunity to treat myself. I might walk over to you a few times today, telling you to drop your pants, yank out the plug, and watch my cum drip out of your ass. And if you run out, well, I can just deposit a new load, can't I?"

This was heaven, Cornell decided, even if it contained a little bit of hell as well. His mind was as confused as his body about the wave of arousal and humiliation that rolled through him. Wasn't it amazing how you could hear something, while eagerly looking forward to it at the same time?

And so he answered the only way he could, with the only words he could come up with that were a suitable reaction. "Thank you, Daddy."

22

Their first week together as daddy and boy was everything Rhys could have hoped for. It was incredible how things had fallen into place in ways Rhys had never thought possible. He still got a rush every time Cornell called him *Daddy*, and he could see that same thrill in his boy's eyes.

And Cornell was his boy, his sweet, perfect boy. Every doubt Rhys might've had about whether it would work, considering the age difference, had been wiped away by how they'd both taken to their roles, their dynamic. They matched like two halves of a whole.

He'd finished up his last days at his job, leaving behind an unhappy supervisor. The man had hoped Rhys would forfeit his rights to his accrued leave, but there was no way he would spend more time away from Cornell than he absolutely had to. He'd written up notes on all his patients for whomever they'd be transferred to, had called a few regulars to say goodbye, and walked out with zero regrets.

Being at home had been wonderful. He took care of Cornell in every way he could: cooking for him, making sure he did his exercises, took his medicine and vitamins, got enough sleep, you name it. He also pampered him whenever he could with his touch, and Cornell soaked it all up.

That didn't mean he and Cornell spent every waking hour together, because after all, Rhys did have a business to start. So he'd been disciplined in setting up a new day rhythm for both of them, with him starting up the mornings with Cornell, inspecting him after his shower and providing him with his healthy breakfast.

After that, he retreated into his office to hash out all the necessary details to get his solo practice up and running. He was a week from launching officially, and he already had his first appointments booked, which thrilled him. Ford's sub Shawn had been looking for a new physical therapist, one who understood more about the lifestyle and his desire to serve his Dom. That made Rhys a perfect match, and he couldn't wait to see how he could help him. He loved working with veterans, and the fact that Shawn was a sub was even more perfect.

In between all the business stuff, which admittedly, was somewhat boring, he checked in on Cornell throughout the day. They shared lunch together, and whenever he was in the mood, there was always time for a quick *encounter*. Rhys smiled as he thought of one particularly dirty blow job where he'd snuck up on Cornell, who had been napping on the couch, and had woken him up by sucking him off as fast as he could. The man had practically needed another nap after coming that hard, which had made Rhys smile.

Then there was the other side of their dynamic, the side that at first wasn't as obvious in a daddy-boy relationship. He'd picked up on Cornell's penchant for soft humiliation kink almost instantly, even before they'd gotten involved. That, combined with the man's deep desire to please his

Daddy and his joy whenever he could serve him, made for some of their more kinky encounters.

That first day, he had kept him plugged the entire day, and Cornell had blushed fiercely every time Rhys had asked him to bare his ass. But the fact that his dick had been hard every single time was all the proof Rhys had needed he was fully on board with this. He'd taken him twice before he'd finally allowed him to come, and after that, Cornell had been pretty much useless the rest of the day, too worn out.

Rhys loved it, this sexy yet sweet dynamic they had going. It kept surprising him, how easily he could read Cornell and how readily Cornell submitted to him on his part. It was like they were two pieces of a puzzle that fit perfectly together, and already, Rhys couldn't imagine his life without him. That was a scary realization after such a short time, but every time he thought that, he reminded himself of what Ford had said. This was not a new, fast relationship. This had been years in the making.

Cornell had slowly taken on more household responsibilities, even though Rhys hadn't specifically asked him to. Cornell had commented that since Rhys was working and he wasn't at the moment, there was no reason why he couldn't do things around the house. So he'd been doing the laundry, performing some basic cleaning duties, and he'd kept the beds made, the house tidy, and had even done some small repairs here and there.

Rhys still cooked, maybe because they both knew that was his forte, but also because he loved taking care of Cornell that way. They also continued his daily massages and exercises, and Rhys was thrilled to see his mobility improve by the day. Bending his knees was still hard, but he could walk around the house now with much more ease, and he didn't tire as quickly.

In short, things were going far better than Rhys could have ever hoped. One of the highlights of his day was his daily inspection of Cornell in the mornings and making him breakfast. It was the perfect combination of taking care of him, mixed in with that underlayer of humiliation they both loved so much.

Sometimes, he fucked him. Other times, he was in the mood for a blow job, or he would suck Cornell off. He liked to keep him on his toes and change it up every day, but they always shared some kind of intimacy in the morning. They hadn't discussed it, but it wasn't hard to see that Cornell loved it as much as Rhys did.

Cornell was waiting for him, as had become standard now, perfectly positioned in their room, his body showing deference for his Daddy. It was interesting to see how they had almost seamlessly merged their previous D/s dynamic with their daddy-boy one and them being boyfriends.

"You look beautiful and perfect as always," Rhys praised him, knowing how much Cornell needed to hear that. And he wasn't lying, taking great pleasure from the way Cornell presented his body.

He kissed him softly on his lips, then allowed the kiss to deepen a little to fulfill his need for more. Besides, he liked Cornell's lips swollen from his kisses. Or glistening with saliva. Then again, smearing his lips with his cum was also highly satisfactory. Oh, who was he kidding? He liked the man's lips, period.

The soft sigh Cornell emitted when he broke off the kiss was music to his soul. "I can't get enough of you, sweetheart," Rhys told him, meaning every word.

He let his hands roam Cornell's body, caressing and stroking, rubbing his nipples between his fingers until they grew hard, which was another small thing he really loved to do. Every day, he was learning more about Cornell's body, like you would learn the intricacies of a delicate instrument. He was still tuning him, adjusting his approach based on his reactions. It was almost eerie, the way he could read him.

"Lift your eyes to me," he told him softly. "I want to see your beautiful baby blues."

Whereas usually, Cornell would obey instantly, now there was a delay. It was a second, maybe two, but Rhys noticed, just like he noticed the slight pout on Cornell's lips. Ah, something was troubling his boy. Now the challenge was to find out what without asking directly.

"What are you in the mood for today, sweetheart? You feel like a quick fuck? A little frotting?" he asked.

Something flashed over Cornell's face before he answered. "Whatever you want, as long as I get to come."

Rhys lifted one eyebrow, waiting silently.

"*Daddy*," Cornell added with a hint of defiance.

Someone was in a mood, Rhys decided. The question was how he should respond. As Dom, he would've instantly punished Cornell for disrespecting him, but what was his role as a Daddy here? He tried to work it out in his head as Cornell stared at him, raising his chin slightly, but enough to warn Rhys this wasn't over yet.

What did Cornell need from him right now? He had to know he was being a brat and that that would have consequences, so what was the outcome he was expecting? It meant he wanted those consequences. Rhys had a pretty good idea where this was leading, but he had to make sure. It wasn't the most subtle way, but he'd be damn sure to get a reaction from Cornell if he was right about this.

"The last time I checked, *I* was in charge of your orgasms, and not you. To remind you, you're now on a twenty-four-hour orgasm denial, so good luck with that. I don't want to see you touching yourself, and if I discover you came without my permission, you'll find the consequences highly unpleasant. Am I making myself clear?"

Cornell's eyes predicted a storm, but Rhys was tuned into every emotion flashing over the man's face, and there had been relief as well. Still, the man wouldn't give in quite so easily.

"With all respect, but that's ridiculous. I told you I was fine with whatever you wanted to do, and now you're gonna punish me for that?"

Oh, it was crystal clear now. He was soliciting, and while as a Dom, Rhys would be damned if he allowed sub to goad him into doing anything, as a Daddy, the rules were different. He put on his stern face, grateful for all the times he'd made himself practice that in the mirror.

"I don't know what your problem is this morning, but this tone will not stand, boy. You just earned yourself a punishment. Go downstairs to the playroom and bring me a paddle."

He shouldn't feel as happy as he did on the inside when he saw Cornell's mouth drop open just a little. Sure, if the man wanted to earn himself a punishment, Rhys would oblige. But he'd damn well make it a real punishment, so Cornell would know that being bratty had consequences.

"A paddle?" Cornell whispered, and all his bravado seemed to be gone.

"Yes, boy, a paddle. I'm pretty sure you know where they are. Now, hurry the fuck up so we can get this over with."

Cornell swallowed visibly. "Yes, Daddy."

He didn't run out of the room, but he left it with enough speed that Rhys was satisfied the man knew he meant business. While he waited for Cornell to return, Rhys looked around the room, quickly assessing how he could best do this. He would've loved to have him over his knee for this, but feared that would still be too much for Cornell's knees, especially in combination with the pain from the paddling. Oh, he wouldn't go all out on him, not for a minor infraction like this, but Cornell had to feel he was being punished. A mild spanking wouldn't do, because that would bring him only pleasure.

In the end, he decided bending over the bed would work best, so he positioned himself next to it and waited for Cornell to come back. To the man's credit, he hadn't picked the smallest paddle, but a medium one. It could pack a wallop if Rhys used it at full force, which he had zero intention of doing.

"Bend over the bed," he told him, keeping his voice stern.

Cornell obeyed instantly, though he did shoot a look of worry in Rhys's direction. Rhys wished he could smile at him and assure him everything would be okay, but that would defy the purpose of this little experiment.

"Why is Daddy disciplining you?" he asked.

"Because I was a brat and wasn't showing you the proper respect," Cornell said, his voice small.

"Do you feel like you deserve to be disciplined for that?"

Cornell's soft "Yes, Daddy" tugged at Rhys's heartstrings enough to almost make him reconsider. Almost, if he hadn't known beyond a shadow of a doubt this was what Cornell needed. They both needed this, to add this new layer to their relationship.

"Five strikes," he told him. "Count them out, please."

He immediately brought down the paddle for the first one, and while he didn't swing it as hard as he could, he did make sure Cornell would feel it. The hiss of pain he let out confirmed he'd succeeded.

"One," Cornell said, his voice muffled.

The second strike was just as hard, but on the other cheek.

"Two."

After that, Rhys went a little softer, hitting each cheek one more time and finishing off with a slap in the middle.

"Five. Thank you, Daddy," Cornell said, his voice choked up.

Rhys followed his instincts and put the paddle down, then gently pulled Cornell up from the bed and gathered him in his arms. "Come sit with me, sweetheart," he said, tugging his hand until Cornell followed him to the sofa chair and sat down on his lap, wincing when his undoubtedly sore cheeks hit Rhys's legs.

Cornell put his cheek against Rhys's shoulder, nuzzling his neck with his lips that were wet from his tears. Rhys allowed him to come down a bit, holding him and caressing his skin wherever he could touch it.

"You made Daddy proud in how you took your discipline, sweetheart. Now, do you want to tell me what happened?"

～

CORNELL HAD MANAGED to stop the flow of tears, but they were still close to the surface, his emotions storming inside him.

"I was angry when I woke up this morning," he said softly, snuggling even closer to Rhys, whose arms instantly tightened around him.

"Were you angry about something specific or upset in general?" Rhys asked, and Cornell loved that the question already implied the acceptance of the second option.

"Just annoyed," Cornell said. "My shoulder hurt, I was

still pissy about the phone call with Sarah yesterday, and I missed Jonas. It was nothing you did," he added.

He'd had another call with his sister, and while it had gone slightly better than their previous one, since at least she hadn't mentioned their parents' money, she'd not been amused to hear Rhys was now officially Cornell's boyfriend. She'd had some choice opinions on that one, and the words *cradle robber* had been mentioned.

"I'm sorry," Rhys said. "It's hard to wake up like that and already feel annoyed and dejected when the day is just starting."

"Yes," Cornell whispered, grateful that Rhys understood. "And my brain went on all kinds of tangents and inner rants, which didn't exactly help either."

Rhys's right hand found that spot on his neck where Cornell loved to be scratched, and he almost purred when he felt those warm fingers touch him so perfectly.

"Were you starting to doubt us?" Rhys asked.

Cornell was ashamed to admit it after everything they had been through already, but he couldn't deny the truth. "I felt like you only wanted me as long as I was perfect, that you would reject me if I ever stopped being what you wanted."

"So you thought you'd test that theory?" Rhys said, and Cornell was relieved to hear a hint of amusement in his voice.

"Not consciously," he said. "I didn't realize that's what I was doing until you dropped the word *paddle*. It was like a cold shower, making me realize what I was doing, but by then it was too late to reverse course."

Rhys was quiet long enough that Cornell started to worry. "Are you upset with me?" he checked.

"Oh no, sweetheart, not at all," Rhys said instantly, and

the warmth in his tone assured Cornell he was speaking the truth. "I was going over what had happened in my head again, now looking at it from your perspective, and I wonder if I handled it the right way."

"You did," Cornell said immediately. "As strange as it sounds, you gave me exactly the proof I needed, even though I didn't know that was what I was seeking."

"But I punished you for what you now admit was acting out of insecurity. How was that what you needed? To be fair, I thought you were debating me on purpose, that you wanted to test out your limits."

Cornell considered it. "You know, I think that's exactly what I was doing, except unconsciously. I needed to know that even if I was a brat, you would be there for me. That you would discipline me, but also forgive me, and that's exactly what you did. You called me out on my behavior, you made me face the consequences, and now I feel like everything is good between us."

"It is," Rhys said, kissing Cornell on his head. "And I'm glad I handled it right. If I ever get it wrong, promise you'll tell me. We're both still figuring out how all of this works, so I'm sure we'll get it wrong at times. If we do, if I do, I need you to call me out on it."

That was a promise Cornell could make. "I will."

They sat quietly for a bit, and then Rhys asked, "How's your ass feel?"

Cornell grinned. "Like I got paddled."

He could feel Rhys chuckle, the sound to reverberating in his chest. "You were, and you deserved it. But it wasn't too much?"

"No, it was perfect. Just enough to make me realize you meant business."

He thought about it, all his encounters with previous

Doms. He'd never been in a position where he could be bratty, where he felt safe enough to act out and know he would be forgiven for it. The older he got, the more aware he'd been how precarious his position was. He had to be perfect, or he would be easily replaced by someone else.

And the six years with Asshole Arnold, they hadn't been any different. Looking back, Cornell had trouble figuring out why he had stayed with him for so long, when even in that relationship, there had always been the pressure to be perfect. He'd known that imperfection would mean losing Arnold, and in the end, that was exactly what had happened, though the irony had been that it had been his age, his body that had caused the imperfection, not his behavior.

"Sweetheart, you can be as bratty as you want, if that's what you need. I'm fine with you asking me outright for a bit of discipline, if you feel that's what you need to ground yourself, or you can implicitly ask for it by acting out. I'll pick up the signs, and I'll give you whatever you need. And if I get it wrong, you always have the option of using your safe word," Rhys said, his voice warm and calm and with all the assurance Cornell needed.

Cornell's eyes watered with the perfection of that answer. He'd had a safe word when he started out in the scene, but in recent years, he'd reverted to the well-known green-yellow-red system. It had happened to him once, that a Dom had to interrupt the scene because he'd forgotten Cornell's safe word, which he'd clearly stated at the beginning of the scene. It had scared the crap out of him, and ever since, he'd decided to use the color system.

But now, things had changed, and it was time to trust again. He didn't want to use his old safe word, which had been linked to Jonas and everything they had shared together. No, he needed something new, something that had meaning for him and Rhys. Within seconds, he'd found it, and he had to smile at how perfect it was.

"My safe word is oatmeal," he said. "And I trust you with all my heart to remember it, Daddy."

His reward was another kiss on his head and then more neck scratches. He sighed with contentment, even though his ass informed him indignantly that being a brat was not smart. Maybe, but he'd loved it just the same.

23

R hys was excited to have Brendan and Raf come over for dinner again. The last time, they'd been interrupted because of Cornell's breakdown, which in hindsight, had proved to be a turning point for him. Plus, Raf hadn't exactly been at his best either, so Rhys hoped that a second attempt would be more successful.

He'd expected Cornell to be nervous, but if he was, he wasn't showing it. Then again, Rhys had just given him a wonderful massage with a happy ending, so there was that. He still loved doing that for him, making the man feel like the most treasured boy on the planet.

The doorbell rang, and Cornell looked up from the book he'd been reading. "They're here, Daddy," he said, stating the obvious, while at the same time signaling he was ready and willing to embrace their dynamic in front of Rhys's friends. Rhys could only hope they would become Cornell's friends as well.

He extended his hand to Cornell and pulled him up from the couch. "Let's greet them properly."

As soon as he saw Raf, he knew his friend was in a much

better place than last time. He gave him a solid hug, then kissed him on his cheek. "How are you doing?" he asked. "You look good."

Raf shot a quick look in his Daddy's direction. "Long story, but we'll catch you up over dinner."

Much to Rhys's surprise, Raf didn't hesitate to hug Cornell as well. "Good to see you again," Raf said. "I hope you're feeling better than last time."

Raf didn't have much of a filter, but Rhys wasn't worried about Cornell's reaction. He knew the man would pick up the genuine concern behind that remark.

He hugged Raf right back and said, "Thank you, I am. I'm glad to see you're doing better too."

Rhys had prepared various small dishes so they could graze more than sit down for a formal dinner. It was more relaxed anyway, and Raf didn't tend to do very well when he had to sit down for a long time. As Rhys had expected, Raf immediately threw a pillow on the floor and settled himself at his Daddy's feet. Brendan's hand found a spot on Raf's head, and Rhys knew that constant contact kept his friend grounded.

"So what's new with you guys?" Rhys asked, gesturing to Cornell to find a spot on the couch next to him. He was pleased when Cornell didn't hesitate to obey and cuddled up against him.

Raf quickly looked at Brendan before turning back to Rhys. "I quit my job," he said.

He'd been a teacher's aide for a kindergarten class, and while Rhys had always felt the job suited him, he also knew it had been stressful for Raf to manage.

"That's quite the decision," he said. "What happened?"

Raf let out a sigh that sounded a bit sad. "It was too hard to manage for me. Between my ADHD and the depressive episodes I've struggled with lately, it was too much for me to work full time. I wasn't getting good reviews from my supervisors, and that only added to my stress."

Brendan looked down at Raf with eyes full of love, and Rhys's heart filled with gratitude that his friend had gotten so lucky. "I asked Raf to move in with me, and he said yes."

Rhys's face broke open in a wide smile. "That's amazing news. I'm so happy for you two."

"I had my last day yesterday," Raf said. "And I already feel so much lighter, knowing I won't have to go back tomorrow."

"So you're not gonna work at all?" Cornell asked, and there was something in his voice that made Rhys sit up and take notice. Not judgment, not even close, but more like...curiosity?

"I'm lucky, because Daddy makes enough to support us both," Raf said. "I may end up doing some administrative work for him, but right now, that's the extent of what I plan to do. He's given me permission to take it easy for a little bit and recover, because I've been under a lot of stress."

"That's wonderful," Cornell said, and Rhys could hear the genuine emotion in his voice. "There's such a pressure from society on the need to work and provide your own income, but I think it's wonderful that you're given the opportunity to take that pressure and stress off your shoulders."

The smile Raf sent him was blinding. "I have the best Daddy in the whole world."

Rhys couldn't help but smile at that statement, his heart almost bursting with happiness for his best friend, so he never expected it when Cornell spoke up and said, "My Daddy is just as awesome."

Rhys couldn't hold back the little gasp of surprise when

Cornell made that simple statement, owning their relationship without blinking. Hell, Rhys couldn't even detect nerves in his voice, nor on his face.

Raf's eyes went wide as he leaned forward. "Rhys is your Daddy?" he asked.

"He is," Cornell said.

"That's so cool," Raf said. "I bet he's a really good Daddy, because he's a lot like Daddy Brendan. Rhys always took really good care of me until I met my Daddy."

And just like that, Raf had accepted them, and one look at Brendan revealed a big smile on the man's face. Rhys hadn't expected any difficulty from them, but it was telling that even Raf, who had zero filter, never even brought up the age difference between them.

They chatted for a long time, conversation flowing easily. At some point, Rhys could see Raf struggling to pay attention, but before he needed to say anything, Brendan pulled him on his lap, handed him a binkie and a little stuffed animal, and told him to get some rest. Raf put his head against his Daddy's broad chest, closed his eyes, and was out like a light.

Rhys offered them the guest room when Brendan said it was time to go, but he indicated he wanted to spend his first full day with Raf at home, which Rhys completely understood. So he and Cornell waved them off, Raf sleepy in his Daddy's arms, and when Rhys closed the door behind them, he spotted a wistful expression on Cornell's face.

"What's on your mind, sweetheart?" he asked. "I can see you're thinking about something. Can you share it with me?"

Cornell smiled at him. "Is it okay if we do this in bed? I want to feel close to you when we talk about this."

Rhys hurried them through their evening routine, then got into bed and held his arms open so Cornell could cuddle close with him. Despite his growing impatience, he waited until the man started talking.

"I don't want to go back to work."

CORNELL REGRETTED SPEAKING SOON as he'd said the words. He was going too fast, bringing this up when they'd been together as daddy and boy for only two weeks. He would scare Rhys away if he kept moving at the speed of light.

"I was wondering about that," Rhys said. "Can you tell me how you feel about it?"

At least his first reaction wasn't shock, Cornell concluded, which relieved some of his instant stress. "For the last few years, my work has been very stressful. I know it sounds rather boring, being an estate lawyer, but I've always loved it. But the firm I work for kept taking on more and more clients, while reducing our support staff. I have a wonderful assistant, but I share him with three other lawyers, and that's just not enough. The pressure to bring on new clients rose and so did the expectation of billable hours. I make great money, but I'm starting to wonder if it's worth it."

"Dad mentioned something about that one of the last times we spoke," Rhys said. "He told me he was worried about you, that you were close to being burnt out."

Cornell smiled at that reminder of how Jonas had fussed over him. He might've been a submissive, but he shared the same caring instincts as his son. "I was, and he was absolutely right about that. In fact, it was one of the reasons why we went to the club that night, because he wanted to see if a good scene would help me relax a little."

Rhys turned his head toward him with one finger. "I

hope the thought that you somehow caused the accident because of that never occurred to you," he said, his voice stern.

"It went through my mind in the first few weeks, but I'm rational enough to know that I had nothing to do with it. Call it fate, call it bad luck, call it being at the wrong place at the wrong time, but whatever it was, it wasn't something I could've prevented," Cornell said, and as he spoke the words, he was happy to feel that he meant them, that he could feel the truth of that statement deep in his soul.

"Good," Rhys said simply. "Just wanted to make sure. Please, continue."

Cornell sighed. "The first few weeks of my recovery, going back to work didn't even occur to me. I was too focused on getting better, on grieving, and on trying to process what had happened. And even after I moved in with you, I barely thought of my job. I know that sounds horribly spoiled, but I figured I had a good excuse, so they couldn't really complain about me being absent. And they didn't, to their credit."

His firm had sent a big wreath to Jonas's funeral. The funeral Cornell hadn't been able to attend, since he'd still been in the hospital, unable to leave his bed, even in a wheelchair. Rhys had arranged for a friend of his to livestream the funeral for Cornell, and he'd watched from his hospital bed as much as he could, for as long as he'd been able to stay awake, heavily drugged as he'd still been.

And ever since, the firm's partners had inquired after him, but never in a pushy way. After the pressure he'd felt in the last years, that had been more than he expected from them. But despite that, he had zero desire to go back.

"Did your dad ever mention I received quite the inheritance from my parents?" he asked Rhys.

Rhys shook his head. "No. I knew they had died, and I assumed you had a little nest egg considering you didn't seem to be in a hurry to get back to work, but that's all I knew."

Cornell took a deep breath and told him about his parents' decision to leave seventy-five percent of their fortune to him, rather than split it evenly between him and his sister. And considering his dad had owned a quite successful car dealership for many years, one that had been bought out when it became clear neither Sarah nor Cornell intended to succeed him, the inheritance had been substantial.

"I am glad it affords you the opportunity to take your time to figure out what you want to do next," Rhys said, his voice warm. "But we both know that we'd rather have our parents back than have all this money."

How true was that? Cornell had always been close with both his parents, even his father, who had struggled a bit when Cornell had come out as gay. But in the end, the man had embraced him fully, and they'd been in close contact till the day he'd died. They'd been very fond of Jonas as well, and Cornell had been relieved they hadn't been alive anymore when Jonas had passed, so they'd been spared that grief. He'd been like a second son to them.

"Yeah, very much so," Cornell said.

"So are you going to quit officially?" Rhys asked.

"I would love to, but I'm asking what you think," Cornell said.

"This is not a decision I can make for you," Rhys said, and he sounded quite resolute. "This falls outside of my purview as your Daddy, don't you think?"

"What if I don't want it to? What if I want you to weigh in on things like this?" Cornell asked, forgetting about his earlier misgivings about speaking up and going too fast until he saw the utter shock on Rhys's face. His stomach dropped. Had he still misjudged Rhys's intentions? Had he really been going too fast?

"Forget about it," he said, feeling himself shut down.

Rhys gripped his chin, forcing him to make eye contact when he wanted nothing more than to look away so Rhys wouldn't see the pain in his eyes. "No, sweetheart, don't do that. Don't lock me out because you think I feel a certain way. Give me a chance to react, okay?"

"I could see the truth on your face," Cornell said miserably. "I'm going too fast, aren't I?"

Rhys seemed to think for a few seconds before he replied. "Sweetheart, it's such a big responsibility you're giving me. I'm blown away that you're willing to let me in on decisions of that magnitude when a few weeks ago, you weren't even sure if you wanted to stay with me."

He had a point, of course, and Cornell wasn't even sure how he could refute it. How could he explain how he now wondered where his distrust for Rhys had ever come from? After everything Rhys had done for him, his reaction to the fact that Rhys hadn't initially told him he was a Dom seemed so out of proportion now. Of course he trusted him. He'd known him his whole life. He was Jonas's son. He was his *Daddy*. Could Rhys not see that?

"Of course I want to stay with you," he latched on to that last bit Rhys had said. "Unless you want me to leave?"

They hadn't even talked about that, he realized with a sinking feeling in his stomach. What if Rhys didn't want things to go this fast? What if he wanted their relationship to develop at a slower, more traditional pace? Normal couples didn't move in right away, the way they had.

Then he caught himself. No, that line of thought didn't

make sense at all. Rhys had wanted a twenty-four seven relationship as much as he had, and they both agreed this was what they wanted. If Rhys had had reservations about Cornell staying with him, he would've spoken up, that much Cornell knew.

"Sweetheart," Rhys said with a twinge of sadness in his voice. "Please tell me you don't think for even one second I don't want you here."

Cornell smiled at him. "One second," he admitted, "but then I caught myself and realized the truth."

With a lightning fast move, Rhys rolled them over until Cornell was on his back, with Rhys on top of him. "Don't you ever doubt that I want you here. And no, my hesitation isn't because I think you're moving too fast for me. I've wanted you for years, sweetheart. Breakneck speed would still be too slow for me. My hesitation is because I'm not sure if we're going too fast for *you*, if at some point your brain is going to catch up with your heart, and you end up regretting some of the decisions that you made on a whim."

It hit Cornell all over again, how long Rhys had had his eye on him, even when Cornell hadn't seen him as anything but Jonas's son. Sure, they'd always gotten along great, and Cornell had definitely thought he was cute as fuck a few times, but it had never gone beyond that. To know that Rhys had wanted him all that time, that was a heady feeling. He couldn't even describe what that did to him, knowing that this wonderful, gorgeous man wanted him, with his damaged body, his limited physical abilities, even his emotional trauma.

"Thank you for looking out for me, Daddy," he said, his voice tearing up as he stared into Rhys's beautiful brown eyes, the same eyes as Jonas. "I love that your first concern is for me. But I really do want your opinion on this."

Rhys nodded, then settled them both on their sides, facing each other. "If your job makes you that stressed and doesn't bring you joy and you can afford financially to quit, then quit. You know I would love nothing more than to have you at home."

Home. The word echoed through Cornell's brain first, then registered on a much deeper level. This was his home. Somewhere in the last few weeks, Jonas's ranch had become Rhys's ranch, and then their home. His home.

"I want to sell my house," he said, and it took him a few seconds to realize that the tears that popped up in Rhys's eyes were good tears, happy tears.

"I love you," Rhys said, looking at Cornell as if he was a rare treasure. "I think I've loved you for years, and the last few weeks, it's only grown deeper. I don't just want to be your Daddy, my sweetheart. I want to be your everything. I want to take care of you for as long as fate allows me to."

Cornell didn't even have to think, never doubting a word Rhys said. All his fears and hesitations were gone, replaced by a deep knowing that Rhys loved him more than anything.

"I love you," he whispered. "All I need to do is look into your eyes to see how much you love me. I want you to be my everything, more than I can express. I'm not the type to jump into a pool when I don't know how deep it is, but you make me want to. I want to quit my job. I want to sell my house. I want to be all in, no holds barred, no reservations. I want to stay here with you, be your boy, and be the happiest I've ever been."

Rhys's kiss was like a feather as it brushed his lips, filled with a reverence that matched the magnitude of Cornell's feelings. "Yes, please."

24

"I have a surprise for you," Daddy said a few days later.

He'd just inspected Cornell, and Cornell had been waiting for the next move, the signal of what they'd be doing to start the day right. He loved it, those precious moments of intimacy between them. Sometimes it was fast and raw, other times Daddy would take his time to drive him crazy, and then there were the days where Daddy would send him to the brink and then tell him he wasn't allowed to come. Cornell still wasn't sure if he hated or loved that. Probably both in equal measure.

One look at his sparkling eyes made Cornell realize this would be a naughty surprise, one he'd end up having mixed feelings about as well. "Do I want to know?" he asked with a laugh.

His punishment—if you could even call it that—was a slap on his ass that echoed through the room. "There's more where that came from," Daddy warned him, but his mouth pulled up in the corners.

"Is that a threat or a promise?" Cornell joked, which earned him another slap, though a much softer one.

"Do I need to bring out the paddle again?" Daddy asked, his eyes narrowing in mock indignity, and Cornell quickly shook his head.

"No, Daddy. Sorry, Daddy."

"Now, are you going to show the proper enthusiasm for my surprise?"

"It's hard to be enthusiastic for something I don't know," Cornell said, "so please show me, Daddy?"

Rhys's eyes were smiling at him, which assured him that he understood this to be playful brattiness, not real disobedience.

Rhys walked over to the dresser and opened the top drawer, where he removed a package. Now Cornell was legitimately intrigued. It was neatly wrapped in bright blue, shiny wrapping paper with a silver bow stuck to it.

"This is for you," Daddy said, and Cornell took it from him.

It was heavier than he had expected, and he started unwrapping it with impatience. As soon as he ripped off the front, he knew, and his stomach swirled with anticipation. His moves grew much slower as he removed the rest of the wrapping paper.

"A cock cage," he whispered. "You bought me a cock cage."

Rhys must've picked up on the slight tremble in his voice, because he immediately lifted Cornell's chin to make him meet his eyes. "It's an experiment, and only if you want it."

Cornell nodded. "I know, Daddy."

He unpacked the cage, holding it in his hand. It was sturdy, heavy, made out of expensive-looking metal. "I've only worn one years ago," he said. He had to clear his throat before he could continue. "With Arnold. It was something he wanted to try, but I didn't like it."

Rhys is jaw tightened. "Then we won't try it."

Cornell put a hand on his arm, meeting his eyes again. "I want to try with you, Daddy. I'm a little apprehensive, but there's also excitement mixed in."

"What happened with Arnold?" Rhys asked, and Cornell thought that was the first time he'd referred to him by just his name. "Why didn't you like it?"

In hindsight, it was so much easier to see. When he'd been in the middle of it, trying to figure out why things weren't working, it had been so much harder.

"He wanted me to wear it for long periods of time, like days and even weeks. It was very much a power issue for him, the fact that he could control me like that."

Rhys cocked his head, looking at him intently. "I'm not in any way choosing his side, but that's not uncommon behavior or motivation for a Dom."

"Granted, but most Doms do it for the right reason, which is to bring their sub pleasure as well. Arnold only did it so he could use me and not have to worry about my pleasure. After all, if I was locked in a cage, he didn't have to spend time making me come."

Rhys's eyes widened, and his mouth hardened. "Cornell, that's absolutely unacceptable," he said, and it had been the first time in days, maybe even weeks, that he'd called him by his actual name. "That man doesn't deserve to call himself a Dom, not with behavior like that."

Cornell let out a sigh. "I know, but I didn't see it at the time. To his credit, he did honor me safe wording out of that, and afterward, I made it a hard limit."

Rhys shook his head. "Honoring a safe word is not to his credit. It's the bare minimum requirement."

Cornell could hear the simmering anger in his voice, and it warmed his heart, because he knew it was on his behalf. "There's a lot I can see now that I didn't see back then. Just to be clear, our relationship wasn't abusive. It never went that far, but he definitely wasn't considerate, and I think it's safe to say that he used me. Jonas, your dad, he pointed it out multiple times, but it took me a long time to realize he was right."

Rhys cupped his cheek, and his brown eyes were filled with worry. "Sweetheart, if this is such a trigger for you, are you sure we should do it? There are so many other things we can try."

Cornell loved him for that, but then again, it was only one more item on a long list of reasons why he loved Rhys. "I want to try it with you, because I know you're not like that. But maybe we should try with a shorter period?"

"God, yes. I wanted to propose you'd wear it for maybe two hours or so, just to get used to it. And if at any time you want to stop, just say the word. I won't ever hold it against you."

Cornell leaned in for a kiss, because he needed his Daddy's lips on his right now. He was rewarded with a soft, sweet kiss that made his heart sing.

"I'm so proud of you for trying," Daddy whispered, and that praise alone was enough for Cornell to know he'd done the right thing.

Then Daddy went to his knees, kneeling in front of Cornell as he handed him the cage. Luckily, he was so nervous that his dick was completely soft, which made it easy to put on. Daddy double-checked it before he snapped it shut and turned the key to lock it.

"You'd better not lose that," Cornell said, his voice wavering a little.

Rhys rose to his feet and smiled, holding up the key. "Not a chance, sweetheart. I've got you. How does it feel?"

Cornell looked down at himself. It was a strange sight to see his cock wrapped up like that. "It looks really small like this," he said, not sure he liked that part.

"Well, you *are* smaller than me," Daddy said.

Cornell's head shot up to protest, but then he saw the laugh on Daddy's lips. He was teasing him, the bastard. "You're mean," he said. "You're a mean Daddy."

Daddy's smile only widened as he held up the key again. "If I were you, I'd be a little nicer to the man who holds the key to your dick."

He had a point there, Cornell had to concede. He looked down at himself again, moving a little to see how the metal would feel against his skin. It had been cold at first, but it was warming up to his body temperature now, and the cage was surprisingly comfortable. It probably would be unless he got hard.

Uh oh. "How exactly were you planning on experimenting, Daddy?" he asked, already knowing he wasn't going to like the answer.

The smile Daddy sent him was downright devious. "Oh, nothing specific. But to make sure it fits correctly, I'll have to keep an eye on it, so I think it's better if you don't get dressed. I've already increased the heating so you won't get cold."

Okay, so he was to walk around naked for a bit. He could do that, even if it embarrassed him to be on display like that. He'd done it before, and Daddy had loved it, so there was that.

"Of course, I'll need to make sure the cage doesn't prohibit you in any way, so we'll have to run some tests."

Cornell decided there was a distinct glee to Daddy's voice he didn't trust at all. "Tests?"

Daddy nodded, his face serious, but his eyes still sparkling. "Nothing big. But of course, I do need to make sure that their claim one can pee while wearing it is accurate. And I need to make sure that I can fuck you with the cage on, so we'll have to run some tests there as well."

Cornell's heart skipped a few beats, and his stomach swirled as much in anticipation as dread. He was *so* fucked.

"LET ME INSPECT YOU, SWEETHEART," Rhys said for the second time that hour.

Cornell shot him a dark look, but he dutifully got up from his chair and presented himself to Rhys. Because he was still seated, Cornell's groin was right at eye level, and wasn't that handy? Rhys leaned forward, making a bit of a show of studying Cornell's dick. He lifted it up, looking at the cage from every side.

"You look so pretty like this," he told him again, waiting for that telltale blush on Cornell's cheeks. Ah, there it was, accompanied by the expected flash of annoyance in his eyes. "Next time, we should accessorize it with some matching nipple clamps."

Oh, Cornell wanted to *hurt* him right now, his eyes shooting daggers. But he didn't say anything, and Rhys admired his self-control.

"Hold position for me while I make a call," he told him.

Cornell's eyes darkened even more as he obeyed, and Rhys took out his phone and called Ford. He'd already texted him to make sure it was an appropriate time.

"Hey, kiddo, what's up?"

It was funny, being called kiddo now didn't bother Rhys anymore. "Hey man, how have you been?"

Ford chuckled. "Better than ever. I found me a sub with a fondness for flogging, and you know how much I love that shit. Did a workout on him yesterday, and the boy was flying a mile high. I got legit muscle pain, man, that's how long it had been. And you?"

Rhys looked at Cornell, standing in front of him with that tight jaw that communicated his inner battle. He stroked his cock through the cage, then his balls, which earned him a pair of narrowed eyes. To warn him, he twisted his right nipple, making him hiss.

Ford laughed. "I know that sound," he said.

"Someone needed a little reminder of what being a good boy entails," Rhys said.

"Your sub?" Ford asked, and Rhys understood he meant Cornell.

"My sweet, perfect boy," he said. "He moved in with me permanently."

Ford whistled between his teeth. "Big steps, baby. I'm happy for you. I take it things are working out between you and Cornell then?"

"I'm his Daddy," Rhys said.

"I'll be damned," Ford said. "I never saw that coming, and yet it makes perfect sense."

"I know the feeling," Rhys said. "It was like everything clicked into place."

"I'm so proud of you, Rhys. That's a big step for someone your age, especially considering the age difference. That makes me happy, man, that you two have found what works for you."

Rhys couldn't help but smile as he looked at Cornell. "I love him so much," he said softly, watching as Cornell's eyes found his, changing into that soft look he knew all too well. Gah, he was getting all mushy inside, but how could he not, when he'd found perfection? "And he loves me too."

"Oh man, you're making me tear up," Ford said. "Congrats. I couldn't be happier for you."

Rhys couldn't be happier either, he thought. His heart was so full, it felt like it would explode. "I gotta go," he said. "I have a boy who needs to know who his Daddy is."

Cornell didn't say anything, but his eyes were hot and heavy on Rhys as he went back to fondling him. Of course he didn't protest, because he loved it as much as Rhys did, just like he'd loved being forced to pee with Cornell casually leaning against the door, watching him. He'd been so turned on and so embarrassed at the same time that it had taken him a few minutes before he'd managed it, after which Rhys had praised him to high heaven for being such a good boy. The look on Cornell's face had shown how mixed up his emotions were about all of it.

"Turn around and bend over for me," he told him. "I want to see how it looks from the backside."

Cornell let out a little gasp, his eyes widening in horror as he stood frozen to the spot. Rhys lifted an eyebrow. "Problem?"

Those cheeks grew fiery red, and how Rhys loved that, reveling in the shuffling of the boy's feet and the slight squirming before he *finally* turned around. He bent over slowly, his legs spread wide enough so Rhys had a perfect view. Cornell couldn't hold that position for long, but that wasn't important. It was the act itself that mattered, the way he had to spread himself open for Rhys, offer up that pink hole for him to see.

"I'm suddenly ravenous," Rhys said, and that was all the warning he gave Cornell before he bent in and buried his face in the man's ass, going straight for his prize. Cornell screamed in surprise, his knees buckling as Rhys's mouth found that sweet hole and kissed it, licked it, then tongued it.

Cornell's legs gave out again, and Rhys let out a grunt of frustration. He pulled back, grabbed Cornell by his waist and pushed him sideways on the couch so he tumbled face-down onto it. "Make yourself comfortable," he told him. "I'm gonna be awhile."

God, he loved pleasuring his boy like this, spreading him wide open and fucking him with his tongue until he had him squirming on the couch. It only took a few minutes to discover that this was the sweetest torture for Cornell, who loved being rimmed, sensitive as he was to touch, but who couldn't maintain an erection with his cock locked up. The *sounds* he made, Rhys drank them all in, spurred on by the frustrated mewls, desperate sighs, until finally, Cornell gave in and started begging for Rhys to take his cage off. And still, Rhys feasted on him, getting almost high on his sounds and suffering.

"Please, Daddy, please take it off... It's too good, I can't take this," Cornell pleaded for the tenth time or so.

Rhys checked the clock. The cage had been on for two hours. That was long enough for a first time. Plus, he wanted Cornell to associate it with pleasure, not with frustration. Not the bad kind, anyway. It had been long enough.

He dug up the key from his pocket. "Turn over for me."

The look on Cornell's face was pure relief. "Oh god, thank you, Daddy."

He had it off in seconds, and Cornell winced as his cock filled instantly. "Please, can I come?"

Rhys knelt next to the couch and took that gorgeous dick into his mouth, wanting to feel his boy come. Cornell's hands fisted his hair none too gently, and he fucked into his mouth, hitting the back of his throat with uncoordinated moves. Rhys gagged a little, but it was fine. This wouldn't take long, not with how on edge Cornell was. Seconds later, Cornell's body spasmed, and he screamed as he came, his whole body shaking with the force of his release.

Rhys stretched out on the couch next to him and held him as he came down, gently rubbing his back as he murmured over and over again how perfect he was and how much he loved him.

EPILOGUE

O*ne Month Later*

RHYS HAD to suppress a deep sigh when his phone rang and he spotted who it was.

"Your mom?" Cornell asked, apparently able to read the annoyance on his face.

"Yeah. I gotta take it."

If he didn't, things would just get worse. She'd tried to contact him plenty of times, and he'd told her he needed time, but that line didn't work anymore, not after a whole month.

"Mom," he said.

It took her a second or two to answer, maybe because she was shocked he was actually picking up this time. "Rhys! Thank you for answering," she said, confirming his thoughts.

"What's up, Mom?" he asked. Granted, it wasn't the

nicest way to restart the conversation, but he still wasn't feeling particularly warm toward her after the way she'd torn into Cornell.

"Erm, okay," she stammered. "I erm... I wanted to ask if I could stop by to see you."

That didn't sound like his overbearing, confident mother at all, and Rhys's heart softened a little. "Let's try a phone conversation first and see how that goes, hmm?" he said.

"Oh, okay," she said, and he could hear the emotions in her voice. For a second, he debated giving in, but then decided she hadn't earned his forgiveness yet. "How are you doing?" she asked.

Well, there was a loaded question. He might as well get this part over with, because if she didn't respond well to this, he'd know where he stood with her. "We're doing very well," he answered, stressing the plural pronoun. "Cornell is recovering well, and we're really happy together."

"It's serious then," she said, her tone slightly cooler than before.

"Very," he said. "In fact, Cornell has permanently moved in with me. We just moved in the last of his stuff yesterday, and his house is already up for sale. Brendan thinks it'll sell fast because it's in such great condition."

"Rhys," she said, and that one word held a world of emotions. "I don't understand this."

"You don't have to," he cut her off before she could say more. "I'm not asking you to. I'm asking that you accept and respect it." He debated telling her about the daddy stuff, then decided that could wait. There was no need to spring everything on her at once. "I love Cornell, and he's as much in love with me, so that's the way it is now. If you have a problem with that, things will get difficult between us."

Cornell came over to snuggle up against him, his wordless way of offering Rhys comfort, and he loved it.

"He loves you?" his mom asked, her tone growing warmer.

"He does. We're happy, Mom. I hope you can want that for us and be happy for us."

He heard her swallow. "Your dad, he..."

He waited for her to finish, but when she stayed silent, he said, "Cornell is convinced Dad would've approved, that his primary concern was consent. Don't you think he would've loved to see Cornell taken care of, happy with a D-Dom?"

He'd almost said *Daddy,* and Cornell's eyes widened in fake shock. They wouldn't be able to keep that part secret for long, but they could grant her some time to get used to them first before they sprang that on her.

She let out a long sigh. "Yeah," she said. "He's got a point there. He would've struggled with it, I think, like I am, but in the end, your happiness would've been the most important thing."

"We *are* happy, Mom," he said, and his thoughts went to the plans he had for their six-month anniversary. He'd wait a little longer, for Cornell's sake, but when it came time to celebrate Cornell's release from the rehabilitation center, he had plans that included a ring and a much more permanent arrangement. He'd waited long enough for his man.

"I'll try," she said. "That's all I can promise. I'll try."

"That's good enough for now," Rhys said, his heart filling with gratitude. "How have you been otherwise?"

The result was another long sigh. "I'm struggling," she said finally. "Your dad's passing hit me hard, and I don't know why. It's changed me, and I don't like who I've become."

"Maybe you should seek some help," Rhys said. "Cornell and I have talked to a grief counselor a few times now, and it's been super helpful for us. I can give you her name if you want?"

"Yeah," she said, and he knew how much that cost his proud mom. "I think that would be good."

They ended the call shortly after.

"It's strange to hear her like that," Cornell said. "I've not ever heard her so insecure and fragile."

"Yeah, I know. I'm glad she's open to seeking help."

Cornell rubbed his cheek against Rhys's chest, one of those gestures he made often, as if to confirm Rhys was still there. "I'm glad you told her about us, that I've moved in."

"You're my everything, sweetheart. I would never try to hide who and what we are."

Cornell lifted his head, and they shared a sweet kiss.

"Which reminds me, I'm done washing all the sheets," Cornell said.

Their eyes met, mirroring each other's mix of joy and sadness at this next step they were taking. "Are you ready to do this?" Rhys asked softly, his heart clenching painfully even as his brain embraced the idea at the same time.

"Yes, Daddy. It's time."

They got up from the couch and walked to the master bedroom hand in hand. They had cleaned it together the last few days, removing most of his dad's things and putting their own stuff in. His clothes had been sorted, both of them opting to keep some shirts they were attached to, and they'd donated the rest to charity. Cornell had gone through his dad's personal effects, including his toys, and even though Rhys had already seen them, he understood this was something Cornell needed to do. It had been hard on him, saying goodbye all over again, but they'd made it through.

The last step had been to wash the sheets that had been on the bed, the sheets that had still smelled like his dad, and he and Cornell had both lost it when they'd held them for the last time. Now they were clean, ready to be used again for new memories.

They made the big king-size bed together, the one Cornell had shared with his dad numerous times. But it didn't feel strange or inappropriate. No, it felt right, like they were honoring him by not pretending that part of their lives had never existed.

Above the bed, they'd hung three pictures that symbolized their history. There was one of his dad and Cornell that Rhys had made a year ago, the two men smiling broadly at the camera, their arms slung across each other's shoulders. Then there was one of Rhys with his dad, taken at his college graduation. His dad's smile had been so broad you couldn't help but smile when you saw it. And lastly, there was a picture of Rhys and Cornell, taken a few days ago by a photographer. They looked so in love, so happy, that it made Rhys's heart do a dance every time he looked at it.

They pulled the covers tight, put the pillows back on, and then found each other again, looking at the bed together. "I think we'll feel sadness in this room for a while, maybe," Rhys said, but Cornell shook his head.

"No, not sadness. Melancholy mixed with gratitude that we got to know him. Happiness that we're able to move forward. Joy for the love we've found with each other," he said, and he sounded like a poet.

Rhys pulled him close, gathering his arms around him and seeking his mouth for a kiss. "Love," he whispered against his lips, leaning his forehead against Cornell's. "So much love."

Cornell's smile lit up Rhys's heart. "Yes, Daddy."

Thank you for reading Firm Hand! I hope you loved Rhys and Cornell as much as I did. What a ride it was for these two.

If you loved this book, please leave a review on Amazon, Goodreads, and/or Bookbub. This is a huge help for an indie author like me since reviews help other readers decide if this is the right book for them and make my books get more visibility on Amazon.

Thank you so much!

PS: did you know I send out a newsletter every Saturday which not only includes news about me and my vastest releases and projects, but also about that weekend's best new releases, 99c deals, and freebies in gay romance? Stock up on awesome MM romances for a bargain price!

Sign up here: http://www.noraphoenix.com/newsletter/

BOOKS FROM NORA PHOENIX

No Shame Series

If you love steamy MM romance with a little twist, you'll love the No Shame series. Sexy, emotional, with a bit of suspense and all the feels. Make sure to read in order, as this is a series with a continuing storyline.

No Filter
No Limits
No Fear
No Shame
No Angel

And for all the fun, grab the No Shame box set which includes all five books plus exclusive bonus chapters and deleted scenes.

Irresistible Omegas Series

An mpreg series with all the heat, epic world building, poly romances (the first two books are MMMM and the rest of the series is MMM), a bit of suspense, and characters that will stay with you for a long time. This is a continuing series, so read in order.

Alpha's Sacrifice
Alpha's Submission
Beta's Surrender
Alpha's Pride
Beta's Strength

Ballsy Boys Series

Sexy porn stars looking for real love! Expect plenty of steam, but all the feels as well. They can be read as stand alones, but are more fun when read in order.

Ballsy (free prequel)
Rebel
Tank
Heart
Campy
Pixie

Ignite Series

An epic dystopian sci-fi trilogy (one book out, two more to follow) where three men have to not only escape a government that wants to jail them for being gay but aliens as well. Slow burn MMM romance.

Ignite

Stand Alones

I also have a few stand alone, so check these out!
   Kissing the Teacher (sexy daddy kink)
   The Time of My Life (first time gay)

MORE ABOUT NORA PHOENIX

Would you like the long or the short version of my bio?

The short? You got it.

I write steamy gay romance books and I love it. I also love reading books. Books are everything.

How was that?

A little more detail? Gotcha.

I started writing my first stories when I was a teen...on a freaking typewriter. I still have these, and they're adorably romantic. And bad, haha. Fear of failing kept me from following my dream to become a romance author, so you can imagine how proud and ecstatic I am that I finally overcame my fears and self doubt and did it. I adore my genre because I love writing and reading about flawed, strong men who are just a tad broken..but find their happy ever after anyway.

My favorite books to read are pretty much all MM/gay romances as long as it has a happy end. Kink is a plus... Aside from that, I also read a lot of nonfiction and not just books on writing. Popular psychology is a favorite topic of mine and so are self help and sociology.

Hobbies? Ain't nobody got time for that. Just kidding. I love traveling, spending time near the ocean, and hiking. But I love books more.

Come hang out with me in my Facebook Group Nora's Nook where I share previews, sneak peeks, freebies, fun stuff, and much more: https://www.facebook.com/groups/norasnook/

My weekly newsletter not only gives you updates, exclusive content, and all the inside news on what I'm working on, but also lists the best new releases, 99c deals, and freebies in gay romance for that weekend. Load up your Kindle for less money! Sign up here: http://www.noraphoenix.com/newsletter/

You can also stalk me on Twitter: @NoraFromBHR

On Instagram:

https://www.instagram.com/nora.phoenix/

On Bookbub:

https://www.bookbub.com/profile/nora-phoenix

ACKNOWLEDGMENTS

The idea for this book came to me while on a trip in Australia. I can't even remember what triggered it, but all of a sudden I had this story in my head...and it wouldn't let go of me.

I wrote the first chapters by hand as I traveled, too excited to wait till I got home. And I even wrote on the looooong plane ride home, in my cramped seat on the plane. By hand. Sometimes you gotta do what you gotta do to get that story on paper!

I'm so happy it's done and these two have their HEA. *starry eyes*

A big thanks to Sloan Johnson from Sloan J Designs who made the super sexy cover for this book. I bought it as a premed but it fits the story perfectly.

My beta readers were amazing as always with their feedback. Kyleen, Amanda, Abbie, Tania, Anna, thank you so much. You made this book better.

Jamie, thanks for doing a fab job on the editing. As always, I learned new things from you, which I so appreciate.

Vicki: you not only alpha read this book, firing me up with your enthusiasm, but you helped type it up, made gorgeous teasers, and as always, functioned as my listening ear and holding hand when needed. If I were prone to getting sappy, I'd say you're the wind beneath my wings, but that could get awkward fast, so let's not indulge in that mushy crap. We're way too snarky for that.

And last but not least, a huge thanks to my Nookies, the wonderful readers in my FB reader group Nora's Nook, and to all my other readers out there. Your love and support means the world to me. Thank you.

Made in the USA
Middletown, DE
15 July 2019